The Empath
BONNIE VANAK

First published in Great Britain 2012
by Mills & Boon,
an imprint of Harlequin (UK) Limited,
Large Print edition 2012
Harlequin (UK) Limited, Eton House,
18-24 Paradise Road, Richmond, Surrey TW9 1SR

© Bonnie Vanak 2007

ISBN: 978 0 263 23034 5

Printed and bound in Great Britain
by CPI Antony Rowe, Chippenham, Wiltshire

Bonnie Vanak fell in love with romance novels during childhood. While cleaning a hall closet, she discovered her mother's cache of paperbacks, and started reading. Thus began a passion for romance and a lifelong dislike of housework. After years of newspaper reporting, Bonnie became a writer for a major international charity that took her to destitute countries such as Haiti and Guatemala to write about famine, disease and other issues affecting the poor. When the emotional strain of her job demanded a diversion, she turned to writing romance novels. Bonnie lives in Florida, with her husband and two dogs, where she happily writes books amid an ever-growing population of dust bunnies. She loves to hear from readers. Visit her website at www.bonnievanak.com or email her at bonnievanak@aol.com

For my beloved Tia, our loyal friend
for 11 years. You will always
live on in our hearts. Special thanks
to my friend Julie Sloan and the Rebs;
Pamela Clare, Jan Zimlich,
Alice Duncan, Alice Gaines,
Mimi Riser and especially
Norah Wilson, who kept urging me
to write this book. And a very special
thanks to my wonderful husband Frank,
and our vet, Dr. James Grubb,
who loves animals as much as we do.

Chapter 1

Death with fangs and long talons stalked him.

The enemy hunted him. Nicolas, the powerful warrior. The pack's best fighter. The ostracized.

Nicolas Keenan lifted his muzzle, sniffed the wind. Caught his pack leader's scent marking a nearby oak tree. His wolf form stiffened with longing. Pack. Home. Family.

But he no longer had a family. Even though he continued to quietly patrol their territory, protecting his people, and even though his loyalty would never die, he'd been banished from the pack.

He was Draicon, werewolves who once used their magick to learn of the earth and its wonders. Now, hunted by the more powerful Morphs, they used their powers in a desperate attempt to survive.

Morphs. The very word made his hackles rise. They had been Draicon like him. Draicon who willingly embraced evil, entering the ranks of the Morphs by killing one of their own. Nicolas had spent nearly his whole life destroying Morphs. When some in his pack turned, he'd been forced to kill them as well.

He would always be Draicon, Nicolas silently promised, remembering the tiny mark on his neck. He would never surrender to the Morphs' alluring power.

He felt a cooling breeze stir, rustling the leaves and chilling the air. In this part of northern New Mexico, fall draped the trees in vivid colors. Thirty minutes ago, after he'd left his ranch to take a walk in the woods, he'd sensed danger. The familiar warrior instinct surfaced. He'd shifted to lure the enemy away from the pack's homes and hearths.

New scents filled his nostrils. He went absolutely still, smelling evil.

Nicolas caught a faint whiff of rotting seaweed mixed with raw sewage. Enemy. Danger.

Ah, Maggie, what am I dragging you into? What if they find you as well?

He reached out, silently slipped into her thoughts. Mitosis. Carcinogenic cells. She was studying a sample under the microscope. He slipped out, not wanting to jar her concentration. Margaret Sinclair, the pack's long-lost empath. The Draicon foretold to destroy the Morph leader, she was the pack's last hope and Nicolas's destined mate. She was safe. For now.

In the branches of a sprawling oak, a brown deer sat cloaked from view. A shaft of moonlight dappled dying oak and maple leaves with silver. Dead undergrowth soaked in the evening dew. In the distance, a doe crashed through brush. His ears pricked forward.

They were coming. Once solitary, the enemy had combined their numbers. Nicolas didn't dare shift. Not now. His change left trace elements of magick, clear as muddied paw prints to his enemies.

Standing still, he inhaled the air. The scent grew fainter. A new smell filled his senses. Body odor. Fake deer scent. Stale beer. Humans. Loud, obnoxious voices crashed through the woods.

"There! Did you see that wolf? Let's get him!"

The humans who had spotted him earlier had taken chase. Out to bag anything tonight. Such as Wolf de la Nicolas.

No choice now. Had to risk it. Nicolas shifted, muscles bulging, stretching, bones lengthening.

Fur melted away. Wolfskin vanished, replaced by bronzed human flesh.

Naked man meets eager hunters with loaded rifles. Not good. Summoning clothing by magick would show his presence to the enemy like a lighthouse beacon. He didn't have to use his power this time. Instead, he dove for the rotting tree trunk and the clothing stockpiled beneath the sprawling roots. Damian had laid similar caches all over pack territory for emergencies like this. He dressed, grabbed the whiskey bottle, gave a liberal splash over his bright orange clothing.

Nicolas sank down against the tree and waited. He chuckled, glancing at the half-filled amber bottle. "I never drink anything less than twelve-year-old scotch, Damian, you cheapskate."

Shouting victoriously, the hunters crashed through the woods like clumsy oxen. He smelled cruelty heaving with every excited breath.

They entered the clearing. Pale silver light from the full moon struck their camouflage outfits. Nicolas hiccupped loudly. He raised the bottle in a drunken salute.

"Here's to my shooting a twelve-point rack today!"

Disbelief flashed over their faces. The men shifted their rifles, narrowed their gazes. "Get lost," the shorter one in plaid asserted. "We paid good money to hunt on this land."

Ignoring them, Nicolas pretended to belt a few swallows.

The fat one snorted, shifted his rifle. His potbelly sagged over olive trousers like jowls. "Listen mister, you're trespassing. Get out, before we toss you out. We're on the tail of a lone wolf."

Grinning at them, he dropped the whiskey and made to leave. And then the scent slammed into him like a locomotive.

They were coming straight in his direction.

He went absolutely still. Hair rose along the back of his neck. He flexed his muscles and stood. "Leave," he growled. "They're coming."

But the hunters simply gawked. "What the hell is wrong with your voice?" one demanded.

"Run," Nicolas warned.

Too late. They entered the tiny glen, not bothering to cloak their numbers. Shuffling forward, they advanced, disguised as human beings. The enemy resembled young women, sullen teenagers, elderly people and businessmen in suits. But for their scent, they looked perfectly normal. The scent of rotting seaweed and raw sewage slammed into him. Damn. Hordes of them. Too many to fight alone. His mind strategized. Surprise remained his best defense. Magick would give him away. Silently he cursed, wishing for his daggers.

If he remained blended with the hunters, perhaps the enemy would not see him.

The human hunters turned, saw them. One tipped back his cap, scratched his forehead. "What the hell is this, a party?"

He pointed to a stooped gray-haired man wearing round glasses, leaning on a wood cane. "You lost, Gramps? Nursing home is that way. It's way past your bedtime."

The elderly one lifted his head. Smiled. Gleaming white teeth flashed. Crocodile teeth, sharp, pointed.

"Jesus," whispered the fat hunter. "What the hell is that?"

"Early Halloween party," his friend joked, his voice cracking. "Or cheap dentures?"

Nicolas smelled the men's fear. He knew his enemy smelled it, too. It stank like sour sweat.

"Enough," the elderly mage said softly. He signaled.

They advanced as one unit, like a column of army ants. One by one they shape-shifted, clothing vanishing from their human forms, fur erupting on their bodies. Their magick, dark and powerful, transformed them far easier than Nicolas's powers.

Silent as fog, eyes glowing like hot coals, they prowled forward on four legs. One blinked slowly. Night vision registered the eyes turning black as empty pits.

The eyes, always the eyes, told their true nature, no matter what their form.

Wolf in him rose up, thirsting for blood, action. Caught between revealing himself to outsiders, and needing wolf to attack, he hesitated. Instinct urged him to run, wait for better odds. Humans had caused this evil. Still, he felt a flickering compassion for the hunters. He scanned the approaching enemy for the weak link.

The humans' fear turned to terror. "Holy mother of God," the taller one screamed. "Wolves!"

They fired.

Gunfire crackled. Bullets fell before meeting their target. Jaws agape, the humans stared. Identical masks of fear tightened their faces. The pungent odor of helpless urine filled the air.

In that instant, the Morphs attacked.

Now. Daggers materialized in his hands as he sprang forward to engage them. Six Morphs jumped him. Razor-sharp teeth sank into his neck; claws swiped his legs and torso. Cloth shredded like thin paper. He grunted and swung out with the knives, stabbing their hearts. They died, screaming. He sliced, stabbed again, wincing as their acid blood splashed over him. Again. No use. Each time he struck one down, another materialized. Cloning themselves.

A damn animal army.

Warmth dribbled down his throat. Nicolas ignored the burning pain, struggled with his clothing to shift. The hell with the mortals. They were dead already.

As he tore off his clothing, they fell on him, shifting once more. Fur erupted on their bodies; claws grew, shifting yet again. He cursed their ability to change into any animal form. Enormous brown bears roared. Four slammed him against the tree trunk. Pinned, his arms and legs useless, Nicolas could not summon his magick.

"Good God Almighty," one hunter screamed.

Struggling in the Morphs' grip, Nicolas felt blood drain, bones ache.

The others turned to the human prey. Nicolas struggled harder, wanting to save the hunters' sorry asses. Knowing it was too late.

Jaws yawning open, saliva dripping from their yellowed fangs, the pack converged on the hapless men. Screams mingled with the sounds of tearing flesh. Blood splattered on the oaks, dripping viscous black. The hunters were all dead.

The Morphs shifted into their true shapes. Bent over, skin sagging on bone, more animal than human. Wisps of hair clung to fleshy scalps. Pointed, sharp teeth grinned. Their fetid stench filled the air. They whined, drew in deep breaths.

Absorbing their victims' terror and dying breaths, the Morphs fed on their energy. The Morphs holding him back loosened their grip on his arms. Taking advantage of their distraction, he broke free and shifted. Wolf greeted them, eager for the fight, desperate to carve his claws into them. Surprised, his captors drew back. He lashed out with razor-sharp canines, snarling. He downed one, as the others came for him silently.

There were too many. He had lost too much blood.

"Stop," an authoritative voice ordered. "Leave him be."

Blood trickled down his flanks, warm in the chilly air. Nicolas ignored the stinging pain and the burning in his side. He steadily regarded the Morphs' secret weapon. Confident. Arrogant. Jamie presented a greater threat than the Morphs themselves.

He snarled. Instantly the Morphs closed ranks

around Jamie. They'd die protecting the human who'd formed them into an army. The mortal whose blood manufactured disease and death.

He would not die as wolf. Nicolas shifted back into his human form to address the mortal. Because of Jamie, Damian was dying.

Naked, vulnerable, he refused to cower. "Jamie," he uttered. "Your time will come."

Low, amused laughter rippled through the air. Jamie pushed past the glowering bodyguards. "You can barely stand. We'll destroy your leader, Nicolas. We already have, thanks to your help."

Nicolas remained silent. Disobeying pack rules, he'd taught Jamie magick and she used it to join the Morphs and increase her powers. From her blood, they'd manufactured a disease that was killing his leader.

Another Morph shifted back into human form. Greasy brown hair, empty eyes, cruel twist to his mouth. Kane. The leader. Saliva dripped from Kane's parted lips. Talons grew from his fingernails.

Nicolas tensed as Kane approached.

"Nicolas," the Morph leader drawled. "Join us. You know you want to."

"I'll die first," he growled.

"I have powers you'll never have as a Draicon,

Nicolas. Join us and see." The Morph spread his long, thin arms. "I can take to the air as an eagle, swim the seas as a shark, race through the jungle as a jaguar. Can you do the same?"

Nicolas steeled his spine. "And you smell like the bottom of a garbage can. No thanks. I'd rather be a corpse. Then again, you are a corpse. No, something less pleasant." He added colorful verbiage comparing Kane to a natural bodily function.

But Kane only laughed. "Words can't hurt me. But you can. Do you dare?"

Nicolas remained silent, hands clenched into fists.

"Let's kill him," one Morph suggested.

"No," Kane countered. "Do not touch him. We need him alive for Margaret, if she is the true empath. He'll reawaken her powers when he seeks her to mate."

Dread clawed at Nicolas's chest. He had not feared them, even faced with death. He feared now for Maggie. "You'll never find her. I'll die fighting before you get your claws on her."

Kane flashed an obscene grin. "We already found her, Nicolas. We infected her dog with our new disease. And you can't stay away. The mating urge is claiming you even now. You can't fight your nature."

A mocking snort came from the Morph leader. Nicolas steeled himself against reaching out to strangle Kane. The Morph leader gave a thin, mocking smile.

"Leave the bodies. The law will blame the Draicon. Again." Kane laughed.

Clever twist. More ammunition to hunt wolves, destroy his dwindling pack. Pain racked him. Slumping against the oak tree familiar with his scent and Damian's, he watched the Morphs vanish into the forest. They would continue growing in power and strength, continuing their assaults. He couldn't stop them.

He needed Maggie. Margaret, the empath prophesied to become the force capable of eliminating the Morph leader. His destined mate, who didn't realize she was Draicon.

Dead leaves crunched beneath their feet. He waited until their stench no longer fouled his nostrils. On the wind, silent laughter followed his noiseless crawling out of the glen.

An hour later, his wounds healed, Nicolas hid beneath the recesses of an overhanging rock. He rested, staring at his beloved moon, listening to wind rustle the branches and stir the dead leaves. Hunger scraped his insides. Power he'd lost needed replenishing either by ingesting food, or sharing his body with a woman and absorbing the rich energy emitted during sex.

He needed to hunt. Too weak to change, he ignored the growling of his empty stomach. Must think of other matters. Focus. Softly, he began singing, in desperate hope of easing the agonizing hunger. It didn't work. He switched his thoughts to Maggie.

Sweet, lovely Maggie. His draicara, his destined mate. Naked in the shower when he'd sunk into her mind yesterday.

A wave of desire rocked him as he remembered. Slender figure, full, rounded breasts and that mouth…ah, made for kissing. Nicolas felt his body tighten, thinking of the delicious things her mouth could do. Those legs, slightly padded with muscle, curved, silky smooth. He'd felt the brisk, impersonal glide of her hand as she'd soaped one thigh, bubbles frothing and popping. In her indifferent eyes he'd seen the thatch of dark red curls hiding her cleft, and he'd gone wild.

Nicolas had howled with lust, driven by the fierce need to claim her. Running his hands over her silky flesh, cupping her breasts, watching the nipples harden and peak. Gently parting her female flesh, testing her readiness, feeling that wetness as he slid a finger into her tight sheath. Then spreading those silky thighs wide open, mounting her, her yielding body pressed beneath his hard one, sinking into her wet, waiting flesh…

Hunger abated, replaced by lust as he focused on Margaret. Seeping into her mind like water percolating into the ground.

New agony assailed him. He raised his nose. Wolf inside him silently whined. Lust vanished. Thousands of miles away, he felt her stabbing pain as if it sank into his own chest.

She was crying over the dog again.

Last week, after years of searching, he'd found Maggie by pure accident. He'd been baling hay on his ranch when a wave of grief suddenly slammed into him, sharp as the pitchfork tines. Nicolas had sunk to his knees and moaned.

When he recovered from the initial shock, he'd sorted out the thoughts invading his mind. And realized he'd found his mate. Under extreme duress, a female draicara sometimes subconsciously projected emotions onto her intended mate, as if to summon him to her side at last.

When he'd explored the mental trail she'd sent out, he realized who it was.

Margaret, the pack's missing empath.

Nicolas drew in a deep breath, struggling to maintain his identity even as he now sank fully into hers. Absorbing her, sinking into every cell. Her breath as his. Her heart thudding rapidly, increasing his heart rate.

Her emotions his own.

Sweat erupted on his brow. His inner wolf whimpered, anxious to calm the spreading agony, human emotions twining with raw animal pain. So alone, as if all the world were oblivious.

He didn't like feeling like this—open, vulnerable and exposed. Nicolas reminded himself it was Maggie, not him. Unlike his draicara, he could guard his emotions.

She perched over the sink, clasping it with whitened knuckles. Tension strained the heart-shaped face reflected in the wavy mirror. Her full, pouty mouth thinned with pain. Nicolas felt as if poison had seeped into his very bones.

Tears streamed down her cheeks.

Trying to hold them back—oh, she tried—so as not to upset the animal she carefully tended. But the grief, it washed over her in cresting waves. She hung her head over the sink and sobbed.

Nicolas struggled to hold back his own tears.

Finally she splashed cold water on her face, and dried it. Forced a wobbly smile on her face, and went out to tend to her patient. The little brown dog lifted her head.

Across the white tile floor of Maggie's kitchen, a small brown cockroach scurried, then went still. He tensed, for the roach might be a Morph in disguise come to kill her. But it did not show any signs of shifting. After a minute he relaxed. Just an ordinary insect.

Nicolas felt Maggie's natural disgust. He figured she'd scream, slam down the broom. Instead, he felt her stride over to the loathsome insect. She fumbled for a jar on the counter, trapped it, turned the jar over. Just as quickly, she released the roach outside. Through Maggie's eyes, Nicolas watched it crawl over the white beach sands.

His jaw went slack.

From its fluffy pillow, he heard the dog she'd named Misha bark weakly in protest. Damn straight, dog, Nicolas agreed. *I'd kill it, too.*

"You know the rules, Misha. Everything lives," Maggie said softly. "Even roaches. I swore never to hurt another living thing. Ever."

Damn. This was going to be far harder than he'd ever imagined. How the hell could he turn this woman into a cocked weapon ready to kill Morphs when she was rescuing bugs?

Nicolas drew in another deep breath, severed the connection so cleanly he could almost hear the snap. He dropped his head into the thick cushion of dead leaves and moss.

He didn't want to break away. Part of him wanted to remain. Comfort her. Enfold her in his strong embrace and never let go.

Those emotions were his own, he thought grimly. Dangerous emotions but natural. Every male Draicon was born with the instinct to protect his mate. Even though his particular mate had no idea of his existence or that of his people. Their people.

Minutes passed. Or was it hours? A familiar scent approached noiselessly. Moonlight gilded a pair of polished brown boots. Naked and vulnerable, he sat up to face his leader.

"You look like crap," Damian observed. The soft New Orleans drawl he'd acquired from a childhood in the bayou accented his words. "They came for you again because you were protecting us. Why do you insist on staying when you know you're banished?"

Nicolas made no reply. He knew Damian had

smelled the death, heard the screams. He had sensed what happened.

"Nicolas...one day one will kill you. If you stay," Damian said gently.

"I won't abandon you, Dai. You need me. The pack needs me." He grated out the words, locking gazes with the older male.

As Damian's beta, Nicolas was responsible for carrying out the leader's orders. He was the pack's best hunter. When the pack had been in danger of being eliminated by the Morphs, Nicolas had stepped in and taught them the best way to destroy the enemy. He had studied the Morphs' weak spots and succeeded in destroying hundreds. Nicolas, the killing machine.

He knew nothing else.

Pale green eyes observed him silently. Damian waved his hands. A covered metal plate materialized on the ground before Nicolas. Nicolas sprang forward as Damian winced.

"Dammit, you shouldn't be doing this. Not in your condition. Don't waste your energy."

His leader offered a rueful smile, dragged in a breath. Sweat glistened on his brow. With the flair of a gourmet chef, Damian whipped off the plate's cover.

"*Voila.* I knew you needed food. Or sex." The

pack leader regarded Nicolas with a level look. "But you know the rules."

No sex with pack females. Not for Nicolas, the banished. What irony. Damian often joked about Nicolas's "harem," the unmated, sexually experienced pack females eager to copulate with him. After a Morph fight, he'd pace before those presenting themselves to him. Dark eyes brooding, his muscular body tense and aggressive, he'd select one for the night. Then he'd claim her, using her sexual heat to restore his lost energy.

Now no pack female could touch him.

Salivating, Nicolas eyed the bloodied, raw meat. He shot a worried glance at Damian's pale face, the flash of pain in his green eyes.

"Wolf it down," Damian advised, a half smile touching his mouth at the old joke.

His hunger a live, writhing need, Nicolas hesitated. Trying to disguise his weakness before his leader, he couldn't hold back his howling need for energy. Damian delicately turned his back. Grateful, Nicolas abandoned any pretense. Picking up the elk steak with his hands, he ripped into the meat. Wiping his mouth with the back of his hand, he then replaced the cover. It clanged against the metal plate.

"Thank you," Nicolas managed to say.

Stronger now, he used his magick to cover his nudity with jeans, a black T-shirt and boots. Damian turned. He sat on his haunches, silent.

"Dai, you're getting worse." The matter-of-fact statement cloaked his concern.

"I have time." Damian's cocky grin seemed forced. "Two months, maybe, at the rate my body is deteriorating…." He shrugged, glancing away.

Two months and Damian would be dead? After the agony, the cancerlike disease racking his body with pain ate its way through his internal organs. Nicolas clenched his fists. Dammit. He had to find Maggie. Fast.

"Dai…" His throat closed with emotion. Nicolas clamped a lid on his feelings and arranged a blank look on his face.

Damian seemed to understand, for he waved a hand, dismissing the topic. Never one to complain, more concerned about the pack.

"Tell me about Margaret." The name slipped out in a soft slur. *Mah-gah-rhett.* "You made contact with her again. I can tell by your tears. Her emotions are yours, Nicolas. She was crying." His sharp green gaze focused on dried tears streaking Nicolas's cheeks.

Nicolas scrubbed his face with a clenched fist. "The dog is dying." Always the dog, as Maggie sought a logical solution to a problem caused by something not logical in the human world. Then, in private, the tears would flow, because she could not heal the animal she loved.

"Ah. Her pet. Difficult."

"A friend. Not a pet. She can't cure Misha. She's trying to find the mutation in the cells. The Morphs infected the dog."

Damian rubbed the back of his neck absently. "A test of Margaret's powers to draw her out. They've found her."

Nicolas drew in another breath, feeling his lungs expand with clean, pure air. The dog had been Maggie's constant companion for five years. Serving as canine nurse, she also helped her calm the animals she treated.

Now Misha was dying, succumbing to a new disease that baffled Maggie.

The very same disease eating away at Damian's insides.

He felt an ache reverberate down to his very soul, his spirit crying out to be with hers. He threw back his head, feeling the beast emerge, the wolf howling to be released, and allowed to run. To avoid the pain. Find a dark place and seek comfort.

He could not, just as he could not sever the tie between himself and Maggie.

"She's unaware of her true identity." Nicolas stated it as fact. "I discovered that much by mind-bonding with her. Something happened when her parents died, and she blocked out all prior memories. She thinks she's mortal, not Draicon. Convincing her will be difficult."

"You know your duty, Nicolas. You must mate with her soon and bring her home. Before the Morphs destroy her."

Damian stood, leaning his six-foot-tall body against a tree. Beneath the casual air lurked coiled tension, power. Ready to spring into action, if necessary. Their leader never released his guard. Or trusted easily, outside of his pack.

"I know. I know the risks." To him and to Maggie. "But if it means saving you…"

"Forget me." Damian made a slashing gesture. "It's too late. But if she can heal our people when the Morphs infect them, that's all that matters."

"I'll get her here in time," Nicolas said fiercely. "Don't doubt it. Trust me."

Emotion flared in Damian's eyes. "It's not good for you to face this alone. You need our people."

Nicolas lifted his head, regarding him calmly. "You know that's impossible. They blame me for what happened to Jamie. As they should. When I get Maggie, then I'll return. Until then..."

The casual lift of his shoulders hid his pain. For the good of the pack, Damian had banished him. Maggie was his way back to acceptance, back to the warmth and comfort of his family.

Maggie was much more. Maggie was the weapon destined to vanquish Kane. Her healing touch could cure the dying Damian.

"Do it," Damian said softly. "Make her yours." He watched Nicolas stand, and went to embrace him in the usual brotherly fashion, then pulled back.

"I can't touch you," he said thickly.

"I know," Nicolas agreed. His scent would mark Damian, whose word was law, but the pack would question. Whisper. Worry.

"May the moon spirit guide and protect you on your journey," his leader said in the formal blessing. "Stay safe, stay strong."

A thick lump rose in his throat. "Up yours," Nicolas said cheerfully, hiding his emotions.

Damian flashed another half grin. More pain knifed through Nicolas as he watched his friend slip into the woods, heading back home.

Home for him no longer.

He drew in another breath, began softly singing

to himself and trotted in the opposite direction. Maggie, Maggie. He needed to get to Florida.

Every day the danger of Maggie being exposed intensified. Visits to her veterinarian clinic resulted in calmer animals. Maggie had a special healing ability, like a horse whisperer. Only it wasn't her voice.

But her hands, her soothing touch.

Maggie was an empath, born once every 100 years. She was their last hope. She belonged with the pack, her family.

He'd mate with her, his hard male flesh sinking into her female softness, his warrior's aggression sinking into her gentleness. Male and female, exchanging powers, becoming one. He'd perform his duty, then mold her into the warrior they needed to fight their enemy. And bring her home, even if she fought and kicked and screamed the whole way.

She had no choice.

Just like him.

Chapter 2

Maggie Sinclair forced herself to concentrate as she stared into the microscope for what seemed like the thousandth time.

Still there. The ugly reality met her weary eyes. Blink, and the cells did not change. A physical impossibility, yet, she could not deny it. The cell samples were black, misshapen like oblong ink blotches.

She had no idea what was killing her beloved Misha. All the academic research proved useless.

X-rays had revealed a large mass in Misha's stomach. Blood samples showed cell mutation similar to cancer. Yet not cancer.

Maggie rubbed her reddened eyes, trying to contain the tears.

Misha had been her true companion for five

years. The long bouts of loneliness she'd felt vanished when she'd adopted the dog from a shelter. Misha had been an abused puppy, and came to her snarling and suspicious. Maggie won her trust and now the dog offered unconditional love and trust. Misha curled up on her lap after a tough day at the office, and licked her face. She was more than a pet. She was a friend.

Twenty-four hours without sleep didn't help. Last night Misha was restless. Maggie stayed up, stroking her whimpering pet. As with other animals she'd treated, her touch soothed.

She'd dozed off, then awakened to the feeling of someone pounding a rail spike into her body. The pain subsided then vanished. Always seemed to happen after a difficult case. Since real sleep proved impossible, Maggie resigned herself to downing a fresh pot of Blue Mountain, and went back to work.

Three weeks without answers. Three weeks of leaving her lucrative practice on the mainland to her partner, Mark Anderson, and holing up in the beach house on Estero Island like a sand hermit.

Three weeks of drawing blood, testing samples, consulting journals, articles, Internet Web sites. Nothing. Not a clue.

She didn't dare show her findings to colleagues. This was too weird. Too... Witchy.

I don't believe in witches. I don't. I don't. I don't.

She believed in science, pure and simple. Logic. Nothing else.

Late afternoon sunlight streamed into the improvised lab on the house's second floor. Papers, charts and notes littered a long white table, along with beakers, syringes, test tubes and slides. On the cool tile floor, Misha slept fitfully.

Maggie stared out the window. Sun-worshippers strolled at the gulf's edge. Coconut palms ringing her beachfront home rustled in the wind. The burning blue sky promised another balmy afternoon in southwest Florida.

Momentary envy filled her. Mindless of the air-conditioning, she slid open the window to inhale the brine. She longed to be as insouciant as the tourists, nothing more to worry about than ruining their Birkenstocks in the saltwater.

She couldn't be insouciant. Whatever was killing Misha could kill other animals, maybe even humans. Maggie suspected she had discovered a new, dreadful disease. She couldn't risk it spreading to others, or turning Misha over to become a lab experiment by others. So she had quarantined her pet in the beach house, determined to find answers for herself.

Enough daydreaming. Back to work.

She removed the slide from the microscope. Maggie took a drop of blood obtained from a healthy shih tzu at her practice. Using a Beral pipette, she added the blood to a fresh slide containing Misha's infected cells. Maggie covered the slide, placed it under the microscope.

Maggie fumbled for a tape recorder, clicked the record button as she bent over to peer into the microscope again.

"The tumor lies in the submucosa, infiltrating the lamina propria. Cellular morphology not characteristic of known tumors. The nuclei are indistinguishable. No nestlike appearance as in the fibrovascular stroma."

A clatter sounded as Maggie dropped the instrument onto the scarred tabletop. The tape whirled, silently continuing to record her next words.

"Oh my God!"

Misha lifted her head, whined at the loud outburst. Maggie stepped back. Rubbed her eyes again. Oh God. It couldn't be…surely she was exhausted, seeing things.

Dread surfaced as she forced herself to examine the clump of cells. Bracing her hands on the table, she studied the sample.

Blackened cells that had been separate, like individual drops of ink, bonded together as if pulled by invisible magnets. They surrounded the single drop of healthy blood, corralling it. Then absorbed it, sucking it into their mass. And grew.

They spread, forming a giant singular cell. As her shocked gaze watched, the singular cell divided. And again.

Cloning itself.

Cells taken from Misha's stomach tumor were growing exponentially and forming a new organism. Growing, spreading to the edges of the slide.

It couldn't be. Not happening. Somatic cells, even those mutated by cancer, couldn't do this. Yet here it was, dividing and multiplying and growing to form…living tissue.

With a cry of disgust, she grabbed the slide, dropped it into a beaker of alcohol. Maggie stared, watching the now clearly demarcated black mass sink down into the liquid.

A sharp buzz made her cry out in alarm. *Get a grip, Mags.* Maggie sucked down a trembling breath. She covered the beaker with a towel and pasted on a shaky smile. Her sneakers thumped on the staircase as she headed for the door.

It had better not be Mark. He had agreed to take over the whole caseload while she begged off six week's leave. But he'd phoned, whining about the work piling up.

Mark must never know how ill Misha was or he would insist on taking her pet and quarantining Misha at the office. She had to find answers herself. Misha would not be turned into a living experiment, poked and prodded by fascinated colleagues.

Maggie looked out the door's scope. A blond little girl in a pink shorts set clutched the handle of a small red wagon. The wagon held a steel cage containing a rabbit.

Tammy Whittaker, seven, from next door. Tammy's mother was a fussy, carefully groomed woman who insisted on calling Maggie "Miss Sinclair" instead of "Doctor." Vets weren't real doctors, she had said, sniffing that she couldn't understand why anyone with a medical inclination would choose to treat filthy animals.

Dropping the curtain, Maggie felt a flutter of alarm. She only wanted to be left alone to muse over this latest frightening find.

The trilling buzz sounded again. With a sigh, she opened the door. Tammy Whittaker looked up at Maggie. Hope flickered in her huge brown eyes. "Hi, Dr. Sinclair. This is Herman, my rabbit."

"Honey, I'm awfully busy...."

Tammy's face screwed up. Her mouth wobbled precariously. "Herman's hurt. Please, Dr. Sinclair, can you fix him? I have ten dollars I saved from my allowance. My mother says she won't waste money on a stupid rabbit."

The little girl's woeful expression twisted Maggie's heart. She went outside and picked up the cage containing the chocolate-colored rabbit.

"Come on, Tammy. Let's see what's wrong with Herman."

Inside the spacious living room, Maggie set down the cage. She removed the large French lop from the cage and set him on the tiled floor. Herman weakly hopped. His back left leg flopped. Broken, probably.

A terrible suspicion crested over Maggie. "Tammy, how did this happen?"

Her gaze flicked away. "I forget to lock the door sometimes. He got out. Mom said he got his leg caught."

Maggie gnawed at her lower lip. Outside of her own dog, she hadn't examined an animal in over two months. Doing so caused odd images to flash through her mind, as if she could envision the source of the animal's injury. Feel its past and pain.

Just an overactive imagination. It was only her great desire to heal, causing her to envision the injury's source.

Yet the fledgling ability had grown stronger over the past six months. Maggie had solved the problem by leaving the initial exams to Mark, in exchange for doing the clinic's paperwork.

"I thought your mother didn't like animals."

Sniffling, Tammy explained her friend Bobby had given her Herman when his family moved away. "It was either me or Sally. Sally has a big yard with a fence, but she's got a hamster. Mom didn't want him, but Dad said I could keep him if Herman stayed in the cage. Please, can you make him better? He's hurting."

Maggie gently stroked the quivering rabbit. Images poured through her mind like movie screen captions: Fear. Pain. Cage door open. Freedom. Good smells. Food nearby. White grass. Urge to void. Tall human. Screams. Pointed shoe. Hurt. Fear. Hide.

Tammy's mother had kicked it in a rage for the droppings on her immaculate white wool rug.

Biting back a startled cry, she jerked her hand away. Maggie turned, hiding her reaction from Tammy.

"Is Herman going to be okay?" Tammy asked.

"He'll be fine. I need to get the medicine to fix him."

Maggie pushed a weary hand through her hair as she went upstairs to her office. She headed for a locked white cabinet and combed through it for the necessary supplies.

The odd ability to envision the source of an animal's pain hadn't vanished. It was growing stronger.

No. She hadn't felt the animal's pain, nor seen what happened. Besides, Iona Whittaker was fastidious, but cruel...? Ridiculous. Herman probably broke his leg...

Falling down the stairs, a deep male voice asked.

Maggie gasped, nearly dropping a box of bandages. First hallucinations, now voices? Definitely, too little sleep.

Science, not speculation. Cell mitosis. She formed images of cells, dividing, new life growing. Her mind processed the information at hand. Rabbit, broken foot caused probably by angry woman with a ruined carpet. Yes, Iona Whittaker could be cruel. People were.

Businesslike, she stacked emergency medical supplies on a tray. Splint, bandages, tape, medicine, syringe, needle, medication, prescription pad.

Downstairs, she injected Herman with a mild sedative, asked Tammy questions about school to divert the girl's worries. Very gently, she bound the rabbit's broken leg. Maggie settled Herman back into his cage. She inhaled the scent of fresh cedar shavings and gave the bunny a reassuring pat.

"Such a pretty chocolate color," Maggie murmured.

Tammy brightened. "Herman's like an Easter bunny."

Easter bunny. Delicious, biting into a chocolate bunny.

Rabbit. Fresh. Tasty. Raw, bloodied meat. Dinner. Energy.

Shocked, she analyzed her thoughts. Where did that come from? One minute, daydreaming about a sugar rush, the next, salivating over meat.

"I'll give you some pills." She scribbled instructions on the pad. Herman. Injured rabbit. Sweet little rabbit.

Prey. Thrill of the kill, snapping bones, sinking fangs into fresh, delicious meat…

Maggie shoved aside the hungry thoughts. Giving Tammy instructions on how to administer the medication, she smiled.

"Herman has been well cared for. He has good muscle tone," she noted, trying not to think of meat. Good meat, not tough, just right. Laced with tasty fat…

Maggie hastily stood, grabbed the cage. Sweat beaded on her brow. *I'm going insane. First feeling images and pain, then hearing voices, and now, thinking of pet rabbits as dinner?*

At the door, Maggie gently pushed aside Tammy's offering of crumbled dollar bills. "Instead of paying me, I need a favor. Herman looks a little cramped in his cage. I bet he'd love a nice, big yard. Why don't you give him to Sally? You can visit him, and it will make your mother happy." *And keep that bitch from hurting him again.*

Tammy's lips curled up, then she glanced down at Herman. "All right, Dr. Sinclair. I guess it's only fair to share him."

"Yes, it is."

Placing the cage on her little red wagon, Tammy turned. Her brow wrinkled. "Are you okay, Dr. Sinclair? You look funny."

I bet. "I'm fine. Go home, call Sally."

Maggie waved, closed the door then fled up-stairs to grab sleep before she imagined anything else.

She fell asleep upstairs on her king-sized bed, dreaming of warm breath against the nape of her neck, hard muscles holding her fast.

White teeth erotically scraping her flesh, fol-lowed by a long, slow lick. Wetness pooled be-tween her legs. She stirred. Maggie moaned as two large hands, dark hair dusting the backs, slid over her trembling thighs. Sliding them open. Dark eyes staring at wet female flesh.

You want my tongue. There.

Her vagina clenched, aching. Empty. Needing. Hot. *Please.*

What do you want?

You. Inside me. Please. Fill me. Forever.

I'll give you everything you want. And more. My Maggie.

She jerked awake with a start, clutching the sheet. Sweat dampened her lace panties, the ribbed lilac sleep shirt. He had been inside her, again. Her dream lover.

His presence lingered, like the slow stroke of a man's hand upon a woman's naked skin. Tender as a lover's caress, edged with desire. Demanding. Hot. Broad shoulders, hard muscles, crisp stubble abrading the soft skin of her throat as he kissed his way down her body.

Maggie stood on wobbly legs. She ran a hand through her curls. Two hours' sleep gave no rest. She'd been tormented with edgy, erotic dreams, leaving her restless and yearning.

Late afternoon sun streamed through the sliding glass windows as she went downstairs. Maggie headed for the adjoining kitchen. Misha lay on the cool tile. With a false smile and a cheeriness she did not feel, she stooped down to pet her dog.

"Hey there, Misha, babe. Feel like eating a little dinner?"

A brown tail thumped madly against the floor. Hope rose, fed by desperation. From the fridge, Maggie fished out chicken livers. She cooked them over the electric range, chattering the whole time, filling empty space with words the dog did not understand, but were soothing.

Maggie set the dish on the floor. Misha sniffed, licked a piece. Hope rose. It sank as Misha walked away.

No appetite. Maggie, acquainted with the dying process, could not deny what her heart, and her mind, knew. Misha looked at her with mournful brown eyes as if to apologize. Maggie shoved the liver into the fridge.

She patted her friend's head. "It's okay, baby, I never did like liver, either. Yuck."

The long brown tail thumped weakly against the tile. Misha reached up, licked her face.

Fighting tears, Maggie washed the few dishes in the sink. Routine dulled the raw pain in her chest, allowed her to pretend everything was normal.

The sun began setting, turning the brilliant blue sky to flame-red and orange. Maggie pulled open the large glass slider. Warm currents of air drifted inside, scented with brine. She stared at the expanse of white sugary sand stretching before her, the blue gulf beyond.

Laughter rippled from the Tiki Bar down the beach. Tourists and natives gathered there for traditional sunset drinks, and to watch the spectacular vista of sunset sinking into the water. Maggie disliked crowds and socializing, preferring to remain alone. Besides, she couldn't afford to waste Misha's remaining time.

Being alone didn't bother her these past weeks. She needed privacy. Yet lately, when the night stole over the sky, and the moon rose high, she itched. To run wild and free.

She stared out onto the sugar sands in utter desolation. A raging restlessness seized her. This time of night seemed hers, the darkness falling, the wind blowing.

Palm tree fronds rustled in secret communication with each other. Raucous laughter from the Tiki Bar drifted over the sands. It sounded like fun. *I'm so damn alone.*

You are not alone.

Maggie whipped her head around. Wind tossed her hair as she searched into the gathering twilight. Nothing but wind and distant laughter. But someone was here.

"Get a grip, Mags," she whispered. Too much time alone, then the erotic dream, stirred her imagination.

But she could *smell* him? Pine, earth, a woodsy pleasing scent tugged her in a nostalgic way.

I'm here, the same, deep voice assured in her mind. Quiet, nonthreatening. Maggie wrapped her arms about herself. *Maybe I'm insane.*

Only those of us craving absolute power turn, losing their minds, what's left of their souls.

A subtle note of warning threaded through it. She shivered.

Do you smell that? Be careful.

This was too weird. Maggie went to cut off her

imaginary friend by thinking of cell mitosis. She stopped. The heels of the wind brought a faint but foul odor.

Like rotting seaweed at low tide mixed with raw sewage. Except this stench carried nothing natural about it. Maggie fingered the chunky turquoise bracelet on her wrist. Grappling with control, she decided to indulge this voice, a fragment left over from her dream. A strong male presence, wanting to protect her.

You're wearing turquoise. Good.

Turquoise fends off evil seaweed?

No. But it fends off an evil werewolf. For a while.

Maybe I should wear silver as well. Fend off rotting seaweed and werewolves.

Silver? That doesn't stop them. I've tried.

Fear spilled through her like ice water. Tiny hairs on the nape of her neck saluted the air.

You've nothing to fear. I'm here now. But don't remove the bracelet.

The quiet, masculine voice settled her raging nerves. Maggie rubbed her arms, reasoning this internal monologue was a stress reliever.

Superman saves the day. And turquoise is the kryptonite to fend off the Big Bad...

Wolf.

Ridiculous. Wolves in Florida? Only in bars. Her imagination was running amok, result of being alone too long.

She needed company. The pull of human laughter from the Tiki Bar tugged at her like a siren song. Maggie glanced at the dog lying drowsily on the tile. "I'm going out for a bit, Misha. Just a drink and sunset. Stay here and guard the house. And if any burglars break in, try not to lick them to death, deal?"

The dog raised her brown head, then slumped back to the tile. A lump clogged Maggie's throat. She locked the sliders, went to the bathroom and brushed her hair. Dark purple shadows lined deep hollows beneath her eyes. She thought about cosmetics, decided she wasn't getting married today. Giving a cursory glance at the turquoise bracelet, she sniffed.

No more imaginary voices. Unhooking the clasp, she let it fall to the counter with a clatter. For a moment, a heavy sigh echoed in her mind.

Ridiculous.

After changing into white linen shorts, a turquoise sleeveless blouse and Birkenstocks, she set off down the beach.

Sand sank into her toes. Maggie slipped out of her sandals, wriggled her toes with delight. Sandals swinging from one hand, she ambled toward the trilling laughter and clinking glasses.

Minutes later, she stood before the thatched hut bar. Buxom women in tight shorts and tighter T-shirts clustered about the bar like bees around a honeycomb. Younger men in wild tropical prints and khaki shorts buzzed around them. Some grizzled salty types downed beer and roared at off-color jokes. She recognized only one person. John, a client, was engaged in serious conversation with a taller man.

Doubts assailed her. What was she doing here? She didn't drink. But something propelled her forward. Reasoning too many solitary days and nights isolated in her grief caused this yearning, she opted for the company. Maggie shouldered her resolve, slipped into her sandals again and approached.

The bar was elbow to elbow, people sitting on the wood benches, smoking, talking, laughing. Maggie sauntered to the counter with more confidence than she felt. Had she been so alone all this time she'd forgotten how to order a drink?

Then he caught her eye. Maggie's heart hammered out an erratic beat. She stared.

A black T-shirt stretched taut over broad, muscled shoulders. Faded denim jeans hugged lean hips, molded to muscular thighs the size of tree trunks. Dark bristles shadowed his taut jawline. He had arresting features, a strong nose, firm, sensual mouth and silky black brows. A hank of inky hair hung over his forehead, spilled down past his collar. But his eyes, oh, they commanded her attention. Expressive and dark brown, they were soulful and deep. They observed the bar scene a little sadly, and he held himself aloof.

As if he, too, did not truly belong here.

Biceps bulged as he lifted his beer and drank. Fascinated, she watched his throat muscles work. He wiped his mouth with the back of one hand.

His gaze swung around, captured hers. For a moment Maggie forgot to breathe. Her hand fled to her throat. Arousal, sharp and deep, flooded her. A deep throb began between her legs.

You're pathetic. Getting all hot and bothered over a stranger at a bar.

Maggie jerked her gaze away, shouldered her way to the bar. Trying to squish between the bodies crowding the bar, she barely managed to push through. Why the hell was she here, anyway? Ready to flee for the safety of home and hearth, she started to turn when a deep male voice interjected.

"Room here."

Tall, dark and gorgeous gestured to the empty seat beside him. She hesitated.

"Grab it before it, or the sunset, is gone."

His mouth, chiseled and full, quirked in a charming half smile. Maggie mustered a smile and joined him. What the hell. She needed this.

"Drink?" he asked. His voice was deep, smooth, the burn of whiskey sliding down a parched throat.

She didn't like strangers buying drinks for her. The man arched a silky black brow. "You buy. I get the bartender's attention. Deal?"

Fair enough. "Pinot noir."

"Good choice," he murmured. The stranger signaled. A bartender floated over as if jerked by invisible strings and a minute later, a rounded glass of ruby liquid sat before Maggie.

The stranger lifted his glass. "Here's to the beauty of nature," he murmured.

They clinked, drank. Maggie savored the rich taste on her tongue. Awkwardness came over her. So long since she'd conversed with a total stranger other than clients. And such a gorgeous one. She struggled for conversational openers. Cell mitosis wouldn't do.

"I usually don't like crowds of strangers, but the scenery in my room was boring. How many times can you watch hurricane storm stories on the Weather Channel without wanting to drown yourself in the bathtub?" the man said.

Maggie gave a reluctant smile. "I tried drowning myself in the bathtub once after watching one, but I had just returned from the hairdresser and had a good hair day for once."

He laughed. "Here's to good hair days."

Maggie clinked glasses. She took another brief swallow. *Here we go again, what do you do, do you come here often...*

"Baths are overrated. Too much water, unless you share."

Maggie stole another glance at his firm chin and the delicious sprinkling of stubble. His mouth was full and sensual. Most striking were the eyes, dark brown with swirls of caramel. Enticing. Hypnotic.

He tipped his glass toward her. "Nicolas Keenan, here by way of New Mexico."

Maggie smiled. "Maggie Sinclair, here by way of the beach."

She stuck out a palm to shake. Businesslike, how's it going? But he picked up her hand instead. His palm was warm, a little calloused and swallowed hers.

Electricity shot through her, pure current that

sizzled. Never had she felt such deep, primitive emotion. Dark eyes met hers as Nicolas brought her hand to his mouth.

He brushed his lips against her knuckles. A brief, but intoxicating kiss. Maggie fought a wave of sudden lust. Her body tingled pleasantly. He let her hand rest in his, then released it. Wordlessly, she sipped more wine. For a long minute, she felt as if they were alone, two strangers sharing space and more.

"Are you here vacationing?"

Nicolas gave a slow smile. "Out to see a friend. She doesn't know I'm coming." White teeth flashed. "It's a surprise."

Lucky girl, Maggie thought with an odd pang of jealousy. "Just a friend?"

His steady gaze burned into hers. "And we will be more than friends before the night ends. I'm a very determined man."

"Do you always get what you want?"

"Always," he hinted softly.

Maggie wished someone would want her. She pushed back at her unruly curls. "I'm usually persistent at what I want, but some things are beyond my control." She lifted her shoulders in a careless shrug. "But that's life."

"Sometimes what we think is beyond our control isn't. We just need a little help," he observed.

She had the oddest feeling they'd met before. Kismet. Maggie sipped more wine. "Lovely sunset."

Nicolas nodded. "There is such power and energy on this earth. Only now are most people beginning to understand their world, and live in harmony with the elements."

"You sound like one of those snotty hybrid drivers who has solar panels and cooks with his own methane emissions."

Horrified, Maggie bit her lip. But Nicolas laughed. "I drive a truck," he countered, warm brown eyes twinkling. "I have a ranch in northern New Mexico and hybrids can't carry bales of hay. I do have solar panels on the roof, only because I hate paying for electricity. And I never fart. Ever."

He winked. Maggie laughed her first real laugh in weeks.

"But I do host lovely candlelight dinners…when I meet a special lady."

Tension eased, replaced with something more intense and far more sexual. Wine made her bold. "I bet you even seduce by candlelight. To save power and be romantic at the same time."

"Not all women. But there's one special one I would definitely seduce by candlelight," he said softly.

Daringly, she set her wineglass down, met his smoldering gaze. "And how would you do it? Seduce her? What if she didn't want to be seduced?" she challenged.

"It wouldn't matter. Because when I set my eye on something I want, I can be quite ruthless. I would pursue her endlessly, until she surrendered to me."

She saw in the swirling depths of his dark eyes his determination—the relentless energy of the hunter pursuing what he wanted. A little shiver snaked down her spine.

"And once you caught her? Why should she surrender?"

"I would tell her she's the only woman in the world for me, someone special sent just for me. That I would die unless I made love to her, and how perfect she is, how absolutely lovely. I would coax a smile to her sad face, kiss away her fears and whisper to her that there was nothing to fear. I would take very, very good care of her," he murmured.

This man, he sounded so familiar. Must be her alcohol-doused brain. Maggie moistened her mouth, tossed her hair. Flirting couldn't hurt. When was the last time she'd flirted?

"How good?" Maggie challenged. "Because you'd have to be good. Very, very good."

He leaned closer, until she could count the black bristles shadowing his jaw. His smoke-and-whiskey voice dropped to a husky murmur. "Trust me. I would be good. Very, very good."

Heat coursed through her. Maggie sank into his liquid gaze, the dark vortex pulling her down. He looked at her as if she were that woman, and he wanted to love her all over until she sobbed for mercy.

She drained her wine, focused on the crimson-gold sun swallowed by the horizon. "It's so beautiful. So right. I love this time of night. Dusk."

"The edge of night filled with promise." His hooded eyes regarded her. "There's one sight in nature I find more stirring than a spectacular sunset."

"That is?"

"A full moon."

She nodded. "Yes, a full moon can be quite inspiring, can't it?"

A soft laugh rumbled from his deep chest. "Yes," he said, gazing at her intently. "Indeed, it can be quite...inspiring."

Chapter 3

Her delectable aroma drove Nicolas mindless.

Primitive lust coursed through him. Her scent hovered on his tongue. Female, musky, aroused. Exciting. Nicolas picked up the brown bottle of beer, took a long swig. The icy liquid slid down his throat but did not cool.

Liquor would not quench his thirst. Only Maggie would now. Sweet, delicious Maggie, the taste of her flooding his senses.

He'd heard of the driving relentlessness of the mating urge when werewolves found their draicara. "When you find her, watch out. Catching her scent turns you totally animal. You forget everything. You just want to rip her clothes off and mount her," one of the newly mated pack males had said.

Nicolas had always scoffed at such mindless

loss of control. As the pack's fiercest warrior, he prided himself on his restraint. All those times he'd bedded scores of women after a hunt, releasing savage energy built from fighting Morphs, he'd never lost control.

Now he knew the other male hadn't exaggerated. He'd expected his draicara to be attractive. The chemistry strong, but not this explosive. Not as if the entire world had faded, and the sun's last rays shone exclusively on her.

A nimbus of silky dark red curls framed her heart-shaped face, pert nose and soft, rosy cheeks. Her large, expressive eyes werc the blue of a quiet lake. Her mouth, ah, her mouth! Full, soft and inviting.

Maggie stole a glance at him. Smiled. She tossed her head and moistened her lips. Desire darkened her eyes.

Oh, yes. She was feeling it, too.

Nicolas's body tightened pleasantly as he imagined the things he could teach her to do with that lovely mouth.

Shorter than he'd envisioned, Maggie barely cleared his chin. Her figure was a bit too thin, her cheeks slightly hollow. He'd fatten her up, personally hunt her fresh game. His gaze flicked to her full breasts. He imagined cupping them in his eager palms, testing their heavy weight. Enjoying her little moans of excitement as he gently stroked his thumbs over the pearling nipples. Then bending his head to taste, he'd swirl his tongue over one. Oh, yes.

Maggie frowned. Two lines, facial punctuation marks, formed between her silky dark brows. Nicolas was utterly charmed.

"Be right back," his sexual fantasy murmured.

She sprang off the bench, nearly spilling her wine. Drunk with lust, he eyed the white linen shorts hugging the tempting halves of her rounded bottom. His hands itched to squeeze. He imagined feeling the smooth skin of her plump ass caressing him as he mounted her from behind and drove into her in the traditional mating position.

Not the first time. Werewolf sex could be quite rough, too intense and passionate for her first time. Threading through Maggie's female arousal was the distinct impression of innocence. Sexy, yes. Enticing. Oh, yeah. But experienced. No way. He'd bet a raw steak on her being a virgin.

He imagined gently initiating her in making love. Slow, sensual caresses. Perhaps a hot oil massage, his fingers sliding over her silky skin, caressing and stroking, delving into her secret hollows and making her writhe and plead. Slow for her first time, with lots of orgasms to compensate for taking her virginity. Then finally, igniting her passion and tangling together with her in hot, raw animal sex. He grew hard as granite, thinking about it.

Blood thrummed hotly in his veins. Nicolas hungrily watched Maggie walk toward two men.

What the hell?

Fists clenched, they fumed at each other. One, bristling sharp as the spikes on his crew cut, boasted muscles worthy of a veteran WWE wrestler. The other was leaner, but tall and wiry. They looked ready for a fight.

They *were* going to fight!

He swiveled, realized the crowd had quieted. They stared at the men, expecting action. He focused on the scowling men. And Maggie, his Maggie, was hurrying up as one drew back his fist.

Nicolas leapt off the bench. He bolted toward them, muscles tensed as he prepared to defend his draicara.

Maggie stepped between the pair snarling like angry dogs. She placed a hand on each man's arm. Her honey-smooth voice rippled in soothing tones. "Stop it. John, you don't want to hurt this man. Whatever it is, you can work through it without hitting each other. You don't want to hurt each other. Listen to me. You're here for a good time. Calm down. It's all right."

Serenity radiated from her. Maggie's aura of peace extinguished the tension between the hot-tempered men like a bucket of ice water on a campfire. The two looked at each other, tension fading from their bodies. This is silly, their expressions said. Why are we doing this?

Nicolas ground to a halt between the pair. They backed off. "Lay a hand on her and I'll tear you apart," he growled.

Not giving them a chance to think it over, he wrapped his fingers firmly about Maggie's wrist and tugged her back to their seats. Admiration for her courage and spunk filled him. Deep inside she possessed the qualities to battle the Morphs. Nicolas bit back frustration. First though, he must teach her to make war, not peace.

Better yet, make love. Then make war.

"What are you doing?" she protested.

"Saving your sweet little ass."

He herded her back to the bar, barked an order for another pinot noir to the bartender. Nothing for him. He couldn't risk another sip. Not if he had to stand ready and protect her from breaking up fights where she could get hurt.

Defiance snapped in her sea-blue eyes as they resumed their seats. The bartender set the wine down.

Nicolas pinned her with a censured look. "What the hell were you doing? They outweigh you by a hundred pounds."

Maggie lifted her stubborn little chin. "I don't like violence. John has already been jailed for getting into one fight. And what right do you have to interfere?"

"Same right you do." Only more, he thought grimly. No way in hell would he allow her to endanger herself needlessly. "I had no desire to see you take a punch in the face."

Her expression softened. "And I had no desire to see them fight. Fistfights serve no purpose."

"They serve a great purpose when the fist is headed at your face. A man has to do what he must to protect his own."

Her lovely mouth wobbled. "Sometimes a man is better off turning and walking away than risking violence. Men can die from a fight."

"And there are those who seek nothing but a fight. You don't turn and walk away from them. Because they'll hunt you down and rip you into pieces while you're singing the praises of peace and harmony. What would you do then, Maggie?"

Her gaze grew distant. "I'd try to negotiate. Beg for my life, if necessary. And escape. Run." Her voice dropped. "Anything...but fight."

"There is no compromise. No negotiation. Run and they'll run faster after you. Plead and they'll ignore you. You must kill. Or be killed. Rules of the jungle, Maggie."

"This isn't a jungle."

"Everywhere is a jungle. The covering is just different." Nicolas braced his hands on the bar, scanning the crowd. The rose-gold sun had sunk into the gulf. Dark shadows spread over the sand. On the beach, the men playing volleyball laughed as they ceased the game.

Nicolas studied Maggie. Instinct urged him to see inside. Get an idea of her emotions. No. No invasion.

Her hand shook as she picked up the wineglass. Ruby liquid sloshed over the rim. Droplets splattered on the laminated counter, quivered, dark as blood. Nicolas fought a rising premonition. He gently touched her wrist, marveling at the heat sizzling between them.

"Are you okay, Maggie?"

Expression distant, guarded, she gulped down

the wine. Nicolas kept quiet. Finally, she took a deep breath. Her voice cracked.

"I shouldn't have...have come here. I knew this was a mistake. I just wanted...a little diversion. Some company. I've been working so hard."

He didn't invade her thoughts. Nicolas read her expression instead. It said she wanted to retreat to the safety of her four walls, where she didn't have to encounter fistfights.

"What kind of work do you do?" He kept his tone casual. Inside, he ached at her wild look, like a cornered animal.

Enthusiasm chased away dark shadows from her eyes. She began talking about her practice as a veterinarian. Nicolas fired one question after another. Kept her talking, distracted her from leaving. He learned she'd been raised by a parade of indifferent foster parents after her mother and father died when she was twelve. Only after she turned fourteen did she finally have affectionate foster parents. Her foster father was a physician and encouraged Maggie's studies.

"I skipped grades and graduated high school at sixteen and went to college. My foster father wanted me to major in premed and I was desperate to please him because he had been so good to me. It was almost...like having a real father."

Her tiny sigh pierced him like a dart.

"I thought they both loved me as if I were their real child, until my second year of school when I knew I wanted to become a veterinarian. My foster father threatened to stop paying my tuition if I changed majors. Animal doctors weren't as skilled as real doctors."

Maggie's gaze dropped to the counter. "I couldn't force myself to comply with his wishes so they cut off all contact with me. It was challenging, but I had a few scholarships and worked through school as a phlebotomist."

Nicolas steeled himself against the rising urge to take her hand and give it a comforting squeeze. "Your foster father was wrong. It takes a special skill, and empathy to treat animals. Animals don't talk, and can't communicate with words as to what's wrong." He gave a wry smile. "But in many ways, they're easier to be around than people."

A little laugh escaped her. "You think so, too? I had to force myself out to come here. Sometimes I don't want to be around people, especially men. They can be such wolves."

Nicolas raised a questioning brow.

"Not you. You don't have that wolfish demeanor. I like you. No one else would have cared if one of those men hit me. And you're very cute," she blurted out.

A radiant flush tinted her cheeks. Nicolas was utterly enchanted.

"I've studied wolves, you know," she confessed.

He raised a dark brow. "Oh?"

"As an undergrad. My major was zoology. I spent a summer out West working with a conservation program relocating wolves. It was fascinating watching them work as a pack. Real teamwork. Did you know that, in a pack, the beta wolf is responsible for ensuring the alpha male's orders are carried out?"

"I've heard something about that," he murmured.

She cocked her head, looking adorable. "I'm babbling. It's the wine. I shouldn't have had that second glass."

Pulling out a wad of bills from her pocket, she tossed them down on the bar. Maggie stood on wobbly legs, swaying like a palm tree in a head wind. Nicolas stood, laid a hand on her shoulder.

"I'll take you home."

Auburn curls flew as she shook her head. "I'll be fine. It's just a short stagger down the beach."

"Then I'll stagger with you." He took her

elbow, steadying her as she slogged through the soft sand.

"Besides, I have to keep you safe from the Big Bad Wolf." Nicolas winked. Maggie laughed. It was a gurgling laugh that reminded him of crystalline streams tumbling over rocks.

Wind combed through her hair. Darkness thickened, draping the beach in ebony. Yellowish light from beachfront homes and towering condominium buildings cast oblong pools on the sand. Above them, a canopy of stars glittered like tiny jewels. A sailboat, blue light bobbing atop its mast, drifted as it headed south for the inlet.

He guided her around an abandoned beach bucket threatening to trip her. Had Maggie ignored her night vision, or did the fact she never experienced the change dim her wolf senses?

Sand kicked up in little eddies as they walked. They wended through a small stand of palms. Maggie paused before a tidy, two-story whitewashed house. "Thank you for seeing me home."

She leaned against a swaybacked palm trunk, lacing her hands behind her. Clearly in no hurry to say goodbye, leaving him standing in the dark. His night vision showed interest flaring in her deep blue eyes.

She didn't want to end the evening. Neither did he.

"Been my pleasure, Dr. Maggie." He sketched a courtly bow. Straightening, he winked. She laughed again, stopped, searching his face.

"It's odd but I feel like we've met before tonight."

"Perhaps we're destined to be together," he said softly, watching her.

Nicolas placed a hand on the trunk, above her head. Leaned just a little closer. Close enough to drink in her delicious aroma. Spice. Something fresh, floral like wildflowers. And the gut-clenching scent of female arousal.

That adorable frown line dented her brow. "You said you came here to visit a friend, and that she'd be more than a friend before the night ends."

"I did," he said softly. Nicolas brushed away a lock of silky hair from her cheek. "It's you, Maggie. I came here to seduce you."

She drew in a deep breath, blue eyes darkening. "You're very charming. Are you like this with all woman?"

"Just you. Only you, Maggie." He cupped her chin, tilted her head up to meet his penetrating gaze. "You're the only one for me."

Her lush mouth parted. "It's odd. I truly do feel like we know each other. As if it's meant to be. Do you believe in destiny? One person, your missing half, destined to be with you? But what are the chances of it happening?"

"I do. You know what they say. You have to kiss a lot of wolves to find Mr. Right," he murmured.

"I thought it was kiss a lot of frogs?"

He shot her a cocky grin. "Would you rather kiss a frog?"

"No," she said, a little breathlessly. Nicolas watched the pulse beat at the base of her throat. Fast. Faster. "I'd rather…kiss you."

Against the coconut tree's rough bark, he braced his hands on either side of her, pressing her against the tree. "What do you want, Maggie? This?"

He lowered his head, and his mouth claimed hers.

It felt electric, hot, as if all his nerve endings centered on the contact between their lips. He savored the tangy taste of wine and her innocence. Her mouth was pliant, soft and silky beneath his. Nicolas cupped the back of her head, deepened the kiss. His tongue plunged into her parted mouth, thrust, imitating the sex act. She hesitated, reached out in turn, flicking her tongue over his.

He drank in her essence, her spice, tasting her life, all her hopes, dreams.

Passions.

Nicolas felt himself flowing into her, his internal essence trickling like water into her spirit. First contact...prelude to mating, when they'd exchange magick powers, and become fully one. Each lost half joined as in Old Times, before the Draicon split themselves in half to willingly lessen their powers before they became too powerful. Too dark. Too...evil.

Nicolas groaned as she writhed against him, pressing her hips against his. Maggie. His Maggie. His free hand stroked her body, teased, explored.

Sweetness. Spice. His hand delved between her thighs, cupped her in hard possessiveness. Nicolas rubbed, wanting to give her hot pleasure. She whimpered, twisted, ground her hips against him. Maggie pressed closer to him. As if she couldn't wait to get inside him.

He withdrew his hand, his groin growing hard and heavy. Nicolas brought his fingers up, inhaled her delicious female scent. Bringing his index finger to his mouth, he gave it a long, slow lick. As if licking her.

Her wide gaze held his. Maggie moistened her kiss-swollen lips.

He gazed at her, dark, fierce. Wanting.

In minutes he'd have her, shorts stripped off, panties shredded, her slender legs spread open. Tasting her, bringing her to one shattering climax after another. Then, when she was wet and ready for him, he would sink his hard cock into her, sealing their bond of the flesh.

Every male instinct screamed yes. Nicolas reached for her again.

And caught a scent that rocked him back on his heels. Not delicious, aroused female spice.

Something dark, evil. Like a rotting corpse.

A Morph.

Trembling, Maggie fell back against the palm. One kiss. One soul-stopping press of his warm, wet mouth against hers. Feeling that hard, muscled body mold against her. In that moment, she went from guarded, slightly drunk but distant Maggie to Super Hormonal Woman. Able to leap his male body in a single bound.

She'd never been this sexual. Men interested her, but thought her too intelligent, too unapproachable. Too prudish when she refused to go to bed with them.

Now, dealing with a man she'd met barely an hour ago, her hormones were hopping like water drops on a hot skillet. The guy radiated sexuality like a beacon.

Practical to the bone, Maggie knew it was only nature dousing her with a flood of arousal to make up for the long months she'd avoided men while focusing on her work. Nature versus Overworked Single Businesswoman. Hormones on nature's side. Score…tonight.

Maggie blinked as Nicolas lifted his head. He appeared to sniff the air. The dim yellow glow from her porch light revealed his expression shifting from fierce desire to wary speculation.

He moved so quickly she had no time to react. Strong fingers laced about her upper arm in an unyielding grip. "Get inside," he urged, and steered her toward the front entrance.

Whoa. A bit fast. But wasn't this what she wanted? Maggie, the practical, weighed the consequences of sleeping with Nicolas, a total stranger. Okay, a cute total stranger. Condoms? She had none. Maybe he had some in his wallet. Right. New ones. She swiped a glance at his bulging crotch.

Her internal traffic light flashed yellow. *Caution.* Yet everything inside yearned to join with him. She felt caught in the helpless grip of sexual arousal. Why not sleep with him? She was a virgin, not out of moral principle, but sheer disinterest. No man had ever made her feel interested enough. Until now.

What was she waiting for? She'd been a virgin for twenty-seven years. If she waited any longer, they might as well bronze her and slap her on the shelf.

Green light. Go. Go. Go, her body urged.

Maggie gave up, and decided to cave in to her body's insistent demands. They reached the front door. She fumbled for the key in her shorts pocket.

"Hurry, Maggie," he ordered.

When the door was unlocked, Nicolas nearly ran inside, dragging her with him. Gently, but firmly, he put her behind him as he shut the door and clicked the dead bolt home.

Maggie flicked on the wall switch. Light splashed over his face, showing ruthless features hard as granite. He studied the living room. Suddenly shy, she fumbled with the buttons of her blouse. This seemed so effortless in movies and romance novels.

Nicolas turned back to her. Surprise flared as he watched her slowly part the halves of her blouse, revealing the lacy cups of her bra.

Surprise was not the emotion she'd hoped for. Maggie clapped the blouse shut.

"Ah, Maggie." His unshaven jaw worked, as if he struggled for control. "Later. When there's time," he said softly.

Grim-faced, Nicolas strode over to the sliding glass doors and drew the blinds shut. Maggie followed, totally flummoxed.

Whump! Something launched itself with lightning speed against the slider. A low screech hurt her ears, raking against her nerves like fingernails against slate. Maggie winced, but Nicolas only splayed his hands against the wooden blinds.

"You'll not get her, evil one," he mused, nearly to himself. "You'll have to kill me to get to her now. And Kane will not allow me to die."

He glanced at her. "Stay away from the windows. They can eventually find a way in, but don't make yourself a visible target. I'm going outside." He started for the front door.

They? "Who are they? Nicolas, what's going on? Nicolas!"

He halted, slowly turned.

"What's wrong? What was that that hit my sliders?"

"You don't want to know. Not now."

Slowly, she understood. He'd dragged her inside to escape…something. But there couldn't be anything outside. This was too weird. Logic said Nicolas was flaky. Surely he looked a bit dangerous, with that wild, searching look in his dark eyes, the grim set of his mouth.

An old college course in behavioral science surfaced. Maggie studied her would-be lover. "Is there something out there that can hurt me, Nicolas? What is it?"

He glanced right, as if searching in the distance. "It's not something that can hurt you. It's something that *will* hurt you. It can sneak up on you before you take a single step."

"You're telling the truth," she realized. "But Nicolas, if there's something out there…"

He kissed her lips—a brief, intense kiss. "It's just a small problem I must take care of. Lock the door behind me. And avoid the windows."

Maggie put a hand to her spinning head, watching in dumbstruck disbelief as he padded out the front door. She bolted it behind him, her thoughts a maelstrom.

Hormones forgotten, she hugged herself. Odd

noises. Threats. Danger. A stranger in a bar who evoked a feeling of déjà vu, whom she wanted to sleep with almost instantly. It made no sense. Yet deep inside, it did.

Memories pushed to the surface, clamoring to be heard. *No. I will not,* she thought wildly. Cell mitosis. Division. Creation. Life.

Misha, dying.

Maggie went to check on Misha. The dog slept on her pillow in the corner by the china cabinet. She squatted down, stroked her pet. *If only I could take away your pain, sweetheart, I would. I'd do anything to make you well again.*

Misha's breathing was labored. Grief gripped Maggie like an iron fist. Soon, she'd have to make the decision. Did she do the humane thing as Mark insisted and euthanize her beloved friend before the pain became too intense? Maggie pressed shaking hands to her temples. She needed more time for research.

Time was a luxury she lacked.

Maggie went into the living room to wait.

In minutes he returned, locking the door behind him. Three long, bloodied gashes furrowed his right cheek as if something with claws had swiped him. Staring, she lurched to her feet.

"Problem solved," he announced.

"What was it?" Maggie went to him, her stomach lurching at the blood on his face. Blood, except for in her practice, always nauseated her. She could perform surgery on injured animals and treat the worst wounds, but on humans, it had always sickened her.

"Let me take care of this. I have a firstaid kit."

Nicolas shook his head. "It's nothing. I heal fast."

Unable to tear her gaze away from his cheek, she couldn't fight the sinking feeling something sinister had lurked outside. "What attacked you?"

"Just a little stray problem. I took care of it."

She worried her bottom lip. "I've got questions…."

"And I have answers, which I'll share, when the time is right." He smiled, lifting the darkness from his expression.

She lifted her chin, met his gaze head-on. "No, Nicolas. I want answers. Right now."

Chapter 4

Maggie wanted answers he could not give. Not now. Not in her present inebriated state. He needed her alert. Yet perhaps this was best. Her inhibitions gone, maybe she'd stop clinging to logic and believe. The Morph's claws had sunk into his cheek, but he'd dispatched the enemy easily. Now the lacerations barely stung. By tomorrow they would vanish.

She folded her arms across her stomach. The move served to thrust her breasts at him in a delectable invitation. His gaze dropped to the inviting valley between the lacy cups.

Nicolas longed to run his tongue there. Chart new territory.

"Nicolas? What was out there?"

He raised his gaze to meet hers. He'd feed her some information, see how she reacted.

"Sit, Maggie." He steered her over to the plush floral couch. She sat, rather unsteadily.

"What attacked your door, and what I took care of, was a creature called a Morph. A shape-shifter."

She gave him a blank stare. He pressed on. "It uses dark magick to change into any kind of animal form and seeks to destroy. It feeds off the energy and fear of a dying victim. It needs constant energy to stay alive and work magick. The slower the victim dies, or the more fear the person produces, the richer the food source."

He paused, studying the disbelief dawning in her eyes.

"It's after you, Maggie."

Maggie rubbed her temples. "I *must* be drunk. Did you say shape-shifters?"

"Morphs. They shift into different animal shapes."

She laughed. "Shape-shifters who change into animals. Right. And they want me for, what? Free medical care since I'm a vet?"

"They want you because you're the only one who can defeat and destroy them, Maggie. You're extraordinary."

"That's me. Maggie the Super Destroyer of Shape-shifters!" Her blouse gaped open again, showing a delicious cleft of creamy skin. Nicolas felt his groin grow even heavier. He steeled against it. Control, control. Now was not the time.

"You don't believe me. But you will, soon enough. Just as you sense we have something between us." He took her hand, running his thumb lightly over her knuckles. She shivered at his touch. A pulse throbbed in her neck.

"I don't believe in shape-shifters. Or magic. The sexual chemistry between us? Basic human biology." Her mouth thinned as she yanked her hand away. "I'm a researcher, a doctor of veterinary medicine. So if you're trying to convince me of anything as nonsensical as this Morph creature, it defies human logic. I need evidence."

Nicolas remembered how the Morphs had torn the hunters to pieces. "Don't underestimate them, Maggie. Morphs are far from nonsensical."

Maggie, the scientist, the unbeliever. If he revealed more, she'd grow even more wary. She wanted empirical evidence.

He wanted to pick her up, and run off with her. Get her out of danger before the Morphs attacked. Not yet. She was still safe. Since she hadn't displayed any empath powers, the Morphs lacked proof she was the Draicon destined to destroy them.

He gauged his plan. Tell her to pack now, get the dog in the car and run, and she'd not only balk, but put up such a fuss she'd attract unwanted attention.

She needed to see to believe.

He'd dispatched the Morph scout easily, killing him before he cloned. Scouts worked in pairs. In the morning, when it was supposed to check in, another would appear. After intense study of their patterns, he knew what to expect.

Chances were a Morph wouldn't appear before morning. But he wouldn't leave her alone.

He could mate with her now. But their first time together, he wanted all night. Take it long and slow, not fast and hurried, with the threat of a Morph appearing at her door.

Besides, Maggie needed evidence that the Morphs existed. Nicolas smiled grimly.

She'd see plenty tomorrow morning. He felt certain of it.

Maggie's swimming head couldn't process everything. First, the raging desire stripped away all coherent thought, leaving nothing but the urgent need to rub her naked body against this man. Then there was the odd feeling of danger and Nicolas's mysterious vanishing act.

Now his assertion that a creature stalked her?

It was too fantastic. Yet a tiny part of her warned he told the truth. She ignored that voice. If he were truthful, everything she'd built for herself would collapse into rubble. Her life was ordinary, organized and carefully planned. It allowed no room for the whimsical and mysterious.

No room for childish beliefs such as magic. Magic with a *C*, not a *K*, she thought.

Maggie clenched her fists. *No*, she said silently. *It's not possible. I only believe in what I can control, or accept that which is beyond my control.*

Some diseases were beyond her control. Death. Misha, dying.

A small whimpering drew her attention. Maggie jumped from the couch, and staggered into the kitchen. Nicolas followed as she bent down, stroked the newly awakened Misha with a trembling hand. The dog raised her head, regarded Nicolas. Her tail beat the air like a metronome as she licked his hand.

"She doesn't take well to strangers lately," Maggie said, her heart leaping for joy. This was the most life Misha had shown in days.

"I'm a dog person," Nicolas murmured, rubbing behind Misha's ears.

Maybe now she could finally coax Misha

into eating. From the refrigerator, she fished out a plastic tub and tore off the lid. She squatted before the dog, holding out a small piece of cooked chicken. "Look, Misha, your favorite. Please, eat for me. Please, baby. You can do it."

The dog reached for the chicken. Wild hope arose. Then a strong male hand seized Maggie's wrist, pulling the food away. Anger flooded her. "What are you doing?"

Nicolas was studying Misha with an intent look.

"Don't."

Maggie's mouth flattened. "She's very ill. This is the first food she's shown interest in."

He stroked Misha's head. "What are you feeding her?"

What business was it of his? Yet Misha acted animated, continuing to wag her tail as he rubbed behind her ears. Certainly he had a way with animals.

"Protein. The…mass acts like a cancer. Cancer doesn't feed well on protein, so I have her on a diet of eggs, meat, poultry, white fish, with raw vegetables and…"

"Stop feeding her. It's not cancer."

Maggie stared. "What?"

Nicolas leaned forward as Misha licked his

hand. "The disease is different. It feeds off energy. Any food provides Misha with energy, which the diseased cells use to multiply and spread. She's literally starving to death when she eats and feeding her makes the disease spread."

She slapped the food container on the floor. Misha whined. Nicolas arched a brow.

"Starving to death when I feed her? What do you propose I do, let her not eat and hope that will help? She's dying, dammit! She's dying and there's not a damn thing I can do. All my research has been useless. I'm a vet and I can cure other people's animals, but not my own dog."

Maggie pressed a trembling hand to her face. No more tears. The gentle pressure of a hand squeezing her shoulder made her look up. Nicolas's expression softened.

"Maggie, I'm sure you've done everything for her. I can tell how much you love her. Don't give up. Modern science can't fight ancient, dark magick. Hasn't your research shown this disease to behave abnormally, unlike anything you've ever seen?"

She remembered how the cells divided when she added a drop of healthy dog blood. How they seemed to almost...

Eat it.

Maggie closed her eyes in disbelief. It made no sense. None. Science demanded logic, answers, evaluation. What Nicolas proposed was pure nonsense.

Her eyes flew open. She jerked away from him and went to the fridge, shoving the container back inside. "If Misha has a new type of disease, there's a perfectly logical explanation for it."

Nicolas stood and parked a lean hip against the arched doorway. "You trusted I was telling the truth before when the Morph was outside. Trust me now, Maggie. Go with your instincts."

A bitter laugh escaped. "That wasn't instinct. It was pure behavioral science. You looked right when I asked you if there was something out there that could hurt me. That indicates you were remembering. If you had looked left, it would have told me you were making up a lie. The eyes reveal more than most people realize."

"And so does what's deep inside a person." Nicolas advanced. "Don't look to science, Maggie. Look inside. Stop being logical. Logic has nothing to do with it."

He ran a thumb across her cheek. "Logic has nothing to do with this. These feelings we shared toward each other when we met. I know you have them. Don't fear them. They're perfectly natural and expected. Just like your parents shared."

Maggie studied him, obliquely noticing the lacerations on his face had shrunk. *I must be drunk,* she rationalized. Wounds didn't heal that fast. Instead, she focused on the swirling caramel of his brown eyes. Faint memories tugged. Parents. Forest and mountains. Familiar warmth of friends, love, strong bonds. Her father affectionately licking her mother...

Licking?

"It's plain, simple biology," she asserted, struggling with her emotions as he swept his thumb over her jawline. "Sexual attraction, nature's means of propagating the species."

His eyes darkened. "Have you ever wanted to propagate like this?"

Maggie put a hand to her swimming head. "No," she admitted. "It's the wine. Alcohol lowers inhibitions. Which is why women sleep with men they just met."

Nicolas bent his head toward her. With one hand, he caught her curls, swept them back from her ear. Warm breath feathered over her cheek. Maggie caught his very male, woodsy scent, reminding her of pine forests and wildness. "Is that why you kissed me? Why you began removing your blouse? Two glasses of pinot noir?"

His mouth nuzzled her neck. Maggie moaned as he nipped it, then delivered a soothing lick. Her hands anchored on his shoulders. Thoughts of magic, strange creatures and danger evaporated like raindrops on a hot Florida blacktop.

Nicolas set her back. His gaze burned into hers. "Not wine, Maggie. We both know it."

"Yes," she breathed.

Nicolas cupped her face, bent his head as if to kiss her. Then he uttered almost a growl, and jerked away.

"No. Not now," he muttered.

His dark brows pulled together in a frown. Her body left aching and yearning, Maggie shouldered her pride and buttoned the blouse.

"I think you should go. I'm tired." Maggie managed to force the words out.

"I think I should stay," he said quietly, his gaze searching hers. "You shouldn't be alone now. It's too dangerous here."

"From whatever was outside? How do you expect me to believe in something I can't see?" She collapsed onto the couch.

"Do you think I was lying, Maggie? Do you think something wasn't trying to get inside?"

The little hairs on the back of her neck rose. "I believe you believe that there are such creatures, Nicolas. But asking me to swallow a story about a magical creature that shape-shifts...? You might as well ask me to believe in something as silly as werewolves. Maybe it's them I need to fear. It's nearly a full moon." She threw back her head, gave a short, fake howl.

One dark brow lifted again. "Not bad," he drawled. "But in time, you'll do better."

He paced over to the door, checked the locks. Next he checked the windows, shut the curtains. Maggie rubbed her arms, her confused, muzzy emotions raging. "Nicolas, what are you doing?"

He shot her a hooded look from beneath long, dark lashes. "I need to secure your house."

"Against what?"

"Against anything needing to get inside. I'm staying the night, Maggie."

"You don't act...interested."

In answer he cupped her face, drew her toward him. Nicolas kissed her, a warm authoritative kiss. His tongue swept over her lips, danced inside as she opened to him. He groaned and tore himself away. Breathing ragged, eyes dark and wild, he visibly fought to control himself.

Elated, yet confused, she licked her lips and touched his arm. "Then why not?"

"Now isn't a good time, Maggie." Nicolas drew in a deep breath. "I want...time. I want to make love to you more than I want my next breath. All night long. When I know it's safe."

"I feel perfectly safe."

He shot her a level look. "You're also intoxicated."

Disappointment mingled with newfound respect. Another man would simply take advantage of her being drunk, and happily walk off without caring he might have left behind a package awaiting delivery in nine months.

"Go to sleep, Maggie. I'll protect you."

From what? Whatever mythical creature that attacked him? Or against himself?

Maggie curled up with a yawn. Something warm and soft fell over her a minute later. A blanket.

"Good night, Mags," he murmured. He shot her a faintly exasperated look. "I told you not to remove the bracelet. But you didn't listen. Perhaps you will now."

Confusion at his words faded with the tender kiss he pressed against her cheek. Maggie yawned and snuggled into the couch, pulling the blanket over her. Just a minute's rest, then she'd escort him out. She closed her eyes to the image of Nicolas, silently standing guard by the sliding glass doors, as if keeping watch.

Sunlight speared the white tile floor the next morning as she slowly awakened. Maggie stared at the small clock radio on the bedside table in bleary confusion. How could she have slept until ten o'clock? Jackhammers slammed into her skull. Damn. No wonder she had no inclination to drink. Hangovers were a bitch. She sat up slowly, gritting her teeth against the nausea, then headed for the bathroom.

When she emerged, memories of last night surfaced. A low groan rippled from her lips. What a fool she'd been.

No sign of Nicolas. He must have carried her upstairs and then left. The blinds, closed last night, now were open, the windows uncovered.

Just as well. Never before had she been so edgy, wanting, ready to leap into bed with a stranger. One she'd met at a bar! Maggie rubbed her face, wincing at her aching head. No more alcohol. Not even a thimble of sherry.

Still, she couldn't erase his strong, impassioned

face from her thoughts. He remained embedded there like fingerprints.

She went into the kitchen, checked on Misha. The dog greeted her with a wagging tail and ambled outside as Maggie opened the sliding glass doors. No trouble walking, more energy than she'd exhibited. When Misha returned, she lay down on the cool tile.

Troubled, Maggie measured out coffee and poured it into her automatic coffeemaker. Misha hadn't eaten yesterday and acted livelier.

Nicolas had warned feeding Misha would spread the disease.

Ridiculous. A disease that fed off the energy produced by food? Maggie headed for the bathroom for a shower to clear her muzzy brain.

To her amazement, Misha followed her up the stairs. The dog wagged her tail, lay down by the bathroom door. Maggie's spirits lifted.

Half an hour later, she emerged from the bathroom, her hair damp and curly. She coaxed Misha into her lab and drew another sample of blood. Misha watched with large brown eyes as Maggie studied the sample underneath the microscope.

There were fewer black cells in the blood sample than the previous day. Maggie glanced down at her dog. "Nicolas can't be right. This is just a coincidence."

Misha yawned and laid her head down.

"Okay, sweetie, stay there. I think you deserve a nap after climbing those stairs."

Downstairs, Maggie poured coffee into a china mug, added sugar and pulled open the sliders. She stepped out onto the patio. The mirrored surface of the gulf rippled sea-blue this morning, reflecting the cloudless sky. On the mile-wide beach, green and royal blue umbrellas blossomed to greet the day. People walked along the surf, some jogging, others ambling or shell hunting.

The air smelled briny. No breeze rustled the spindly palm trees. Musing over last night's strange events, and the odd findings in Misha's blood this morning, Maggie stared out at the beach. Something caught her eye.

She squatted down and studied the white sugar sand. A man's large footprints, slightly scuffed as if he'd been tussling with something. Other tracks caught her attention.

Deep gouges in the sand. Large sinister prints, clearly reptilian. Alligators inhabited the freshwater marshes to the west. The tracks were distinctly reptilian.

Turning around she studied her sliding doors. Gooseflesh erupted along her bare arms.

Deep slashes scored the glass, as if a creature with razor sharp claws raked over her door. A creature clamoring to get inside.

"Nothing around here could have made these marks," she mused aloud.

"Only the Morphs."

Maggie jumped, spilling hot coffee on the concrete.

Clad in jeans and a gray T-shirt, Nicolas stood on the sand a few feet away. "Sorry I startled you." The smooth, even features looked apologetic. His full, chiseled mouth twisted.

Suddenly shy because of her brazen behavior last night, Maggie stole a glance at him. His dark hair was slightly mussed. A hank of it fell over his forehead, giving him a boyish look.

"Good morning, Maggie. I trust you slept well."

Feeling awkward, she studied her coffee cup as if it contained all the answers in the world. "I woke this morning and you were gone. I thought you'd gone…."

"Left for good?" Nicolas ran a finger along the tracks. "I went back to my room to pack."

"So you're leaving." An odd pang filled her. At least he'd returned to say goodbye, more than

most men would offer after spending the night.
What irony. The first man to spend the night and
he didn't even sleep with her.

"Not yet. I had to come back and see you."

His genuine smile lifted her spirits. Warmth infused her as she drank in the sight of him. She
gestured with her cup.

"Want some coffee? Freshly made."

"I don't drink coffee. But thanks."

He flashed another friendly smile.

*Sorry we couldn't mate last night. I couldn't
take the chance with the Morphs endangering
you.*

Maggie studied him, puzzled. That voice inside
her head again. She'd felt the distinct, faint invasion. Post-alcoholic hangover. The voice from
yesterday, her overactive imagination sprout-
ing up. She studied his heavily muscled body,
the way his faded jeans hugged his hard thighs,
the shadow of stubble on his lean jaw. A thought
crossed her own mind.

*Oh, yeah. I'd jump your bones in a minute.
Drunk or not.*

Now a huge grin spread over his face. As if he
were reading her mind. Impossible.

Something else was wrong. Maggie looked at

his cheek. The wounds from last night were gone. Another impossibility.

He rubbed his cheek. "I told you, I heal fast."

Probably some amazing liquid healing solvent. Maggie shrugged it off and gestured to the sand. "I was just examining the tracks. Some animal was roaming around here last night."

"No creature from around here made these," he observed.

Nicolas squatted down, studied the odd tracks.

Maggie set down her mug on a glass-topped table. Staring at the marks, she felt a touch of unease crawl up her spine.

"Alligators. That's all. Unusual, but not impossible."

"Alligators didn't claw your glass." Nicolas traced the outline of one track. "Morph. It shifted into another form for the attack, a much larger and more powerful predator capable of clawing its way through. The window must not be ordinary."

"It's hurricane-proof, so the manufacturer said. Can withstand one-hundred-twenty-mile-per-hour winds." She examined the jagged marks, tracing the gouges on the glass. Shifting? Hammers pounded her skull. Maggie pressed clammy fingers to her head.

Nicolas went behind her and gently laid his hands on her throbbing temples. He began a steady massage. She stiffened as he nestled behind her.

"Relax," he murmured. "I'll take good care of you."

Tension fled. Maggie leaned back, relishing his soothing touch. He's leaving, her disappointed hormones reminded.

She jerked away. "If you're leaving, Nicolas, you should go. I appreciate your returning to say goodbye, but it wasn't necessary. I have a lot of work to do."

"I didn't return to say goodbye." Nicolas nodded toward the tracks. "Another Morph tried getting inside your home, Maggie. Look at the signs. The tracks, the glass. Whatever comes into contact with them faces danger. Look at the grass."

Maggie never tended the landscaping, but this morning the tough Bermuda grass appeared blackened and shriveled, as if seared with flame.

"Dragon's breath," Nicolas said softly.

Maggie laughed. "And I thought I was the one drinking too much last night."

He aimed her a level look. "We must leave, before it returns."

This was too sudden, too intense. "You want me to leave, Nicolas? With you? Why?"

His ebony gaze sought hers. "It's not safe here for you. Not now. Their magick is too powerful and potent and you're too vulnerable right now."

Magic. Mystery. Not for her, the practical and analytical. "Nicolas, I don't believe in magic. I'll call the authorities, let them know something tried to break in." Maggie shrugged. "This house has withstood hurricanes. I think it can resist other elements of nature. Whatever you think they are."

Nicolas shoved a hand through his thick, dark locks. "The Morphs aren't an element of nature. They will find a way inside. The one this morning was testing your defenses, discovering the best way to gain access. Do you see that ant?"

Maggie watched a red ant the size of a dime march across the aluminum railing separating her porch from the sand. Shocked, she leaned closer.

"Is that what I think it is?" she mused aloud.

"What *do* you think it is?"

"Wow. It can't be…but it is. Not native. How did it get here?" Fascinated, she studied the insect, which went still. "Hey there, fellow. I've seen these in books, but never this close."

Nicolas gave a blank stare as Maggie picked up

a pen on the nearby glass-topped table. Using it as a pointer, she directed it at the ant's head. "Hmm. Massive pincers, must be a soldier. The females are the largest in the world. They can colonize in numbers up to twenty-two million. Hunt mainly at night, by sensing the carbon dioxide that their prey breathes. *Dorylus helvolus.*"

Her mouth curved into a sheepish grin.

"Sorry. I studied entomology. It's a driver, or army ant. Native to Africa. The only ants recorded to have eaten people. What is he doing here? Maybe he came on a shipment."

Maggie frowned, thinking. "I need to alert the Florida department of agriculture. I'll keep him alive until they arrive and conduct an investigation, determine if..."

Nicolas moved with blinding speed, his palm slamming down on the ant. Maggie's jaw dropped in astonishment.

"What did you do that for?" she cried out.

Nicolas lifted his palm. Horrified, she stared. On the flat of his palm was a quarter-sized burn. Blackish blood from the crushed ant dripped to the concrete. It sizzled as it hit.

"Morph blood turns to acid. That's what makes killing them difficult." Nicolas grimaced.

He was injured. Instantly Maggie rushed over

to him, clucked anxiously over his hand. Instinct welled deep inside her. Must remove the pain, the hurt, the injury. She placed her palm over the ugly burn mark. She closed her eyes, drawing from a force deep inside. Heal. Heal.

Maggie screamed as searing pain like hot coals sank into her palm. She staggered, nearly losing contact. Something forced her to hold on. Gritting her teeth, she drew in air, riding through the waves of pain. Ancient chants sang in her mind.

The pain eased, then stopped. Maggie's eyes opened as Nicolas yanked his hand away. He led her over to a lounge chair. She fell onto it, her breath coming in ragged gasps.

Never had she felt so weak, so stricken. Nicolas sank down beside her. "It's true," he said softly. "The legend is true. You are the empath."

Chapter 5

Memories flickered like movie images. Small palms on deep wounds gushing blood from her father's chest...please, Daddy, please live... Maggie forced them away. Nightmare images culled from a dark past. It didn't matter. What mattered was here and now.

Nicolas took her palm and turned it over. There was a quarter-sized burn marking it. As her astounded eyes watched, it slowly faded, then vanished.

He pulled her upward. "We must leave. The Morphs will know you're the one."

She put the now healed hand to her temple. It couldn't be possible. It wasn't really happening, was it? Like Misha's illness. Blood absorbed by blackened cells.

Maybe I do believe in witches.

"Nicolas, what happened to me?"

He caressed her cheek, his touch gentle and soothing. "What should have happened long ago, had you not suppressed it. Probably a defense mechanism until recently, and then it became too strong to suppress. Have you ever noticed some of the animals you've healed have recovered re-markably? Or had their pain cease? It would probably be a dog."

"It's hard to tell. Animals, especially dogs, are very good at hiding pain." She searched her memory. "Yes," she breathed. "A dog, with cancer. He was on chemo. I put my hands on him and wanted to take away his pain so bad that I felt like I was actually bonding with the dog, like I could see the disease inside me. It hurt, deep inside, but I just thought it was emotional."

He gathered both of her hands into his, study-ing them, rubbing his thumbs over her knuckles. "Your touch, Maggie. It heals, when you want it to. You take the pain and injury and disease inside you and eradicate it. Did the dog heal?"

"It seemed almost…like magic."

"It was you, Maggie." Nicolas's mouth flat-tened. "But it could have been the chemotherapy, so the Morphs weren't sure. They've been watch-ing, waiting for a moment like this." His grip tightened on her hands as he stood, pulling her with him. "Get inside, pack your things. We're leaving."

"I've just discovered this new skill and you want to bolt...."

"Before they come back. And kill you."

A rill of fear seized her. Maggie fought it. It made no sense that someone wanted to kill her for healing.

"I'm not running, Nicolas. There's no danger. No one knows about this but you and me and nothing's coming for me."

He released her, his dark eyes stormy as he gazed out onto the sand. "You're wrong. They know. And they're already here."

Maggie craned her neck, saw two large brownish specks against the blinding white sand. Bull ants? Maybe. "Nicolas, those are probably bull ants, they're native to Florida...."

Her voice trailed off as he wrapped his fingers about her wrist, tugging her inside. Nicolas closed and locked the sliding glass doors. He shut the blinds. "Where are your car keys?"

Her gaze flicked toward the kitchen. He ran there, returned, pocketing the keys to her SUV. "Go upstairs. Hurry. Pack only your research ma-

terials and anything essential. Forget clothing,"
he said, his voice a whiplash of command.

Panic welled up. She quelled it, resorting to
rationalizations. Fine, get a few things together,
give herself a chance to think, stall him. Her
world was tilting crazily. She felt caught between
ecstasy at her newfound ability to heal and the
feeling that everything was sliding out from
beneath her. Trailed by Nicolas, Maggie went
upstairs to her office as he helped her gather
notebooks and research materials. He carried a
carton downstairs, past the polished oak table in
the hallway.

"I'll take these out to your SUV," Nicolas said.

This was insane. A stranger she'd just met had
commandeered her life. She'd healed his palm.
More study was needed on this fascinating revelation of her healing abilities. What threat was
there? She saw nothing, felt no danger.

Maybe she could heal Misha. With one touch.
She needed more time. Maggie rubbed her temples.

Nicolas came inside, his jaw tight. "Are you
almost ready?"

Maggie folded her arms across her chest. "I'm
not leaving. If I have this unique ability to heal,
then let's use it. I can test it out, try different

things. And how can these…things be dangerous? Maybe you had a severe allergic reaction to
them. I'm a vet, Nicolas. I treat animals. I'm not
afraid of any animal."

His gaze narrowed. "You should be."

"Nicolas, maybe there is something different
about me. But honestly, telling me there are creatures after me, wanting to kill me? It's insane!"

Maggie shrieked as he scooped her up, depos-
ited her firmly over one broad shoulder.

"Put me down! Nicolas! Don't be irrational.
There's nothing out there that can hurt me."

"Oh. You want evidence. Empirical evidence."

She bounced against the hard muscle of his
body as he trotted over to the sliding glass doors.
The blinds were shut. "If you see proof, will you
come with me willingly?"

"Killer ants? Yes," she muttered.

Nicolas opened the blinds. Upside down on his
shoulder she couldn't see anything but the outline of his firm buttocks encased in the worn
jeans. "Here's your proof. They've found you and
they're trying to get inside. And soon, they will."

He slowly lowered her to her feet. Maggie faced
the window. Her heart dropped to her stomach.
"Oh, God. Oh, God."

The two large glass sliding windows previously

had shown a serene vista of blue gulf waters, beachgoers and white sugar sands. But now the view was totally blocked.

The sliding windows were covered with a red, crawling mass of army ants.

She couldn't move.

As she watched in horror, one ant squeezed through a small crack where the glass met the sliding frame. It dropped to the floor, marched toward her with military precision. Suddenly it stopped. It began twisting, writhing.

Growing.

"Dammit Maggie, it's shifting! Kill it before it gets too big," Nicolas roared.

The ant grew to the size of a quarter. Then a silver dollar. Immobilized by her long-ago vow to never hurt another living creature, she stared. Nicolas made an impatient sound, picked up a nearby phone book. It slammed on the ant with a loud *thwack*.

The phone book twitched. Another ant wriggled through the crack, dropped to the floor.

Nicolas grabbed her wrist. "We have to get out of here, now!" he ordered.

Jerked out of inaction, she followed. A weak bark from upstairs kicked her memory. Fear wrapped icy tentacles around her heart.

"Misha's still upstairs!"

Maggie scrambled for the steps, heart hammering as she ran into the lab.

Little sunlight filtered into the darkened room. Maggie fumbled for the switch. Light flooded the room. The same dark mass crawled over the windows. But she'd left the windows open to enjoy the breeze.

Ants had bitten through the screen, and were pouring inside like water through a leaky dike. A thick, red stream swarmed over her worktable, down the table leg. A boiling mass of biting army ants marched toward her dog. Trapped against the wall, Misha yipped and shrank back against the invading force.

Red-hot anger erased fear. Maggie picked up the closest object, a medical textbook.

"Get away from my dog, dammit!" she screamed, running for Misha. From the doorway, Nicolas yelled something. She ignored him, slammed the textbook down on the ants. Again. And again. More ants piled onto the room. Maggie reached down, grabbed a terrified Misha as Nicolas ran forward.

"Take her." She thrust Misha at Nicolas.

"Burn them, Maggie. Fire is the only thing that will slow them down," he shouted, running out of the room with Misha. He set the dog down in the hallway out of harm's way.

Maggie spotted a bottle of alcohol. Her shaking fingers twisted the cap as the ants marched in her direction.

She opened the bottle, tossed the contents on them. Matches, matches, where were the damn matches? On the table, she spotted a lighter she used for igniting the Bunsen burner. She picked it up.

One ant leapt, landing on her wrist. Its fangs sank down. She screamed, dropped the lighter. Ants immediately swarmed over it. Instinctively, Maggie went to slap a hand on her wrist.

"Don't do that!"

Nicolas appeared at her side, drawing her away from the table. He very carefully picked it off her hand, flicked the ant away.

"Their blood will burn you." His wild gaze whipped around the room. "Do you have any more alcohol?"

Maggie ran to the room's opposite side, jerked open a metal cabinet. Supplies tumbled out as she pawed through the shelves, locating another bottle. She tossed it to him.

Alcohol sloshed over the rippling pile of ants as Nicolas uncapped the bottle and waved it over them. He reached over, grabbed the lighter she'd dropped.

Nicolas grimaced as several ants jumped on his hand and began biting.

Cold horror filled her as they began gnawing on his exposed skin. Blood droplets welled, splashed onto the table like red tears.

"Oh, God." Acid bile rose in her throat.

The ants were eating Nicolas alive.

He grimly ignored them, flicked the lighter and tossed it on the table.

A whoosh of blue-orange flames blossomed, raced along the ant trail, eagerly licking the alcohol.

"Go to hell," he growled.

High-pitched squeals hurt her ears as flames burned the ants. Nicolas flicked off the ones on his hand as he grabbed Misha and herded Maggie down the stairs. They raced out the door. Maggie paused, glanced over her shoulder.

Army ants poured down the sliding glass doors in a red stream. Nicolas placed Misha on a blanket in the backseat and then slid into the driver's seat of her Ford Escape as she slammed the front door. She slid into the passenger's side.

Maggie's hands shook as she fumbled with her seat belt. Nicolas accelerated out of the driveway. Rubber squealed, blue smoke billowed. He hooked a right and drove south, jaw tense as he stared straight ahead.

Inside, she shook violently, her heart thudding in an erratic cadence. Blood dripped from the open, ragged lacerations on Nicolas's right hand. Risking his own life, he'd saved Misha. Tension rode his jaw. Nicolas hurt, but wasn't about to show the pain. A mixture of gratitude and confusion poured over her.

Whatever he was, whoever he was, he was wounded. And she had the ability to heal.

"You're hurt. Let me help you," she said, reaching for him.

He shook his head, ebony hair sailing about his head. "No! It's too dangerous to heal me here."

Not taking his eyes off the road, he lifted his hand to his mouth. Maggie gaped at him as he ran his tongue over the back. Like…an animal licking its wound.

Who was he? *What* was he?

The driving need to heal drowned out reason and logic. Nicolas was injured. She would see if her newfound skill still worked.

She seized his wrist. Nicolas tried jerking away, but she placed her hand over the seeping wounds and he could not shake her free. It felt as if they were locked together.

Palm trembling, Maggie closed her eyes, concentrated. Absorbing his pain as hers. Seeing flesh close upon itself, blood ceasing to flow. Heal, heal. Ancient chants buried deep inside her resonated through her body.

The electric jolt slammed into her. Burning pain tore into her hand. Prepared this time, she grit her teeth, rode through it.

After a minute she cautiously lifted her hand. Nicolas's wounds were gone. They appeared on the back of her hand. As she watched in dumbfounded amazement, the wounds vanished.

"Dammit, Maggie! I told you no. Do you realize how stupid that was?" He angled his head toward her in a stern glare. "Do you ever do as you're told?"

"Thank you, Maggie," she snapped. "Why, you're welcome, Nicolas."

His jaw tightened as he turned his attention back toward the road, zipping past cars as if they were on a NASCAR track instead of the highway. "You just left a spectral trail of magick as bright as neon for the Morphs to follow. It's damn hard enough to lose them without you making it easier. Each time you use your healing powers, the magick leaves behind particles like a smoke signal."

Maggie wrinkled her brow. "This is biological and has to be studied scientifically. There's no such thing as magic."

"And I suppose the ants shape-shifting back at your house were experiencing a pure biological reaction?" Nicolas snorted. "Listen to me, Maggie. From now on, do as I say. The rules have changed. If you want to live, you obey me, period. Understand?"

"I'm not yours to order around, Nicolas. We have nothing between us. You have no right," she retorted.

He turned, startling her with a fierce, possessive look. "I have the right more than any other male."

"You sound like an animal fighting over a female in heat." Sarcasm laced her tone.

"If I must fight for you, I will," he said darkly. A low growl grumbled in his deep chest as he bared his teeth. For a wild moment she saw his canines…lengthen? Ridiculous.

Stress caused her imagination to run amok.

Maggie shifted her thoughts to her newfound healing ability. It deserved more study. If only she could truly heal not just small wounds, but larger ones. Diseases. She needed a microscope, samples of her blood. Maybe there was a gene that caused this amazing ability. Chromosome work, detailed analysis.

Misha. Maybe she could even heal her dog. Maggie gasped.

He glanced at her. "What?"

"I need to find out where this ability came from. How can I control it? Is it temporary? And if it's biological, why did it surface now? Or maybe I ingested something recently." She began ticking possibilities off on her fingers, and then laughed. His brows knit together.

"I just got attacked by a legion of killer army ants, barely escaped and my house is burning down. My home that I spent every last penny on is turning into ash. I'm on the run, to where? And all I can think about right now is setting up a microscope so I can analyze where this ability comes from."

A half smile quirked his lips. "Don't try it again, not until I say it's safe. Study it all you want after we get you the hell away from the Morphs."

Her pique at his bossiness faded as she considered her enormous predicament. If the neighbors saw the fire, called emergency services and the ants were still there…

"I have to let someone know I'm not home," she choked out. "My neighbors will see the smoke. If the firefighters go inside and the ants attack them…"

She retrieved her cell, flipped the lid and went to dial 911. Nicolas grabbed her wrist.

"No. Your home isn't near the neighbors. There's no danger of the fire spreading to anyone else's home."

Ignoring him, Maggie wrenched away her hand. "Those things, they'll kill…"

"The Morphs won't appear as army ants anymore. They'll have vanished. That's how they work. They're not animals. They think like humans. They'll blend in. Their goal isn't to kill everyone. Just you and me."

"Forget magical shape-shifting ants. When someone sees the fire, they'll think I'm still inside and try to rescue me." Maggie punched in a number. "I'll call Iona, Tammy's mother. My neighbor. Just to let her know I'm not home."

Nicolas jaw tightened. She ignored it. Iona's normally languid voice answered on the first ring. Maggie wasted no words. "Iona? It's Dr. Sinclair. I'm driving back to the beach house with my dog, Misha. I have a hall closet to fix, and I was wondering if I could borrow your husband's drill when I got home?"

"Drill? That sounds convincing," he muttered.

Maggie glared at him.

"Miss Sinclair, I do wish you'd be more responsible instead of just running off without leaving word. Your cousin has been quite anxious about you. You should have made better arrangements if you knew you were going to be gone."

Maggie's jaw dropped. "My cousin? I don't…"

Nicolas shot her a sharp look.

"Your cousin! David, the one you invited to stay with you for the next two weeks? You told him you'd be at home and he came here, very concerned because he was waiting outside quite a while."

"But…"

"Wait. He's here. He wants to talk to you."

"Put your phone on speaker," Nicolas ordered. "I want to hear this guy."

Maggie pressed the Speaker button. In the background she heard Iona hand the phone over, then someone clearing his throat and speaking. "Yes, thank you, Mrs. Whittaker. Could you be so kind as to get me another glass of water? Yes, this Florida heat, my, in October, I thought it would be cooler. Yes, with ice, thank you."

She dimly heard the distant click of heels on tile.

"Margaret Sinclair." The throaty whisper held a hint of screech, fingernails on slate.

Maggie gripped the phone so hard her knuckles whitened.

"Run, Margaret. Run away. We'll hunt you. We'll find you. And watch you die, very, very slowly. We like it...slow. The better to eat your energy, my dear," the whisper came.

The connection clicked off, leaving the angry buzz of a dial tone.

Chapter 6

Maggie dropped the phone as if red-hot coals suddenly seared her palm.

Nicolas steered the vehicle around a slow-moving BMW, sped through an intersection as the light turned red. She barely registered it. Someone wanted her dead. A distant memory flickered. Threats. Angry voices.

Blood, turning the sidewalk red as it ran…

She pressed fingers against her temples, fighting distant images. Memories? No. Not memories. Horrific images, two people lying on the ground, blood seeping from their wounds. Anger, so fierce it clouded everything, everything, a hazy red until the roaring in her ears echoed with a howl…

No! Her heart hammered with fear and dread.

No nightmares. Not again. Breath caught in her lungs. Maggie gulped for air, feeling panic well up.

Nicolas cut to the right, pulled into a grocery store parking lot and into an empty space. Leaving the engine running, he turned to her. She barely registered the concern flaring in his eyes, the worry denting his brow. He cupped her face, forcing her to turn toward him.

"Maggie, dammit, say something," he urged.

Dragging in a deep lungful of air, she fought for composure. Calm now. Calm.

"Something." She gave a shaky laugh. "This can't be happening. It's not real."

His voice gentled. "Trust me, Mags, it's real enough. They'll kill anything to further their purpose. That's why they were after Misha upstairs. Not because they wanted her energy. They wanted to kill her because she means so much to you. They'd feed off your grief, your fear."

Maggie cast a worried glance backward at Misha, who kept licking her front paw as she always did when distressed. Logic. Attack any problem with calm, sensible logic. Analyze. Pick it apart slowly. No emotions. Somewhere inside, ancient instincts clamored for attention. She squelched them. *Think, Maggie, think.*

"I don't understand, Nicolas. It doesn't make sense. Why would they kill me?"

Nicolas rubbed his thumb over her trembling hand. "Listen to me, Maggie, and stop trying to make sense out of what seems impossible. Think back to your childhood, when magick and myth were more real than the corporeal. Morphs shift into animal forms, retaining their human intelligence. When it's more convenient for them to blend, they shift into human form. They're masters of disguise. They can appear as old men, young men. In part, that's what makes them so damn difficult to kill. But they must shift into their true forms to absorb the energy of their dying victims. Believe me, it's true."

Believe him? It sounded too fantastical. *No, I don't.*

She strove for answers as if the creatures were a new species.

"Are there females? Can they breed?"

"There are a few females, but they can't breed. Morphs can clone themselves. They learned how to organize themselves into a functioning army, thanks to Jamie, a mortal who recently joined them. That's why they've become more dangerous. Kane, the Morph leader, coaxed them into joining him in a pack so they could be more effective in destroying us."

Nicolas squeezed her hand, his deep voice soft and reassuring. "And why I have to protect you, Mags. Trust me, I'll keep you safe. I'm telling you the truth about all of this."

Surely the voice on the phone was a prank, some kind of sick joke. And the ants, an unnatural phenomenon, but creatures capable of shape-shifting? Impossible.

And why would anyone hurt her?

This.

Maggie spread open her palms and studied them. A tidal wave of emotions washed over her. Confusion. Fear. All threaded with an odd elation in the realization of her newfound powers.

I can heal living tissue.

Her scientific mind roiled over the information. She raced over the knowledge, finding solace in this extraordinary news that soared with possibilities for life. Not death. She stared at the palm that had healed Nicolas's wound. Not a trace of injury, not even a pink scar.

"Are you all right?"

No time to panic, turn into a mass of hysteria. Not her style, anyway. Maggie nodded, trembling as his knuckles grazed her cheek in a tender gesture. As much as his bossiness irked her, his gentleness made her melt.

Who was this man? Was she safe with him? What if he had instigated all this?

She thought about unhitching her seat belt and jumping out, but just as the thought entered her mind, he shifted into Reverse and backed out. Nicolas headed back on the highway again, driving south. The sharp, even edges of his profile showed a taut jaw, mouth flattened to a tight slash. Eyes straight ahead, he drove, only the rasping sound of Misha licking her front paw filling the empty silence between them. Gradually she became aware of her surroundings as he sped southbound. Alarm tugged at her as they passed familiar landmarks. Naples. The Books-a-Million with its blue-and-white striped awning. Soon they'd pass Tin City, the popular tourist shopping spot. Then where?

Trepidation filled her. Forget the phone threat and the creatures invading her home. She was in her vehicle with a stranger she'd just met yesterday. Was he her enemy as much as these strange Morph creatures?

"Nicolas, where are you taking me?"

No answer, but his fingers tightened on the steering wheel. Too much happened, too fast.

No time to think, act logically. Now she paid the price. Maggie glanced back at Misha. *Oh, boy, we're in trouble, hon. In a car with a stranger who talks of these witchy things, and I just go along blindly. How could I? Stupid, stupid, Mags! What do you know about this guy? For all you know he could be an axe murderer, a serial killer.*

An image flashed...herself, on the roadside, her naked, battered body sprawled in the grass for some tourist to discover.

"It's not in my nature to hurt you," Nicolas said softly in his whiskey-smooth voice. "Naked and sprawled on the grass, maybe, after I've loved you like you've never been loved before. And what I want to do with you would leave you dead tired."

He was reading her mind. How could he? She swallowed, fear clawing its way down her spine anew. "Nicolas, I told you, it was wine and chemistry. Mere sexual attraction. Biology."

"We have more between us than you realize. Not biology. Just us. And when I get you to a safe place, I plan on picking up where I left off last night. All night. Kissing you all over. Everywhere. When I'm done, you'll be exhausted and limp with pleasure. There won't be one single inch of your lovely body that I haven't claimed with my mouth."

Blurring roadside slipped by as she riveted her gaze to the passing ground, unable to respond. In one day they had gone from potential lovers to potential lovers on the lam.

Nicolas turned his head and shot her a look of pure heat. Electric current sizzled between them. Her insides clenched with desire. She studied his full, sculpted mouth, the hard curve of his jaw, the thick sweep of silky hair feathering his collar, his ebony brows. Darkly handsome. Brooding. Dangerous? Maybe.

"Nicolas, what do you want with me?"

"I want *you,* Maggie. I want you safe. Then I plan on getting you naked and making love to you until you simply can't move an inch. And you don't want to, either."

Maybe not an axe murderer. Just a sex fiend.

"A sex fiend only for you. I can't even remember the color of the eyes of the last woman I had sex with." He didn't even look at her. "But I remember yours. They're blue. A deep, deep blue, like the depths of a peaceful, still lake."

Startled, she pressed against the door. He must be a psychological expert and be able to read facial expressions. Hell, one of her patients, a cop, told her most psychics did it. What the hell had she gotten involved with? The strain of the past days looked like a holiday compared to the fresh danger she faced. Maybe she could jump...how fast were they going? And what about Misha? She didn't look back, didn't dare give him any indication what she thought.

"I don't need you to look at your dog to tell me what you're thinking. All I need is to tap into your mind."

His voice was softer, as if he didn't want to scare her off. Too late. Maggie felt her stomach pitch and roll. Sweat dampened her palms.

"Would you please let go of the door handle? I don't want you to accidentally fall out. You're too important, Mags."

"Important to you? Why?"

"Important to me, and others. I'm not about to let anything happen to you. Relax. If I had planned to hurt you, wouldn't I have done so last night instead of now?" He tapped the steering wheel. His fingers were long, solid looking. Dark hairs dusted the back of his hand.

"You're a medical researcher, Maggie. Logically, would I have deliberately put myself in danger if I were a threat to you?"

Not necessarily. But too many ingredients in this odd mixture were still unknown, like an illness she still had to diagnose. His words made sense. What made less sense was her deep longing to believe and trust him. As if he were a long-lost friend. A hint of beard shadowed his jawline, though it was still morning and he'd looked freshly shaven. The plain T-shirt molded to his muscled chest. Her gaze flicked down to the faded, tight jeans hugging his stone-hard thighs. Nicolas's exposed skin was tanned, probably from working the ranch he said he owned back in New Mexico. Or did he?

She didn't know whether to trust him or run for her hide. Maggie studied the passing landscape. Still southbound, but headed where?

For now, she'd go along, while they were speeding and it proved too dangerous to leap from the car. Slowly her fingers unfurled from their death grip on the door handle. Wincing, she exercised them.

"Why are you calling me 'Mags'? No one's called me that since childhood. Only my parents did."

"Maybe more than your parents did. What do you remember of your early childhood?"

Maggie searched memories, stopped. This thread was starting to worry her.

"Never mind. If calling you Mags makes you uncomfortable, I won't do it."

She'd almost prefer him as cold and uncaring. It made her choices easier. She could easily cut and run first chance she got. This kind of compassion proved more dangerous than if he'd wielded a knife because then she'd know what she fought against. Part of her badly wanted to trust because she needed an anchor in this crazy sea of surreal happenings. The truth hit Maggie. She had no family and no real friends to worry about her, wonder where she had gone.

The realization left her feeling cold and lonely. Would anyone ever care?

"I care," he said softly.

"Will you stop doing that?" she protested.

"Stop what?"

He gave her a charming smile. All teeth. Gleaming white teeth, like a wolf. A dimple dented his right cheek. She squirmed from the sudden heat curling through her body.

"How can you read my mind? It doesn't make sense."

"Does any of this make sense? Not if you're ensnared in the practical and logical. Let go of all you've embraced so far, Maggie. Let yourself go. Feel. Believe in possibilities. Not science and empirical evidence and facts. Imagine the possibilities of what could happen, and what could go right, and wrong, if magick ruled the world. Everything you've denied."

Nicolas angled his head toward her. "Everything you've felt about me, Maggie. Does it make sense? It's not sexual chemistry, not the typical male-female kind. It's deeper, more important and lasting. You didn't run with me because the Morphs invaded your home and nearly killed your dog. You ran because your instinct told you I'm your best damn chance of keeping safe. And I am."

He drew in an audible breath. "Because I will, to my last dying breath. It's ingrained into me as much as your empath abilities are genetically programmed into you. It's what will ultimately bind us together. You and I, Maggie, are destined to be together. So relax and stop questioning everything. In time, it will all make sense."

Maggie closed her eyes, trying to make sense of what seemed like utter nonsense. She didn't believe in karma, the tooth fairy or soul mates.

What she believed in most right now was self-preservation. Having escaped one danger, she now had to get herself out of another one. Was Nicolas a knight to the rescue or a wolf in sheep's clothing who wanted to hurt her? She couldn't risk it. Not now.

First chance she had, she'd escape.

Tension tightened his body as Nicolas followed U.S. Highway 19 as it turned into U.S. 41, eastbound toward Miami. Beside him, Maggie looked as if she feared he'd whip out a knife and start carving her up like a Thanksgiving turkey.

The only instrument he wanted to whip out he had an equally difficult time controlling as much as he did Maggie. The sexual attraction between them hadn't cooled with the present danger. Rather, the more time he spent with Maggie, the more his need to mate grew. The encroaching full moon didn't help, either.

Why had he thought that his future mate would be as eager to acquiesce to his demands as the pack's females? Nicolas had only to flick a finger and they scrambled to obey. Sexually jaded, he'd idly wished for a mate who would challenge him in bed and out.

Now he feared his wish was granted. Her rock-solid stubbornness intrigued him. Frustrated him. She had the fight in her, but he must prove himself dominant. Never could he allow himself to become vulnerable. Weak. Weak Draicons were dangerous ones. He had to remain in control and strong.

Fleeting thoughts of his past zipped through his mind. Nicolas tensed his muscles. There was no room in his life for compassion and emotions.

He knew what was best for Maggie. He'd been Damian's beta who ensured his leader's commands were carried out. With Maggie at his side, he'd resume his position, and together they'd fight their enemies and defeat them.

After teaching her to fight. He bit back a frustrated growl. The approach of the full moon and his own sexual frustration clawed at him. First he had to get her safe.

His thoughts drifted to their destination. Before he'd left, Damian promised to send a pack member to the safe house in Melbourne. The home in Florida had a strong shield against Morphs. Homesickness washed over him. The pack member Damian sent had to be female, sympathetic and understanding in order to willingly associate with Nicolas. Perhaps it was motherly, single Katia who always babysat for other members. The female companionship would be good for Maggie. Katia could introduce the softer side of pack life to Maggie.

Certainly he couldn't. He was the pack's fiercest killer. Nicolas felt the familiar frozen ice inside him. For once, he'd like to know the security of peace. He pushed aside the wistfulness. Such things were for females and other males. It was too late for him. He was Damian's perfect killing machine and could expect nothing more.

His Draicon senses on alert, he scanned the road. Urban concrete jungles faded, giving way to brush and trees, then water. The Everglades.

Punching a button, he rolled down his window. Wind combed through his hair, kissed his cheek. He drew in a clean, fresh lungful, reveling in the sharp, refreshing smell.

The two-lane highway cut across the Everglades like a knife slicing through cake. He'd specifically mapped out this route. Maggie might think their escape was happenstance. It wasn't.

Silence dripped between them. He thought about probing her mind, then abandoned the idea. He didn't want to creep in there like an ant sneaking into…

Shock slammed into him. Nicolas gripped the steering wheel. Dammit! How could he be so careless? He'd forgotten in the rush… He scanned the windshield, the dashboard, looking for tiny invaders.

"What's wrong?"

"Look around the inside for ants. I forgot to check the SUV for hitchhikers." He blew out a breath. "They'll probably be in the form of ants, but see any insect, kill it."

Maggie's brow puckered in a frown he would have found adorable under normal circumstances. Then his supersensitive hearing picked it out. A tiny whine, like a mosquito. A fly buzzed toward the dashboard, smacked against the windshield as if testing for a way out.

A decoy? Possibly, distracting him from the real invader.

He tried listening for the whine, but heard only the fly's insistent buzzing. Nicolas gestured to it. "Kill it, Maggie, before it can shift and kill us."

"It can't be one of those things! It would have attacked us by now. It's just an ordinary fly, trying to get out." She pressed her window button. "Go away, little fellow."

Before he could react, the fly buzzed outside. Nicolas grit his teeth. When they stopped, he'd check the car.

"You're a cliché. You wouldn't kill a fly. Morphs can also cloak themselves as fleas on your dog," he snarled. "Do you kill fleas?"

She gave a serene smile. "No, I don't. Misha has never had a flea. I use natural remedies."

Training Maggie to kill would prove very tough.

About halfway across the Everglades, Nicolas slowed, and pulled over along the grassy patch bordering the road's northern side. Three cars were parked on the grass. People sat by the canal paralleling the highway. He parked a distance from the cars, including his target—a silver Chevy.

Maggie's huge blue eyes widened. "Why are we stopping now?"

"We're switching cars. This one has our scent all over it. I need to check it out, too, make sure we didn't invite any intruders along. We're going to change clothes as well." He switched off the engine, pulled his shirt over his head and tossed it aside.

A small intake of breath alerted him to her reaction. She stared at his chest the way he'd seen pack females eyeing him after he'd returned from a fight and needed a quick coupling. Her pink tongue moistened her wide, mobile mouth. His gaze locked to those lips, remembering their taste and texture beneath the urgent press of his own.

Now wasn't the time. But her reaction sent desire arrowing through him. Nicolas caught the scent of warm female skin. He wanted her. Flesh to flesh, skin against skin, her body soft and yielding beneath his. He wanted her so bad his whole body shook with the longing.

If he didn't take her soon, he'd lose control.

Desire whipped him. The beast inside roared for release, to dominate and claim. Nicolas gave a soft growl as his hungry gaze swept over the pert thrust of her breasts against her shirt. Her gaze collided with his and he glimpsed her stark longing.

"Nicolas…" Her voice was sultry and he doubted she even realized it.

"Do as I say," he said brusquely. "Get undressed."

I'd love to get naked with you. Oh, please. Yes…

Oh, God! What the hell am I doing?!

She'd been eyeballing him like a starving woman ogling steak. Flustered, Maggie flushed. Levelheaded Maggie, all right. What had happened to the woman who never even kissed on the first date? Now she was ready to climb all over Nicolas just because he removed his shirt. Sucking in a breath, she forced herself to look at his face.

Nicolas couldn't be trusted. She barely knew him.

As if he sensed her mood change, he gave her a level look. He reached into the backseat and grabbed a bundle of clothing. "Put these on. They're your size. Should fit."

At her blank stare he added, "Morphs have a highly developed sense of smell just as we do. This clothing is new."

Arousal fled. He planned this. How else could he know to buy her clothing? Hell, maybe he combed through her closet while she slept, scribbled down her size and orchestrated this whole thing. For all she knew, he might prove more dangerous than the creatures that had tried attacking her.

"Not until you tell me what you plan on doing. Where are we going? Why? Who are you, exactly, and what do you want with me?"

"Maggie, we don't have the time now," he insisted.

"Information, Nicolas, I want information."

"Do as I say, caira. I'm pushing my limit." A pulse leapt wildly in his neck.

"What do you want with me? Maybe you're after me for this new healing ability as much as those things were. Why should I trust you?"

"Because I'm the only one who stands between you and an army of Morphs who would kill you without hesitation. And I have to get you to safety before they find us. Now." Nicolas clenched his jaw and held out his fist. "Give me your jeans, Maggie, or I'll rip them off of you." The glint in his eyes warned he might do it.

"What are you?" she asked. "Why do I sense you deep in my mind? You found me, and it wasn't serendipity."

"No," he said, going still, his eyes searching her face. "All right, I'll tell you what I am. After we get on the move and it's safer. Sitting here, it's easier for them to find us."

She sensed his iron control. What if he did want to keep her safe and failed? What would happen to Misha?

Maggie glanced back at her beloved dog. Nicolas didn't want her healing anyone yet. Tough luck. She kicked off her shoes, tugged at her shirt.

Nicolas nodded in apparent approval and his fingers clasped his jeans zipper. Maggie's gaze dropped to the bulge in the denim. She sucked in a breath. Her trembling hand reached out. A knowing smile touched his mouth.

Stop it, stop it! Think, Maggie, think.

She jerked her hand away, stared at the canal

and a fishing family sitting on folding chairs at the canal's edge. An older woman, hair tied back in a ponytail, gestured wildly at the tug on one line. Caught.

Just like me. I'm like some kind of bait. Is he using me to reel in these things? Will I become a Maggie sacrifice for his purpose? And what of Misha?

Nicolas hadn't removed his jeans. Intensity radiated in his dark gaze.

"Maggie, trust me. I would never use you to lure my enemies. Don't be afraid. You need to change clothing. We have to get rid of anything the Morphs can use to track us."

She reached into the back for Misha and cradled the dog. "And what of her, Nicolas? Are you going to dump Misha into the canal because these things will track us through her?"

"Maggie, I wouldn't hurt her."

How could she trust him? Perhaps it was better to take her chances in the swamp.

Nicolas shook his head slowly. "You're not safe here. They'll find and kill you. It's you they want, Maggie. Not me. Take your chances in the swamp and watch out for the alligators. The Morphs will shift and assume their form as well."

His resigned expression stated it. *You can't trust anyone. I'm your only hope.*

Across the highway, a narrow limestone road cut through the thick brush. Maggie knew this area. She'd been here before on bird-watching expeditions. Alligators populated the miles of brackish water and razor-sharp sawgrass. In the tiny tree islands offering refuge from the swamp were poisonous cottonmouths and pygmy rattlers.

Dangerous animals, yet they seemed tame compared to her current predicament. Where did she take her chances? With Nicolas or the creatures chasing them? Emotion clogged her throat.

Dank water scents drifted through the open window. It pulled at her for some unfathomable reason. Maggie inhaled, wanting to run into the swamp's sheltering arms. The Everglades urged her to run free like an uncaged animal.

"You feel it, don't you? The yearning to let yourself run wild," Nicolas murmured.

He slid a warm palm over her neck. Maggie shivered at his touch, the pull increasing as he gently caressed her. She fought it. Somehow Nicolas sensed her thoughts. Learning toward her, he looked intense. Strong and muscular, solid as a stone wall.

Stone walls could be toppled.

Thoughts of her dog's pain blocked her intentions. Maggie stroked Misha's head.

"She's in pain, Nicolas. So much pain. I need to give her something."

Sympathy entered his gaze. Maggie steeled herself against it and reached into the glove box. Inside, she kept hypodermics and animal tranquilizer. On weekends she rescued frightened and angry strays.

The medicine would go to good use now.

Removing the protective plastic cap with her teeth, she filled the syringe with a large dose of diazepam. Maggie murmured soothingly to her pet, then handed her to Nicolas.

"Let her lie on your lap while I give her this," she instructed.

As expected, his concentration shifted to Misha. Maggie lifted the syringe.

She jammed the needle into the base of Nicolas's neck and depressed the plunger.

A fierce howl rumbled from his chest. His body went stiff. Nicolas turned with a snarl, eyes wild, fingers curled like attacking claws. Maggie shrieked and grabbed Misha and opened the door.

Just then the drug kicked in. Nicolas slumped over the seat. Maggie kicked the door shut and bolted. Heart pounding, she raced across the highway, causing a car to brake hard. Burnt rubber filled her nostrils. Maggie reached the abandoned limestone road. She followed it into the swamp as the brush gave way to sharp sawgrass.

A bay head rose above the swamp like an island. Maggie's Everglades experiences taught her that the thicket of trees and brush offered protection from the heat. Best if all, it offered a good hiding place. She began wading through the ankle-deep water. Smells assaulted her senses, the clean scent of water, the stronger smell of small animals. Sawgrass sliced her arms as she curled them protectively around her dog. Her sneakers squished the periphyton algae covering the ground. Odd how the Everglades amplified her senses. Hearing and smell sharpened. Tree frogs chirped in the distance. Overhead, an egret crackled. Maggie caught the faint scent of a deer.

The bay head wasn't much higher than the water, but she spotted a narrow path cut through the thick brush. Coco plum, red bay and wax myrtle flanked the path. Ferns tickled her nose as she ducked and twisted beneath the overgrowth. In the distance, an airboat droned. Broken branches scraped her hands.

She waded through a shallow stream and climbed up to a small clearing. Someone had cut back the brush to create a living space. Dead leaves and dried branches littered the ground. She settled on the ground against a grayish-brown coco plum tree. Thin sunlight filtered through its sheltering branches and glossy, elliptical-shaped leaves.

Tension eased as she settled Misha on her lap. This felt right, somehow. Maggie pushed aside the niggling thoughts that she belonged here, in the wild.

Nicolas would find her.

But dammit, not before she healed her dog. If today she died, Misha would live. Her pet came first. Misha was her only friend. She had the ability to heal her. She'd use it.

Palms trembling, she stretched them over her dying dog, willing herself to begin the healing process.

Bare-chested, clad only in sneakers and jeans, Nicolas waited for a line of cars to pass. He shook his head as he cleared the drug from his system. Should have known. He'd felt it radiating from her, seen it in her jumping pulse, her hitched breathing. He'd been too damn busy paying attention to his dick to give credence to the signals she put out.

He must arouse the ancient instincts inside her to listen to him and obey. He was pack, accustomed to doling out orders in the group, not herding a lone wolf like Maggie who thought she was human. Nicolas, the pack's fiercest warrior. Nicolas, the one who didn't dare let anyone grow close.

No one ever made him feel this way before. Spinning out of control. Helpless. Aching at her pain, even before he mated with her, and knew all her emotions.

Doubts railed at him. If Maggie made him feel this susceptible, what would happen once he exchanged powers? He pushed aside the thought, concentrated on his mate.

Her focus was centered on the dog.

One action could remind her of her origins. Too risky here, yet if she healed Misha, it didn't matter. The spectral trail her magick kicked up would attract the Morphs far more than his change would. He shoved back a hank of hair as the line of cars finally passed. Nicolas bolted across the road.

He had to do it when she could see him, and hope she'd finally understand.

As he picked up her scent, the thought dimly occurred to him that he'd forgotten to check the car for the source of that tiny mosquitolike whine.

Chapter 7

Nicolas whispered into her mind, murmuring soothing assurances.

Maggie ignored his husky voice baiting her. She closed her eyes to everything around her, the distant call of wading birds, the snort of an alligator moving through the undergrowth. Nothing else mattered except healing her beloved companion.

Images of a whole, healthy Misha ran through her mind. Blackened, dying cells shifting into her own body replaced by healthy cells. Maggie drew in a deep breath and concentrated.

Stabbing pain as fierce as white-hot knives slammed into her. Her hands jerked off the dog. A reflex scream of agony ripped from her lips. Sweat streamed down her temple. In her lap, Misha whimpered and twisted.

Her pet had hidden her agony well.

Tears dripped down her cheeks. Taking on that pain again was like dipping her toes into white-hot lava.

"I'm sorry, baby." Maggie buried her face into her dog's fur. "I just can't. I can't."

Misha whined. Maggie felt her slip further away. The brief, intimate contact had warned her the disease was gaining rapidly. The window of life was slowly closing.

A familiar scent invaded her nostrils. Misha weakly barked a greeting. Nicolas. He'd found her. Maggie bent her head, whispered to stay quiet. But as if scenting a friend, Misha lifted her head and wagged her tail. Maggie knew exactly how much energy that movement cost.

His sneakers sloshed through the stream separating her hiding place from land. For someone with quiet stealth, he made plenty of noise.

The sharp edge of his profile, the straight nose, chiseled chin, came into her sight as she remained motionless. Wind whistled through the leafy covering of branches. Nicolas approached and squatted down, studying her with an intense look. He held out a strong palm.

"Maggie. Come with me. Don't be afraid. Please. I promise, I won't hurt you."

The soothing cadence of his deep voice nearly

lulled her into compliance. Maggie pressed against the tree, ignoring the screaming instincts to obey him. Trust him. Mold herself to him, bond with him as they coupled…

Concern lined his features. He studied Misha. "You tried healing her, didn't you? And it was too much pain. Come with me. I'll take you both to a safe place where you can try again."

Something dark and haunting touched his eyes. "I know what it's like to watch a good friend slowly die and feel all alone. It's the worst feeling in the world. I don't want it to happen to you, caira. Reach out with your feelings, not your mind, and trust me."

For the first time, Maggie opened herself to instinct. It gushed in a tidal wave, washing away sense, logic and reason. She wanted to close the distance between herself and Nicolas. It felt right, as if he were someone she knew in her blood and bones even if they had only met…

Her breath came in sharp, jerky rasps. Yes, this did feel familiar. Why? It made no sense.

"You can't protect me, or Misha," she whispered. "And there is no such thing as magic."

"You're very wrong, Maggie. There is magick in the healing power of your touch, and there is magick in me. I'll show you."

Nicolas stepped back, kicked off his shoes, shed his socks and jeans. Naked, he raised his arms. She watched in astonishment as his body seemed to ripple with power.

One minute, a naked man stood there.

The next, a muscled, large gray wolf had replaced the man.

Panic raced up her spine. No, no, no. Not possible. A little moan fled her lips. Then the wolf turned its head to look at her. It began gracefully loping toward her.

A hysterical scream bubbled in her throat. She backed against the gnarled tree trunk, its roughness jabbing her back. The wolf broached the distance between them.

Immobilized with terror, Maggie sat utterly still. The wolf's muzzle was banded with dark brown fur, the caramel gaze sharp and intelligent. It locked on her like a laser. Good God, it was massive, one hundred and fifty pounds, the jaws possessing crushing strength...

Her terrified gaze whipped back to Misha. The dog's tail beat the air in a furious cadence. Her throat went dry with panic as the wolf slowly turned its massive head and stared at her dog. Setting Misha behind her, Maggie steeled herself.

"Good boy, good boy, it's okay, just leave us

alone, please, please," she chanted in the soothing tone used when dealing with scared or angry animals.

Turning, the wolf locked its eyes on her. Then, to her astonished shock, it gave a small whimper. Her heart went still. The wolf dropped to all fours and crawled toward her submissively.

Wonder replaced fear. Dragging in a deep breath, she smelled an earthy animal smell—wolf and something lingering and familiar. Woodsy, deep pine forest. Nicolas's scent.

It couldn't be.

The wolf stopped a mere foot away. It sniffed her hand, then gave it a gentle lick. The tongue felt like velvet sandpaper, and warm against her quivering hand.

Emboldened, Maggie lifted her hand and touched the luxurious fur. The wolf whined again, and laid its head upon her lap. Deep inside, fear slipped out on four paws, replaced by long-forbidden memories. She stroked the wolf's head, its fur soft and thick beneath her shaking fingers. No reason to fear. This was right.

No. It wasn't. Made no sense.

She squeezed her eyes shut. When she opened them again, Nicolas lay on the loamy earth, her hand woven through his thick, silky hair. Eyes dark as obsidian stared up at her. He was naked.

Maggie gulped down a deep breath as he caught her hand in his warm strong palm.

"It's true, Maggie. Everything I told you. But I knew you had to see for yourself. I am a Draicon, a wolf shape-shifter. My pack is in New Mexico, where I live. I came here to escort you there, because you belong with us, Maggie. With me. I'm your mate and that's why you feel this pull toward me. It's how I can delve into your thoughts, just as you can into mine if you try.

"You're Draicon as well, a wolf and our pack's missing empath. We've been searching for you a long, long time. And now the time has come for you to return to your rightful place, and your home. Long ago our people left our dimension to learn of the earth. We discovered how to manipulate the earth's natural forces and energy. To learn to live in harmony with the earth, we shape-shifted into the form of wolves. Those creatures that pursued you—" his gaze flicked off to the west "—the Morphs, were once Draicon as well, but turned to evil to gain power. They kill for power, absorbing their victims' energy as they die. They can be birds, alligators, any animal shape and can clone themselves into an army to track their prey. They infected Misha with a new disease they created to draw you out, and then kill you."

He reached for his clothing and dressed. "Maggie, we have to leave. Please. Even if it's too much for you to believe now, just believe this. You saw how those creatures were after Misha. Their only desire is to cause pain and fear, and gain power from it."

Nicolas squatted down, held out his arms. "Come here, Misha. You're tired, I can tell. Let me try something."

From behind her, the dog weakly stumbled over to Nicolas. He picked her up, cradled her against his chest. Nicolas waved a hand. Iridescent sparks floated on the air. Awestruck, Maggie watched as he chanted odd words, moving his hand. Ancient memories surged. Her mother, chanting lyrical, soothing words when her father fell ill once....

Nicolas rested a gentle palm on Misha's head. "I can't heal, not like you, Maggie, but I issued a spell to take away the pain. It's only temporary, but it will make her feel better."

Misha stared up at Nicolas with trusting eyes. The heavy weight on Maggie's chest lifted. There had to be something inherently good about a man who loved an animal enough to remove her pain. Maggie stood, dusting off her jeans.

Nicolas stood, holding out Misha. "No, you take her. I trust you with her," she said.

Progress. Trust, the first step. Weaving the spell over Misha and his change had cost him much-needed energy, but seeing Maggie's soft smile was worth it. Nicolas guided her back to the car. He folded Misha into Maggie's arms. The dog slept, her breathing even. Misha was key to Maggie's connection, her grasp on the immediate concern. Her gaze dropped to the dog. "I think she needs a little reassurance," Nicolas murmured. *As do you.*

Maggie took Misha, rested her cheek against her pet. His supersensitive hearing noted her heart rate slow to a more normal rhythm, as he'd expected. Very gently, she set the dog on the blanket on the backseat. She turned to him. The relief on her face made his heart stand still.

They climbed into the front. Her hand rested over his. "Thank you."

Hunger lashed him at the gentle pressure of her touch. Damn, this was much worse than before, weaving magick and paying the price. He didn't want food to replace lost energy. Only Maggie, feeling her hand stroking his head, craving her body next to his.

Forgetting the danger pursuing them, he had only thoughts of her mouth against his. He reached over, braced his arms on either side of her and kissed her.

Nicolas angled his lips over hers and drank in her mouth. His lips were warm, demanding everything, leaving her nothing. The drugging kiss dragged her under a vortex of sudden heat as his tongue thrust past her lips and explored inside. Maggie sagged against the seat and fisted her hands in his T-shirt to pull him closer. He didn't kiss with the consummate skill of a womanizer, but a man desperate only for her.

Her mouth opened wider. Maggie closed her eyes, their tongues tangling and dancing as he intensified the kiss. This wasn't a "hello, let's get to know each other." More like their tongues and lips imitating the sex act.

That thought wasn't hers.

Startled, she twisted away, but he made a strangled sound and cupped her cheeks, holding her still. "Relax, and just feel," his sultry whisper feathered into her mouth.

He kissed her again, his rock-hard body pressed against her yielding one. Maggie felt the soft leather against her back, the plain cotton bra suddenly chafing at her too sensitive, aching nipples. She inhaled Nicolas, his essence, his spirit. A deep, visceral ache throbbed between her legs. Maggie squirmed, needing to satisfy that ache. A little moan fled as she tried to get closer.

Breathing heavily, Nicolas pulled back. He rested his forehead against hers a minute. His hand slid down her hip. Maggie bit back a moan, clutched his muscled forearms.

His fingers unhooked the button of her jeans. The soft purr of the zipper sliding downward filled her ears. Here, in the front seat, was not how she envisioned making love for the first time. But an unbearable heat infused her as if her very skin were on fire. Kicking off her shoes, Maggie raised her hips and wriggled free from the jeans.

"Take off your panties," he murmured.

She stared at the taut, tanned flesh stretching over hard muscle, the dark hair feathering his deep chest. A line marched down his flat belly, dipping into the waistband of his jeans.

A low growl rumbled from his chest as she shimmied out of her panties and tossed them aside. Nicolas nuzzled her neck, his lips skimming over her throat. Maggie writhed, needing him closer. His hand stroked her cotton T-shirt, skimmed over one hip and then delved between her legs. He stroked gently, culling more moisture. She leaned into him as he slid a finger between her aching, hot female flesh. Sweet tension pulsed there. A little moan fled as she clutched his head as he slid lower, feathering kisses over her hot skin, his fingers caressing her below.

The sudden slam of a car door tore them apart like two strong hands. Maggie moaned in disappointed frustration as Nicolas drew back. Outside, a man walked away from a Saturn SUV with a fishing pole in hand.

"Damn," Nicolas muttered, his dark eyes wild. "I forgot myself. Sorry." He dragged in a deep breath. "I need energy. Food. It can't wait. I need to hunt. These woods are filled with small game. Stay here. I'll be back."

Wild erotic need subsided into sheer bewilderment. "You can't be serious. Nicolas, you make no sense. First you're on the run from these things, then you want to make love to me and now you stop and say you have to hunt?"

"I'm a Draicon, as you are, Maggie. Every time I exercise magick or change, I have to replenish lost energy. Think of it as a long-distance runner needing calories for fuel. One way is to have sex and absorb your partner's sexual energy. But not with you. Not now."

His dark gaze stripped her to the bare skin. She shivered with delicious anticipation.

"The fastest way for me to absorb energy is to change and find small game to kill."

Sensual anticipation faded, replaced by revulsion. "Kill small, defenseless animals?"

His jaw worked. "There's not enough time to make love to you now, so I need to hunt. The knowledge will come back to you."

The words caused a mass of confusion. "I'm not like you, Nicolas. I don't know what you are, I don't even know what I am yet...but I don't kill. Ever."

"You'll learn." He gave her a level look. "Don't move until I return. Understand?"

He crossed the highway, muscles moving fluidly beneath the jeans. As she shrugged back into her clothing, Maggie felt rising tension mix with dread. In the backseat, Misha stirred restlessly. She lifted her head and scraped at the door.

The dog had to go outside. Maggie clipped on Misha's leash and went outside with her. She thought about following Nicolas. Bad idea. But...

Misha pulled at the leash, as if eager for a walk. Encouraged, Maggie tugged her toward the direction Nicolas went. In the same bay head where she'd found refuge, she found a pile of abandoned clothing. Nicolas's scent was stamped all over it.

She heard a rustling noise, turned. A large gray wolf stood silently observing her. Its powerful body in animal form was equally muscled in human form. Dread filled her.

Nicolas.

The leash fell to the earth with a clunk. The wolf waded into the shallow stream, washed its muzzle and returned to the clothing. In an eye blink, the wolf vanished and Nicolas stood in its place. He dressed, wiped his mouth with the back of one hand.

"This is what I am, Maggie. What you are. We are wolf. We hunt, and kill. It's the natural order. Just as we kill our enemies. You will learn to destroy them."

Her stomach quivered. "I'm a vet, Nicolas. I heal, not hurt. I swore a vow long ago never to kill. I will not do this, Nicolas. I can't kill Morphs. I'm not like you!"

His gaze softened. "You are one of us, Maggie. You'll see. You can't hide from what you truly are. Soon, you won't be able to deny it, any more than you could prevent killing the Morphs back at your home to protect Misha."

The implication of his words sank in. She had killed. Maggie struggled with her own confusion and fading conviction. She had killed without thought or rationale to save her dog.

"Draicon don't kill for fulfillment, amusement or power, Maggie. We kill for food, or to protect our own, those whom we love. There is nothing wrong with defending those you love," he said, running a finger along her cheek.

Suddenly he went still, his dark eyes searching. His entire body tensed. Maggie looked around and saw nothing. But a foul smell of rotting seaweed and sewage drifted to her nostrils. She'd smelled this back at her house. Her heart raced.

"Dammit, I knew I should have checked the SUV for intruders. Get behind me," he ordered, pushing her to the side. "Take Misha, and if anything happens to me, drive to this place." He issued directions as she stared in growing shock.

Something came lumbering out of the undergrowth.

It looked like a small raccoon with gray fur and a black-ringed tail. Yet before her astonished eyes, it began changing. Growing, elongating. Morphing.

Misha released a terrified yelp, ran to a tree and hid behind it.

The creature crawled on four legs and was squat, scaly and reptilian. Its head was elongated, with rows of sharp, lethal spikes rising from it. Good God, it looked like…a dragon?

It barreled toward them at a blinding rate of speed. A horrified scream died in her throat as it locked its gaze on her like a rifle's red pinpoint laser. Eyes of madness, glowing like fire, gleamed with hatred. Spittle leaked from the corners of its mouth as it opened enormous jaws, showing rows of yellow sharp teeth.

A crackling noise sounded as it hissed, breathing flames.

Nicolas waved his hands. Twin steel daggers caught stray beams of sunlight as they materialized in his hands. As the creature reared back, never losing eye contact with her, Nicolas struck the soft underbelly. A screech of agony clawed in Maggie's ears like nails against slate. The creature sidestepped Nicolas and snaked around. Its jaws snapped, barely missing her.

"Get back, Maggie," Nicolas roared. He struck again, but the daggers glanced off the thick scales of the creature's back.

It turned its head, as if Nicolas were a mere inconvenience. Bloody furrows showed on his bare arm as it raked a giant claw over his skin. Nicolas barely winced. Maggie's stomach gave a sickening lurch at the crimson stream. Blood. Just like that last time...

She moaned, trying to regain a grip. Not now. *You will not collapse,* she willed herself. Somewhere deep inside, she found a reservoir of strength and drew from it.

Nicolas threw himself at the dragonlike thing. It hissed and breathed fire. Flames licked along his shirt but Nicolas waved a hand and they vanished. He reached up with both fists and struck a powerful blow to the creature's head. The beast swayed and toppled. Nicolas jumped atop it, his powerful fists punching the soft, vulnerable snout.

Immobilized by twin emotions of fear and shock, she stuffed a fist into her mouth. Battling this was a resilience, an urge to engage in the fracas as he tussled with the creature. Powerful instincts surfaced as the creature latched onto Nicolas's calf with razor-sharp teeth. He winced and grimly continued fighting. At the sight of bright blood oozing out of Nicolas's leg, she screamed.

The dragon thing looked at her. Suddenly it swung toward the tree and Misha.

The creature started toward her dog. Misha barked, but was trapped by the thicket of undergrowth, so she could not retreat. Jaws open to reveal sharp teeth, the dragon-thing stalked toward the helpless dog. It opened its mouth and hissed, as if to spew fire. Almost automatically, Maggie waved a hand and directed a thought at the flames, dispelling them.

Never again. Ever. You will not hurt my friend or anyone else I love.

A red-hazed fury blocked out everything but the need to protect Misha. She barely became aware of kicking off her sneakers, stripping off her clothing. Barely was aware of the rush of dank air brushing against her naked skin.

All that mattered was getting that thing away from her beloved dog.

"No!" The roar in her throat turned into a snarl. Power rippled through her. All senses sharpened. She could hear the rush of blood through veins, the frantic, terrified beating of Misha's heart, smell the dragon thing's bloodlust, taste the raw urge to protect what was hers. She rushed forward, snarling, to defend Misha. Her jaws snapped in a growl.

"No, Maggie," Nicolas shouted. "Stay back! You're not trained yet! The heart is the only way to kill them."

He sprang to his feet, throwing himself in

front of her as the creature lunged. The blow intended for her throat struck his right side. Nicolas groaned as flesh tore and blood flowed. Maggie turned and growled at the dragon thing. She smelled its fetid odor, felt its glee at inflicting pain and felt the urge to rip. Tear. Defend.

The creature rose up, roared, and just as it started for her, Nicolas struck. His aim was steady and sure, and the daggers he held in both hands sank into the creature's chest. The dragon thing died with a gasping snarl.

Blood flowed over his hands. Nicolas winced, withdrew his daggers. Burns marked his hands, wrists and forearms where the creature's blood had touched him.

Blood. Crimson, flowing blood. Horror overcame her. Maggie whimpered, felt rage leave, replaced by shock. She went to stick a fist into her mouth.

Instead she saw a paw. Claws extended from the soft padding.

Oh, God. Shock tore through her, and just as quickly, she found herself shivering in her bare skin. Skin. Not fur. Human again.

But Nicolas had been right.

She was a *wolf.* She had changed.

No, no! It couldn't be, this wasn't happening…

a memory flickered. Maggie squeezed her eyes shut, trying to block it out. You can't hide from what you truly are, Nicolas had told her.

I can't be, I just can't be like him! She quickly dressed.

"Oh, caira," he said thickly.

Maggie opened her eyes to see concern twining with pain on his face. She winced at the ugly burns on his hands and arms, the blood oozing from the lacerations. A twinge of sympathetic pain laced her.

Morph blood was acid. Maggie pushed aside her own fear, glad for the distraction. Time enough to deal with that horror later. She raked an anxious gaze over him and saw the suffering glaze his dark eyes. His strong jaw tensed so hard it seemed it might shatter.

"Are you all right? It didn't hurt you, did it?"

Shaking her head, Maggie felt a sense of wonder laced with unexpected tenderness.

He had defended her, deliberately thrown himself in front of the creature to keep her safe. No one had ever done that. Not once since her parents' deaths had anyone dared put themselves in danger to protect her. Trembling, she reached up, touched the blackened bruise on his cheek. Pain barely dented her as she absorbed the injury.

Nicolas pushed her hands away. "Draicon heal from such injuries, Maggie. I'll be fine."

She examined his side, saw him flinch even at her gentle touch.

"You can't go on like this," she asserted. Maggie closed her eyes, placed her hands on Nicolas and concentrated on healing his injuries. To her enormous shock, the suffocating pain endured through healing was gone. Instead, the pain was sharp but fleeting, as if she'd bumped her shin on a coffee table.

When she finished, Nicolas touched her face. "Thank you," he said hoarsely. "Maggie, about what happened…"

Her head flew back and forth in a vehement shake. She couldn't deal with that right now. "Stop," she whispered, putting a finger on his lips. "Just hold me."

His arms slid around her waist, drawing her close. She nestled against him, needing the simple contact and comfort of an embrace. Maggie rested her head against his chest as he stroked her hair. His touch felt comforting, gentle.

As she looked up, something enigmatic entered his eyes. His mouth hovered inches away from hers. His lips were firm, full.

Unable to resist, she leaned forward, touching her mouth to his. A groan wrenched from his throat. Nicolas crushed her against him, his mouth moving over hers. Maggie's mouth opened wide as he thrust his tongue inside. She tasted him, warm, strong, a heady combination of cinnamon and male. His scent invaded her mind, spicy, earth and pine, making her want to join with him and roll about on the spongy ground in a fierce, frenzied mating as wild as the surroundings. She rubbed against him, feeling her nipples tauten, warmth flood between her legs. Maggie hooked her hands around his neck.

She wanted him, desperately. More now than even last night after the wine. Needed him, needed this, to banish what had happened. Push aside the dreaded realization of what she was.

It was Nicolas who gently pulled away, set her on her feet. But the pulse throbbing in his neck warned her she'd nearly tipped him over the edge as well.

Sensible Maggie. Whatever happened to that woman? It was the spice of danger, having a knight in shining—denim? Wolf fur?—rush to defend her. Animal attraction.

Real animal attraction. Suppressing a strangled laugh, she gathered the trembling Misha into her arms. She suppressed a shudder as she looked at the dead dragon creature. "I thought you said the Morphs only replicated as existing animals."

"Who said dragons didn't exist?" Nicolas attempted a lopsided smile.

"We can't leave this…thing here."

"You won't have to. Watch."

Astonishment seized her as the dragon began to disintegrate before her eyes. Another memory surfaced. Bodies, blood flowing from them, then watching them crumbling into gray ash. She buried her nose into Misha's fur. It was too much to open that particular door.

She was a Draicon, just like Nicolas. For years she had suppressed everything, even quieting her anger. This was the reason. When someone she loved was threatened, her wolf emerged. She had no control. Her wolf was a caged beast, awaiting the right time to paw to the surface. Maggie gripped Misha, the only centering influence in her wildly spinning world.

Nicolas watched her with his calm steady gaze. Misha wasn't the only centering influence. He had controlled his wolf. If he could do it, perhaps she could learn from him.

In silence she followed him back to the car. He

tossed her the new clothing. They dressed, then he wadded up their old clothing and got out. "Stay here," he ordered.

Nicolas approached the Saturn SUV. The family fishing on the canal had been a distance away from the fight, shielded by the noise of traffic. Maggie envied their blissful ignorance. Her world was rocking back on its sensible heels. Nicolas waved his hands in the same mysterious gesture she'd seen earlier. He opened the back door, threw their clothing on the floor then paced back toward her. He picked up Misha.

"Gather our stuff. We're switching cars and leaving yours here."

Mutely, she obeyed. Nicolas opened the back door of an anonymous-looking Chevy and gently laid Misha on the backseat. Fuzzy dice hung from the rearview mirror. The interior smelled like old tacos and cigarettes. Maggie didn't care. It was safe.

They sat in silence as Nicolas steered the car back onto the highway. Though one hand rested easily on the fur-covered wheel, Nicolas's jawline was tense. Strain etched his features.

She rolled down the window, let the breeze toss her curls as a distraction. Eventually Tamiami Trail turned into Southwest 8th Street. He drove east, then onto the Florida Turnpike and headed north. Maggie watched the stretch of the Dolphin Mall pass in a blur, then the gray-coated Rinker plant on the left. Construction on this coast blossomed like weeds. Ghostly gray melaleuca trees stretched skyward. Hurricane damage tipped some sideways into the water like drunks teetering on their last legs.

Nicolas was a magic creature, a wolf who killed. *So am I.* Maggie shrank from the thought. Dr. Margaret Sinclair, respected veterinarian with a thriving practice, no car payments—no car now, either—and a beach house, now torched in flames, had turned into a wolf.

Her life was spinning wildly on its axis. One day at a time. It was how she survived after watching her parents die, and how she would survive right now.

Maggie squeezed her eyes shut, seeing crimson flow from the dragon creature. Then the scene shifted. Red flowing on a concrete sidewalk, not all her parents' blood...

Nicolas began humming a low, soothing tune. The melody quieted her turbulent feelings.

"I wish I had brought my music," she mused.

She remembered him singing in Italian at the

bar. Nicolas, a killer wolf, liked classical. She shuddered. Killer wolf.

Was she one as well?

Maggie had changed. Turned into a wolf at last to protect her beloved pet. Nicolas knew he should be turning handsprings.

Instead, he felt ripped in half at her abject horror. Her change didn't bring Maggie joy, only terror. He hadn't thought she could twist him in half like this. He didn't like it. Always he had been able to mask his feelings. But Maggie brought everything rushing to the surface. Emotions overwhelmed him: his urgent desire to protect her and her frightened confusion.

Music would dispel the tension. Nicolas reached into the center console, pulled out the CD he'd placed there earlier. He slid it into the player, cranked up the volume and punched a button, advancing to the second song. The lyrical voice filled the SUV, soothing his nerves. Tension vanished, replaced with the deep longing in the song that echoed his own. The haunting baritone filled his senses. His emotions bubbled dangerously close to the surface: all the sorrowful emptiness of being alone, the hope felt since finding Maggie and his deep need of her. He couldn't allow himself to love. Love made one dangerously vulnerable. Nicolas vowed never to become vulnerable.

Maggie tilted her head, her forehead crinkling in an adorable questioning look. "Who is this? It's beautiful."

"Josh Groban, *Gira Con Me.*"

"I've heard him. He has a hit song in English."

"A couple. I prefer the Italian."

Her smile made something in his chest ease.

"I like Italian, too. It's a beautiful language, but every time I hear it…it reminds me of this time when I went on this date…"

Her laugh threaded with a self-deprecating note sounded forced. "When I was an undergrad in Miami, a fellow student took me to the opera and afterward we went to the beach. I guess he wanted to get amorous. He started talking in Italian and just as he tried to kiss me, I blurted out that…that…I told him I didn't kiss on the first date. He seemed to understand and drove me home when I asked, but told everyone the next day never to speak Italian to me because the language made me frigid."

A heated flush covered her face. She looked out the window.

"He sounds like an insecure loser." Nicolas tightened his hands on the steering wheel with the urge to throttle the man who dared to try to kiss his Maggie, then mocked her.

A tremulous smile touched her mobile mouth. "I thought as much, too. But in a way it made me sad because I could never hear opera again without wondering if I were. I've never..." Her hands twisted in her lap. "Been much attracted to men. I thought he was right."

"You didn't hear the right Italian from the right person," he said gently.

"I think you're right." Maggie raised her gaze to his. A thrill of hope raced through him at the equal longing in her own eyes. Was it the romanticism of the rich baritone drifting from the speakers? Or him?

Too much to expect it was him. But he continued humming and the frozen void inside him began to shrink a little.

Chapter 8

It felt like minutes later when the car stopped, and the door opened. Maggie blinked in sleepy confusion as Nicolas squeezed her hand. "Wake up, darling, we're here."

Gray clouds scudded over the sky. Warm air wafted into the car as he opened the door. Disoriented, she studied the elegant white ranch house sitting on an acre-wide lawn. Slash pine trees peppered the yard. It looked remote…better yet, safe. She blinked, studying the small gold watch on her wrist. It was well after three o'clock. Her stomach grumbled a loud protest. A knowing smile touched his mouth.

"We'll get something to eat here."

Nicolas gathered Misha in his arms and escorted Maggie up the curved stone walkway to a set of elegant oak doors with stained glass panes. He twisted open the brass doorknob and ushered her inside. A white-tiled hallway opened to an expansive living room with mint-green furniture, coral walls and floral window hangings. Maggie forced her sleepy brain to clear as Nicolas set Misha down. A delicious scent of grilled meat filled the air, as welcoming as baking cookies.

The eager look on Nicolas's face vanished as a man glided out from an adjoining kitchen. His square face, dark curly hair and wiry body clad in a silk shirt and creased trousers contrasted with the hard look in his steel gray eyes as he studied Nicolas.

"Baylor," Nicolas said thickly. "Why are you here?"

"Damian thought you'd need a little help along the way." The man's frank interest settled on Maggie. "Hello. I'm Baylor, from the New Mexico pack. You must be the long-lost Margaret. I'm delighted to see you again."

Confusion settled over her as his hand gripped hers. "Again?"

"None of us have seen you since you were very young. It's good you're coming home. We've all missed you."

A frisson of warmth filled her. A real family,

one who wanted her, unlike the parade of foster families in childhood. Baylor's smile widened as he swept an admiring gaze over her. He ignored Nicolas, whose fists were clenched.

"You're even more lovely than I imagined," he murmured. Then he looked businesslike.

"Damian sent me because I'm one of the pack's most experienced in fighting Morphs, if they should try to attack while you're here tonight. He trusts me to help keep you safe, Margaret. I'm pack. Family. Draicon, like you are, Margaret, and can be trusted."

The man shot Nicolas a look of disdain. "Unlike others."

Baylor raised her hand to his lips in a courtly gesture. Nicolas wrapped his fingers around her wrist and pulled it down.

"Get your hands off my mate," he warned.

His eyes narrowed to slits as he pushed Maggie behind him. The men silently sized each other up, bristling like combative dogs. Baylor threw up his hands in a gesture of surrender.

"Enough of this. I came here to help. Both of you must be hungry. I have steaks on the grill. So come in and make yourself welcome. Margaret, I arranged for you to sleep in the master bedroom. You'll find it comfortable enough."

Squatting down, Baylor wagged his fingers at Misha. "Who's this? Hey there, little fellow."

"She's Misha. My dog."

"I'll take her into the bedroom for you, Margaret. I'm sure she's special to you."

"I'll do it." Nicolas lifted Misha and narrowed his eyes at Baylor. "Why don't you go into the kitchen and do a little domestic work?"

Baylor gave a flat smile. "Sure. There's time enough later for talk. And we should talk, Nicolas. There've been changes since you left us."

Nicolas cradled Misha in one muscled arm and then slid his other arm about Maggie in a possessive gesture. He shot the other male a hard look readable in any language—*stay away.*

Leaving Maggie to rest, Nicolas closed the bedroom door. When he entered the kitchen, Baylor sat on a wood stool at the granite-topped island.

Nicolas leaned against the doorway. Animosity radiated off the other Draicon in waves. Why the hell had Damian sent his nemesis? Baylor had challenged him in the past for the coveted position as Damian's second in command. He had been the first to point out Nicolas had broken pack rules by teaching magick to Jamie and should be banished. Baylor also said Nicolas posed a subtle threat to the pack, reminding everyone of his origins.

Nicolas wasted no words. "Why are you here?"

"Damian sent me to help keep Margaret safe, and because he wants us to make peace before he dies," Baylor said quietly. "I'm willing if you are, for the pack's sake."

The statement floored him. Nicolas rubbed the heel of his hand into his forehead. "Why would you want that?"

"For Margaret. You're bringing her home. I trust that you're doing it because you want back into the fold. I don't care why. We desperately need her healing powers. One female died of the disease, many more are sick, including Aurelia. The pack is falling apart."

Anguish speared him. Aurelia had been like a mother to him. Now she was dying, as well.

Baylor folded his arms across his chest. "You're the magnet drawing Margaret back to her real home. I doubt she'd come without you, if the biological pull is as strong in her as I suspect. Of course, I could always mate with her before you do and solve the problem that way."

"Lay one hand on her and I'll rip you to shreds."

"Touchy, aren't we? I hear the mating urge gets more intense as the moon grows fuller." Baylor's smile didn't quite reach his eyes. "Pax, then. But I won't fail in my duty to the pack."

The last sentence was a clear insult. Nicolas bristled. "Neither will I. And if you're going to suggest I will, just say it."

"All right." Baylor jumped off the stool. "You broke pack rules. You should stay banished. You're dangerous, Nicolas. You're a loaded weapon and that makes you unpredictable. I kept telling Damian he was making a mistake in taking you into our pack, but he didn't listen. And then you went and taught magick to Jamie, a human, against our rules. Why, Nicolas? Why would you teach a misfit mortal already vulnerable to Morph influence?"

Nicolas said nothing. If he revealed the truth, he broke his promise to Damian. The secret would cause the pack to panic. Silence condemned him, yet he had no choice.

"Same answer you always give." Baylor came toward him. "I can only draw my own conclusions. You're power hungry and wanted to use Jamie to topple Damian from leadership. Only the Morphs got to her before you could. You got your wish, Nicolas. Damian might be dead by the time I fly back. Happy?"

Nicolas closed his eyes in agony.

The other male released a deep sigh. "Fine. Just bring Margaret back, help us find a cure for this disease. I can't say I'd trust you again, but I'll declare a truce if you will."

"I will. But I'm watching my back. I don't relish having a knife stick out of it. Go ahead and challenge me, if you dare."

Nicolas flexed his biceps. Baylor stepped back with a look of watchful respect. The other male knew Nicolas would win.

Only because he was strong. The moment he displayed any weakness, he was toast.

Maggie sat on the bed, Misha in her arms.

She had to try again. The pain-free period Misha had enjoyed turned into restless whimpering. Whatever Nicolas had done hadn't lasted.

Maggie stroked Misha's head. Big brown eyes lifted to meet her gaze. A lead weight compressed her chest. Misha was dying and there wasn't a damn thing left to do. Except heal her. Or do the humane thing, and finally put her to sleep.

Burying her face into the dog's soft brown fur, Maggie choked back a sob. She was losing her best friend, who understood her, loved her unconditionally. She stretched out one hand. It trembled violently. She had the power to heal.

But this? Whatever cancer or strange disease affected Misha? What if she herself died from the attempt? Could she handle the pain?

She can't make the decision for herself. But if she could, what would she tell you? Let me go?

As if sensing her thoughts, Misha looked up. Maggie knew the answer. Misha was ready to die. Even though Maggie wasn't ready to let her go. The only alternative was healing her.

I'd do anything to take away your pain, sweetie. Anything.   I have the power.

"I'm so sorry, sweetheart, if this doesn't work," she whispered in a broken voice. "But I promise you, if it doesn't, you won't be suffering anymore. I'll do it then. I will."

She laid her palms on the dog, envisioned the ugly, thick black mass spreading, growing… growing. Shifting inside her.

Pain like a thousand white-hot knives slammed into her, twisting her vital organs. Maggie moaned in agony. It was too much pain, too much to take on, she couldn't do it. *I'm so sorry, Misha…*

Maggie yanked her palms away as if they had been seared on a stove. She bent her head, moaning a little.

The dog feebly licked her hand as if to say, *I understand.*

Fresh resolve filled her. She had to try harder. Knowing what Misha felt, that bursting, stabbing pain as if someone had grabbed her intestines and given them a vicious twist.

She laid her palms on the dog, this time concentrating, seeing only the disease as she would as a vet. A mass needing extermination, absorbing it into her body, through her skin, her very spirit, seeing Misha stand, wag her tail and bark and run as if she were a puppy again.

Searing agony slammed into her. Maggie bit back a scream and grimly held on, seeing cells made whole again, blackness disappear. Riding through the pain, she focused until the agony became a vortex dragging her down. Darkness rushed up to meet her and she fell into it.

Outside, Baylor busied himself at the grill. He speared a steak, flipped it over. Leaning back in one of the wicker chairs, Nicolas traced the outline of a crystal wineglass. The ruby vintage caught the fading light, almost looked like blood.

He and Baylor had established a tentative peace for Maggie's sake. The Draicon had filled him in on everything he'd missed. Small talk, easing the masculine tension bristling between them.

He folded his arms across his hollow chest. Damn, he missed the pack. His family. He'd do anything for them. He was doing everything, Nicolas reminded himself. Bringing Maggie back to them. Loneliness smashed into him. He hungered for his family. All he'd done to protect the pack, keep them together, and yet he was so distant from them. Alienated.

Always having to prove himself over and over by killing the enemy. He'd secured his position by violence. Maggie would secure hers through gentle healing.

How could they ever mesh their two opposing lifestyles?

By teaching her to accept her heritage, and be the Draicon that killed Kane, the Morph leader. He would teach her to become as violent as he was. The thought troubled him a little.

He thought of the eventual mating bond with Maggie. They'd absorb each other's powers, thoughts and emotions. Maggie had been on her own for years, no closeness of family. He'd sensed the deep loneliness in her. And her gentle nature, unwilling to hurt even a fly. When bonded with her, he'd not only absorb her powers, but every weakness as well. Maggie would benefit from his warrior's strength and fighting knowledge, but what would absorbing her softness do to him? Her gentleness twined with the healing nature of an empath. But it could backfire against him.

For years he'd demonstrated his ability to maintain the enviable position as Damian's trusted second-in-command. Other males challenged his authority and power. Especially Baylor. Even a modicum of weakness would make Nicolas susceptible to a challenge that would send him out of the pack for good.

Nicolas decided to hold back in the mating bond. He could not become weak. Gentle, as Maggie was gentle in her healing ability.

Yet would failing to share all of himself allow him to absorb enough of her empathic abilities? He needed her magick if Maggie failed to heal Damian. The thought kicked him in the teeth.

He stood on the threshold of gaining everything. Or losing it.

The aching emptiness inside him seemed to expand.

It flowered as he listened to Baylor talk about the pack. Homesickness stabbed him. The soft ping of crystal clinking as Baylor set down his glass reminded him of feasts at the enormous banquet table where the pack would celebrate. Nicolas inhaled the wine's scent, relishing the faint citrus tang on his tongue, the smoothness of the vintage.

Maggie tasted like wine, innocence and rising desire. He licked his lips, remembering her tongue tangling with his. Sharp arousal filled him.

"How is she?" Baylor nodded toward the house.

"Pretty damn well, considering twenty-four hours ago, she thought she was human." Admiration for his mate filled him. "Maggie is tough, beneath her gentle demeanor. She's in severe denial, but has a warrior's soul."

"Has she demonstrated her legendary aptitude for destroying the enemy?"

"Not yet. She will. I'll teach her." He drained his glass, set it down and wiped his mouth with his wrist. "When I'm finished, our Maggie will be a little warrior."

"Trained as a hunter?" Baylor shook his head. "What a shame to turn so much beauty into something like you."

Nicolas bristled. "Like me?"

"A killing machine. Sometimes I wonder if you know anything else. Or want anything else."

Nicolas ran a finger down the glass. He

couldn't argue the point, since it was the image he'd always projected. Deep inside, he longed for something more. He knew he could never have it. Not him, Nicolas, the male who needed to command respect. Changing topics, he asked about a subject certain to distract his rival. Baylor enjoyed bragging about his love life.

Slyness entered Baylor's expression as he turned the heat off under the steaks. "Katia and I have been exclusive now since you left. I think she finally realized who was the better male, now that you're gone."

Katia was a lovely young pack member who once serviced Nicolas's sexual needs after he'd returned from fighting Morphs. She had an eye for Baylor, and admired him, but they weren't true mates. She'd confessed that once to Nicolas. Nicolas felt a stab of pity for the male. Some Draicon spent their whole lives searching for their missing halves and never found them. Those Draicon usually settled for mating with others equally lonely.

Baylor gave a nod at the sky. "We went running before I left with the pack, after a few of us ensured our territory was Morph-free. Slept under the stars. Good times."

Awash in memories, Nicolas stared at the setting sun dappling the pines. Long nights running with the moon as family, hunting, then snuggling up together, the familiar smell of wolf pack, engulfing him into drowsy sleepiness. Sex with any pack female he wanted. But the fervent coupling always left him empty and wanting more. Would he ever find fulfillment? Even with his mate, he doubted it. He could never fully share himself and risk her knowing his secret....

A creaking sound snapped him out of his morose thoughts. Nicolas and Baylor turned to see Maggie creep out onto the porch. Alarm filled him at the hurt stamped on her pretty face as she sagged against a pillar.

"I think...it worked," she rasped. "Misha."

Dark shadows smudged her deep blue eyes. Her color was grayish. She staggered forward.

"Maggie, you healed Misha!"

Ignoring the obvious excitement in Baylor's voice, Nicolas went to Maggie as she collapsed into his arms. He held her upright, her heart hammering fast as a hummingbird's.

Baylor frowned. "You must get her to New Mexico immediately. If she healed the dog, she can heal Damian. You have a duty to the pack, Nicolas."

His duty to the pack. Always the pack. What

about his duty to his mate? Nicolas stroked Maggie's sweat-dampened hair. She shivered against him and clutched at his shirt.

"Stay out of this. And leave us alone."

"If you won't take her back, I will." Baylor narrowed his eyes.

"Try it. Lay one hand on her and I'll break your fingers. She's too frail and she's not ready. She just rediscovered she's a Draicon and needs more time. I won't let you endanger her, runt." A snarl rippled through his voice. "We'll do this on my time and hers, not yours."

Peace between them shattered like glass. The Draicon fisted his hands, clearly itching for a fight. "You were banished, Nicolas. Maggie is your only way back into the family and that's why you won't let her go. Fine. But I'm taking the dog. We need her blood. And be forewarned, if you try to stop me, I'll challenge you. I won't make it easy."

Again, Nicholas's position was threatened. He'd always had to prove himself as the best warrior, the fiercest fighter, the most loyal member. The icy void inside him widened. Best to keep to himself. The barrier he always erected to protect his emotions rose like a metal shield.

"Challenge me later, when Maggie's better.

Then we'll see who's the strongest pack member besides Damian," Nicolas growled.

Defiance flashed in Baylor's hard gray eyes. "You're not really pack."

Maggie pulled back, her lower lip wobbling tremulously. "Please, stop fighting. Stop it, just stop," she whispered.

Nicolas shot Baylor a warning look and turned his attention to his mate. Tears shimmered in her deep blue eyes. Pain mirrored there turned them into glacial shards. He touched her mind and recoiled from the burning agony slicing through her.

He lifted her into his arms, her body icy to his touch. Maggie's head lolled backward as if she lacked the strength to hold it upright. Dread speared him as he ran into the bedroom, her legs and arms flopping limply.

Baylor followed, looking angry. "If anything happens to her…"

"Go find all the blankets. She's freezing. I have to get her warm."

Nicolas removed her shoes. He ripped the covers back with one hand and gently laid her down. Dusk thickened. A cool breeze sifted the white gauze curtains at the window. Maggie lay on the bed, shivering so hard the mattress shook.

He laid a hand on her forehead, filled with dread at her skin's cold clamminess.

Curing Misha had cost her dearly. The reaction turned her body feverish, as if she fought off infection. He jammed a hand through his hair. Antibiotics hadn't cured the disease. He doubted it would aid her healing now.

All he could do was watch over her, hope she pulled through. Remembering how thirsty the disease made Damian, he fetched a glass of water from the bathroom across the hall. Maggie didn't respond, only buried herself deeper into the covers.

"Is she going to be okay?"

Baylor sounded concerned as he came into the room and stacked a pile of blankets on the dresser. He stared at Maggie with the same look Nicolas had seen in the mirror. Maggie, their pack's last hope. Nicolas grit his teeth. Like him, Maggie had a duty to the pack.

No one would ever let him forget it, either.

"I'll see to it. Leave us alone."

Resentment flashed on Baylor's face. "You're not mated to her yet, Nicolas. She's not committed to anyone. Get her well, or there will be consequences."

Nicolas raised an eyebrow. "If you're done

barking, go make yourself useful. Go to the store and buy raw meat. She'll need it."

Runt. He watched Baylor stalk away then turned back to Maggie. Her eyes fluttered open. "Nicolas? Nicolas, I'm s-so cold. So c-cold."

He heaped more blankets on the bed, but she continued to shiver violently. Nicolas stripped off his shoes and clothing, tossed back the covers and climbed into bed with her. He wrapped his arms around her torso, pulling her against him. It felt like embracing a block of ice. Nicolas stroked her hair.

"Shh, I'll take care of you, caira. Let me warm you."

Maggie's moans faded as he held her. She felt so good in his arms. He put his chin atop her head, wishing to take away her pain. This was agony, watching someone you cared for suffer. Nicolas rubbed his cheek against her hair, inhaled her scent. Threaded into the smell of light jasmine and sunshine was a darker, sicker scent. The smell of terminal disease.

"Fight it, Mags. Don't let it take you under. You can do it," he encouraged.

For a while he lay there, embracing her, worried the disease would suck her under as it had with Damian. A fierce protective feeling filled him.

He wanted to hold her close and never let go. Run off with her, forgetting pack, family, duty.

Nicolas pushed aside the fantasy, inwardly admonishing himself for a moment of weakness. He concentrated on warming Maggie. Gradually he became aware of a shift in her body temperature. Her skin no longer felt ice-cold. It was working. She was overcoming it.

To give her strength, he wove his thoughts into her mind, memories of good times with the pack, laughter, kinship. His admiration for her strength and how she'd survived for so long on her own. Nicolas fed this to her in images until she moved against him.

"I'm tired," she whispered.

"Then sleep," he soothed.

In his arms, she slept at last. But Nicolas did not close his eyes, keeping guard over her to ensure she was safe. He smoothed a lock of sweat-dampened hair back from her forehead. She looked so fragile and pale, and his heart twisted. If healing Misha from the disease made her this sick, what were the chances of her surviving healing an adult Draicon like Damian?

Would the attempt kill her?

Chapter 9

Maggie awoke to a ravenous hunger obliterating everything else. It seized her by the throat like a living, writhing beast. Swinging her legs over the bed's edge, she nearly tripped over Misha. The dog barked joyfully, wagged her tail. She barely registered the remarkable change. Hunger drove her like a lash.

Her gaze swept about the room, with its lace curtains, polished oak dresser and the mirrored closet doors. Vaguely she remembered Nicolas picking her up, carrying her to bed and curling his big body next to her chilled one.

Where was he?

As if she hadn't eaten in days, her stomach ached. Maggie doubled over, whimpering in confusion. What was wrong with her?

She remembered the wild look in Nicolas's eyes when he'd told her he had to eat fresh meat. Surely this had nothing to do with it. It was hunger, plain and simple.

She raced down the hallway, hooking into the kitchen, following the delicious smell of meat. Nicolas and Baylor sat at opposite ends of the island, regarding each other like enemies across a battlefield. Each ate thick cuts of sirloin that looked bloodred. They looked up.

She needed meat. Now. Meat, full-bodied, red meat. Not cooked. Baylor rose, came toward her with a plate that held a grilled steak big as a truck tire. She ignored it.

Desperately Maggie clawed through the fridge, scouring it, oblivious of her host watching. Oh, God, she had to eat. Now. Maggie found a package of fresh, raw hamburger. She ripped open the cellophane, scooped up handfuls of meat and gulped them down. Mouthful after mouthful she swallowed, relief replacing the hollow pain in her stomach, making this terrible, awful weakness go away, replenishing her strength, her energy.

Energy. Maggie paused, a handful of meat halfway to her mouth. She stared at the red, raw hamburger squeezed in her fist. Glancing up, she saw

Baylor look at her with a frown. Understanding etched Nicolas's features.

Maggie flung the meat far away from her. Hamburger scattered on the elegant, clean white tile, dotting it in red fragments.

"No," she moaned. "This isn't me. I'm not one of you."

"You cannot deny it any longer, Maggie," Nicolas's soft, deep voice gently asserted. "You see, you are one of us. Not human, but wolf. Draicon. You used magick and need to replenish lost energy. It's perfectly normal for us."

It could not be. Not her, the veterinarian, the pragmatic healer who used her talents to ease others' pain. Maggie, who swore never to harm another living creature, a wolf, who hunted and killed prey? She remembered the alluring call of the Everglades, the peaceful feeling she harbored there. Maggie went to the sink. Like Lady Macbeth, she scrubbed her hands over and over.

"I am not one of you," she whispered desperately. "I will never be one of you."

Baylor shot Nicolas an accusing look. "You didn't tell her?"

Ignoring him, Nicolas took a paper towel and gently dried Maggie's hands. He lifted her chin up with one hand. "You already are, caira. It was imprinted on you from the moment of your conception, just as your magick was to be my mate. You can't deny the truth any longer."

He wanted to make her into something she was not. Could not be, ever. Nicolas was violence, death, fighting. She was peace, living and letting live. His strength and power of will threatened everything she'd ever known. Everything she needed to survive in the moment.

Nicolas steered her over to the table and the steak she'd rejected. Stomach lurching, she stared at the food. "It's your brain insisting that what just happened is repulsive, and not you. Stop thinking what you've trained yourself to believe. You have a need, you're hungry. Fill it Maggie. It's good sirloin. Baylor cooked it on the grill."

Methodically she began cutting the meat into tiny pieces, and brought it to her mouth. Maggie began to eat as if she sat in a friend's kitchen. Nicolas talked with Baylor as if all were normal. Normal? What the hell was normal anymore?

Button nose twitching, Misha trotted into the kitchen. Baylor sliced off a few pieces of steak, set them on a plate on the floor. The dog gobbled them down. Maggie ate more steak.

Nicolas watched her through hooded eyes.

"You don't have to eat to replace lost energy

after you use magick. Sex is another alternative," he murmured, his intense gaze searing her with its heat.

Sex, the force driving her toward him. Maggie squeezed her thighs together, remembering the warmth of his hard body pressed against hers last night.

"We either have sex and absorb our partner's sexual energy, or we must eat meat, preferably as raw as possible. Just as your parents did," he continued.

Maggie cut off Nicolas's words with a sharp wave. "Don't talk about my parents. You know nothing about them."

"But we do," Baylor interjected. "Richard and Carla Sinclair. Two years after their formal mating, Carla gave birth to you. The Morphs had started to flush out and destroy the less powerful packs. Carla doubted Damian's ability to protect you. When you were only six, they moved to Florida. They were terrified and wanted to live as low profile as possible.

"We didn't know where they had taken you until recently, when Nicolas had mind-bonded with you. Then we did some research and found out your parents had been killed in a violent mugging when you were twelve."

Baylor stopped, looking puzzled as Maggie pressed a hand to her temple. "Stop it, just stop it," she whispered. "I don't need or want to hear this. My family is my business."

"But we are your family, Maggie. All of us. That's what pack is," Baylor protested.

Nicolas leaned forward. "Hasn't it been lonely these past years since you were orphaned? Haven't you longed to have the closeness of a family again? That's pack, Maggie. That's what you've been missing all this time."

She toyed with her fork. Years of feeling alienated, trying to fit in, trying to find her niche. Even school and achieving a dream of becoming a vet didn't fill the void. Perhaps Nicolas was right.

Despite her resolve to eat like a normal human, Maggie gobbled down the steak. She wiped her lips with the napkin. Nicolas stared at her mouth with the same hunger, causing her to consume the steak. A flush ignited her cheeks.

He picked up Misha, stroking her head, doing a thorough examination at the same time. Nicolas looked into her trusting brown eyes as Misha wagged her tail.

"She's perfectly well. Healthy as a young pup." He set the dog down.

"Then it's true. You are the empath, Margaret. You must return to the pack and heal Damian." Baylor looked excited.

Maggie frowned. "Damian?"

"Our pack leader. The Morphs—Jamie, specifically—infected him with the same disease Misha had. Do you remember Damian, Maggie? He was pack leader when you were little...."

Maggie pressed two fingers to her temple. "He must be very old." All this talk of pack, family, as if she belonged...

"Damian's older than I am," Nicolas cut in smoothly. "He was eighty on his last birthday."

Her head whipped up to see him regard her with a wry smile. "Our kind do not mature until we reach thirteen, like mortals, then we age slowly. Some of us—a very special few—mature before then and gain our powers of change and magick when we're younger. Like you, Maggie."

"I never changed into a wolf when I was younger," she shot back, exasperated. "That's ridiculous to even think...."

Stricken by a flickering memory, she halted in midsentence. Blood. Endless streams, running into the sidewalk. Screams, then silence. Loud cruel laughter as she sobbed, her fingers splayed over cloth turning crimson, her parents lying so still…then hands reaching out to take care of unfinished business…rough hands…a low growl rumbling from her throat…the odd sensation of red-hazed fury imagining fur and fangs ready to tear apart…

Her head snapped up. "Never," she whispered.

Nicolas's expression softened. He took her hand. His palm felt warm, calloused. Little dark hairs peppered the back of his hand. Hands capable of such gentleness, yet strong enough to kill. She had seen him do exactly that.

"Destroying them is the only way, Mags."

"There must be another." She sat back, pressed fingers to her temples. Information. She needed knowledge. "Tell me everything you know about the Morphs. Everything you've tried in eliminating them."

Baylor threw Nicolas a look of grudging respect. "Nicolas taught us that they can be killed in our human form by stabbing them in the heart with daggers or by tearing the heart with our fangs when we change. The close-quarters combat makes them use all their defenses and drains their magick. Before that, we tried everything. You can't shoot them from a distance—their magick deflects the bullets."

Nicolas nodded. "They're difficult to kill because they shift so quickly into any animal form. They can clone themselves to double, even triple, their numbers."

A grim smile touched Baylor's mouth. "We even tried insecticide once when they shifted into a swarm of bees. Didn't work. Their magick is powerful because it's dark."

"But they weren't always so powerful," Maggie thought aloud.

"They were Draicon, wolf, like us." Baylor shot Nicolas a look she didn't understand. "To become Morph, a Draicon kills a relative such as a parent, or a member of their extended family, like an uncle. Then the Draicon absorbs their dying energy and turns into a Morph."

"So they absorb energy just as Draicons do? Must they always kill to do so?"

Nicolas spoke up. "Not always. If they never shifted, they could survive simply by ingesting the energy of fresh meat just as we do. They need the more powerful energy emitted from dying victims to shape-shift constantly into other animal forms."

"Why would a Draicon want to turn evil? What's the attraction?"

Baylor shrugged. "Power over other life-forms. They crave it."

Nicolas shook his head. His gaze grew distant and dreamy. "No, it's not. They can ride the back of the wind as an eagle, race over the golden plains as a wolf, swim the deep seas as swiftly as a shark. The freedom to shift into many forms is what lures them, and the closeness of pack, just as it is for Draicon."

"But they're evil, and twisted, and will never be trusted," Baylor said flatly. "Maggie, what else do you want to know about them?"

Evil had its weaknesses as well. Maggie thought of the angry, violent animals she'd gentled. Once Misha had been a snarling, scared puppy she'd rescued from abuse. Time, love and caring had turned her into a devoted companion. The Morphs were animals as well as magic beings. Maybe the same could work with them to defeat them.

Maggie explained to them how she'd worked with Misha. "Has a Morph ever rejected evil and returned to the pack as a Draicon? Is it possible?"

Baylor gave a derisive snort as Nicolas remained silent. "Once they become Morphs, they remain that way. They've committed the ultimate sin and killed a loved one. There's no going back. And even if there were, you couldn't trust that they wouldn't change their minds and turn

to evil again. It would be like living with a ticking time bomb."

Nicolas made a sharp, cutting gesture. "Enough
of this. Mags, you have to kill Morphs. Period.
There is no other way. I've tangled with enough
of them to know. They relish killing mortals,
Draicon, other animals. They live off fear and
panic. You have to be strong and know that, when
you hunt them down and destroy them, you're
killing evil."

"I can't kill. I just can't. I've spent my adult life
saving animals, not destroying them." She looked
down at her hands, then at Nicolas. "Their blood
is acid. How can you kill them in hand-to-hand
combat? They bleed all over you."

He shrugged. "Draicon heal. You push past the
pain and just focus on the kill. Remember, they're
evil. You're a doctor, Maggie. Think of them as
germs that must be eradicated. They're bacteria
and you're a white blood cell, surrounding the
enemy and destroying them, no matter what your
own personal cost."

"You sound as if you talk from experience.
Has it been at great personal cost to you, Nicolas? What happened? Why are you so focused on
killing them? Have you ever tried reasoning with
these Morphs? Maybe they're not so different…."

His hard laugh sounded bitter. "What, Maggie? Talk them to death? Reason? They're evil and the only way to save the pack is to kill them."

"Maybe it's the only way you know, Nicolas. And that's why you stick to it," she said quietly.

The same shuttered look came over him. "Enough questions. You'll learn soon enough. You're wolf, Maggie. You will destroy the Morphs just as I do. No more arguing. You can't hide from your true nature anymore. Understand?"

Even Baylor looked uneasy at Nicolas's quiet lash of command. She gathered her courage. "I'm not hiding, Nicolas. I have a good life. I heal animals and make people happy when their pets are cured. Can you say the same?"

She turned and left him standing there, but not before glimpsing a flash of loneliness in his dark eyes.

Maggie spent a restless night alone. Her wolf surfaced, howling to run with the waxing moon. At midnight, she'd awoken, nearly tripping over Nicolas when she stepped outside her bedroom. He lay asleep on the floor, as if protecting her. When she'd opened the door, he awoke with a start. The hunger in his gaze matched her own.

Maggie had fought her sexual needs and run back to bed, shaky and unsettled.

She slept late, awakening to sunshine spearing the dark carpet. In the kitchen, Misha stood between Nicolas and Baylor like a referee as they balefully eyed one another. Nicolas turned toward her with a solemn look.

"Maggie, Baylor is leaving for New Mexico this afternoon. We'll meet up with him and the pack in a week or so." He drew in a deep breath. "He's taking Misha."

"No!"

"Misha is cured. There's a possibility our people can make an antidote for the disease from her blood. Our scientists are skilled. They may save Damian." His eyes closed and her heart turned over at the anguish tightening his expression. They opened again, filled with fierce resolve.

"Damian is dying, Maggie, just like Misha was. I know you can't remember him and have no close ties to him as we do, but your pet may be able to work a miracle. I promise she'll be well cared for, and not hurt."

Panic engulfed her. How could she let the only real friend she'd known go?

"What if she's not fully healed and I have to

try again? This power of mine, I haven't had the chance to analyze it, process it and see how it works. I must watch her for a few days."

Nicolas cupped her face, refusing to allow her to jerk away, forcing contact between them as if it would bond them together. "Mags, Misha will be in excellent hands. We need to leave before the Morphs find us. What if the Morphs infect her all over again? Her system can't take the shock. Trust me, sweetheart. It's for the best. She'll be safe with the pack, I promise."

"She's my dog. I'm a doctor of veterinary medicine and I can determine what she needs."

"The Morphs have the capability to shift into any animal shape." His dark gaze grew intense. "Do you understand? Any shape, Maggie. Including that of your own dog. The Morphs would shift into her form, and rip your throat out just as you're holding her like you are now."

Maggie's heart dropped to her stomach. She glanced down at Misha's big brown eyes, her little pink tongue lolling out. It wasn't possible...then again, she'd seen the army ants, watched them grow and shift. And that creature in the swamp... A shudder racked her.

Knowing Misha was safe with the pack prevented the Morphs from using her form against her. He was right, but letting go of her companion felt like having her heart wrenched from her chest.

"Where are we going, Nicolas? Why can't we leave with Baylor?"

Nicolas's face remained impassive. Unlike her, he wasn't easy to read when he wished to put on a poker face. "We're driving to Atlanta, catching a flight from there. You and I need to take a detour first, Maggie. There's a cottage in north Florida that's safe from the Morphs. It's hidden, cloaked in magick. It can't ward them off for good, but we'll be safe there for a little while. We'll stay there while I teach you to fight."

Unreality washed over her. "Fight?"

"Embrace your true destiny, so the legend goes. You're our pack's empath, and you are wolf. And you have to learn to fight like one."

I don't fight. Or kill. Maggie started to say, then remembered how she'd leapt forward and joined the battle when the dragon targeted Misha. How she wished it were days ago and she were alone in her lab, with her research.

Her gaze darted to Misha, who was sniffing the floor for scraps. No. She wouldn't give this up for anything, even her own peace of mind.

Nicolas rubbed her hand, his touch comforting.

"You need to at least learn to defend yourself if you're alone. I'll teach you all I know about the Morphs, their weaknesses, strengths, how best to defeat them. And I can teach you how to control your change so your wolf won't emerge when you least expect it."

Logical. Sensible. She found no argument with his reasoning. Nicolas had proven his intentions when he'd fought the dragon for her. She found no threat emanating from him, only a simmering, banked intensity. Desire twined with a rising fear that if she surrendered to her feelings for him, he'd take her in a direction she had long ago resisted. A journey to something she'd quashed, a path she dreaded.

Though he was noble and brave and risked much to protect her, Nicolas was wrong for her. He embraced the world of magic, fought and killed. He was everything she feared. Everything she'd rejected long ago.

Maggie thought hard. So many changes in the past few days. She needed more time.

"I need another day, Nicolas. You said this house was safe, then I want to set up a temporary lab and study the effects of what happened when I healed Misha. Check her blood. And test mine, see if I can discover if there's any unusual cell mitosis taking place since I started healing."

A frown dented his forehead. She glanced at Baylor. "If you want a cure for Damian, it will be in my blood, not Misha's, since mine contains the healing agent. I'll arrange to ship vials of it to your people, and perhaps then they can produce a temporary antibody."

Baylor looked relieved. "It might work. Still, we'd be better with you there in person."

"She's not going with you," Nicolas asserted.

Tension radiated between the two males. Maggie sought to diffuse it with questions.

"Baylor, Nicolas, I need information. What did your people discover about this disease? All my research has proven inconclusive. How does the disease work?"

Her ploy worked as Nicolas lost his defensive posture. He turned to her, ignoring the other male. "Unfortunately, we've discovered little. We do know it acts much as the Morphs do when they kill their victims. They absorb the dying victim's fear, which produces energy, and makes them stronger. This new disease eats the victim from the inside, absorbing their healthy cells and replacing them with the infected cells. It works somewhat like cancer, but it spreads more rapidly than most cancers. More like a virus. It's probably injected as a virus, then takes over. Even blood transfusions don't work. They make it worse, giving the invading cells a fresh supply of energy. Withholding food slows the process, but the victim could starve."

Baylor cut in. "They created this new disease and decided to go straight for the heart of our pack. They infected our leader. If we lose Damian, I'm afraid the pack will scatter."

"Like killing the queen in an ant colony," Maggie mused. "The colony dies."

Baylor shot Nicolas a look she didn't understand. "The creation of the disease and infection of Damian was his fault. It's why he was banished from the pack. The only way the pack will accept him back is if he brings you back into the fold."

Like pieces of a mosaic falling together, Maggie saw the entire picture begin to shape. "You need me, Nicolas. That's why you came for me."

"I came for you because we need each other. Can you honestly admit that your wolf wouldn't emerge in the future? I can teach you to control your wolf, Maggie."

The only other choice was Baylor, who kept eyeing her as if he expected her to perform tricks. She didn't trust him yet. Baylor hadn't seen her horrified reaction at shifting. She was Draicon, yet not one of them. Not really.

Neither was Nicolas, she sensed.

"How could a disease be your fault, Nicolas?"

Self-loathing filled his face. "I taught magick to Jamie, a mortal, and broke pack rules. Shouldn't have. But I did. The Morphs tempted her to join them and increased her powers of magick, and used her mortal blood to create this new disease. She then infected Damian."

Something was missing. She studied his blank expression. "Why would you break pack rules, Nicolas, when you're so devoted to protecting the pack?"

Broad shoulders lifted in a casual shrug. "I met her in New Orleans on a trip. We connected and I sensed the magick inside her, and decided to teach her to bring it out."

Baylor gave a derisive snort, but she sensed Nicolas withheld information.

"If Damian dies, it's my fault, Maggie. Mine and no one else's."

Something dark and haunted entered his gaze. Deeply touched, Maggie considered. Nicolas could guide her through this horrifying revelation. Maybe he could teach her to leash the beast inside her so she would never change again.

The pull of the full moon taunted her. Maggie hugged herself. Nicolas was the only one who fully understood what she'd experienced. She trusted him. He could teach her to control her wolf. Nothing more.

Maggie silently asserted her vow.

She would never kill. Ever.

Maggie spent the afternoon studying Misha's blood and comparing it to the slides she'd made when the dog was sick. Her pet's blood cells were fully normal. She also drew samples of her own blood, alarmed at a slight anomaly she had never noticed before.

Baylor assured her the house was safe. He did so after lunch, giving her suggestive looks and flirting openly with her. Nicolas kept pulling her away, growling at the other male. His possessiveness seemed at an all-time fever pitch and grew more intense by the hour.

This afternoon, she nearly had to yank them apart when they began circling in a fight position. Baylor slyly suggested Nicolas wasn't really pack and had no right to mate with her. Instinct warned her these were two powerful males competing for the right to claim her. Her wolf howled in agreement. The strongest would prevail, and Nicolas might beat Baylor to a bloody pulp.

But the self that had lived as a human all these years disliked the male posturing and aggressiveness. Nicolas was far too dangerous and wild. They needed to release pent-up energy. So after they calmed down, she suggested a competitive game of one-on-one volleyball. Nicolas and Baylor reluctantly agreed. She played referee, delighted to see them sweat out their hostility.

Now, she rested on the porch while Baylor went into town to ship her blood to New Mexico. Nicolas was patrolling the property's perimeter, checking it for intruders.

Maggie studied the ants scurrying on the redwood planks. She lifted her feet, tucked them beneath her. Only ants. Still, she wasn't taking any chances.

A mockingbird landed on the thick green grass outside the porch. It chirped, looked around, then flew away. Just a mockingbird.

Maggie watched it warily. Birds could pluck out eyes. Peck at flesh.

Relax. Nicolas spoke into her mind in gentle assurances. *There are no Morphs here.*

Uh-huh. How would you know?

You can smell them. Think the worst smell you'd

ever experience, then multiply by ten. That's a Morph.

Cautious, she inhaled. Only the clean, fresh scent of rain, pine and damp earth. Her shoulders loosened a little. She stared at her hands. Healing hands.

Maggie always dismissed her ability to heal quickly from injuries as normal. She'd never suffered anything serious, no broken bones or severe injuries to make her suspicious about her body's natural inclination to heal. Now she'd put it to the ultimate test. Their acid blood burned. Fangs ripped and tore. Claws shredded flesh.

Beneath a towering live oak, three black crows argued and fought like women at a bargain-basement sale over scraps Nicolas had left beneath the tree. Maggie stared at the woods beyond. It looked safe here. Smelled safe.

She didn't feel safe. She wondered if she ever would again.

I'll keep you safe. My Maggie.

His husky whisper did not assure. Rather it sent sensual awareness coursing through her. Who would keep her safe from Nicolas? Her own emotions in a tangle, she wanted to surrender to the erotic web he'd woven over her. How could one man have such a powerful effect on her?

It's meant to be.

"Balderdash,"she scoffed. Feeling better with that brave assertion, she leaned back. Still, the pleasant, yet nagging throb in her loins increased. She wanted to satisfy it.

Maggie knew her own rising desire would not fade. She'd read the weather forecast in today's paper. Full moon tonight.

And she feared, more than anything what it could do to Nicolas or Baylor, what that meant for her.

Early evening, Nicolas returned from prowling the woods for small game. Baylor was still in town. He shifted back into his human form, pulled on his clothing and stalked toward the back porch. Clouds scudded over the sky, driven by a light wind. Silvery light dappled the sugar maple where a wind chime hung. A breeze caressed the chimes, filling the air with gentle music.

He felt anything but gentle. For Maggie's sake, he hoped she had retired, locked the door and wouldn't come out until morning.

But as he reached the porch, he realized he was out of luck. On the outdoor sofa, Maggie lay curled up, one arm tucked beneath her cheek. She was asleep.

Nicolas ground to an abrupt halt and stared. Her scent swam in his nostrils, flowers and feminine arousal. She was hurting as much as he was.

He approached her like the prince in the fairy tale ready to kiss the sleeping princess, but feeling more like the Big Bad Wolf.

Dropping to one knee beside her, he felt his body respond. His hungry gaze caressed each lithe line and curve, her rosy, parted lips, the stray auburn curl tickling her nose.

All mine, he thought in a savage rush of arousal.

"Caira, wake up," he whispered into her ear. Temptation called. He surrendered, giving the lobe a gentle bite, chasing it with a kiss.

A tiny moan assured him she'd awakened. Maggie sat up, rubbing her eyes with a clenched fist. She looked sleepy and tousled and absolutely delicious. Hunger bit at him with sharp teeth.

He didn't want food.

Only Maggie. Now. But… For a moment, he hesitated. Doubts kicked him. What if the exchange of powers occurred this first mating? Very rare, but possible.

It wouldn't happen until they both reached a level of sexual fulfillment. Not tonight. Maggie was new to sex. He'd gently tutor her in making love first, but stay dominant.

The wolf on top rules. An ironic smile touched his mouth at the pack males' old adage.

A soft tinkling of wind chimes awakened Maggie. She blinked, amazed at how well she could see in the darkness. Instantly she smelled him.

Her mate.

Nicolas hovered over her, raw hunger in his gaze.

"Maggie, I need you," he rasped. "Come inside with me, now."

The glint of the full moon on the wind chimes warned her. Full moon. Feelings she long denied surfaced. A wild, primitive call to run free. Wolf.

Wolf tore and ripped and maimed. Killed.

Fully awake now, she glanced at the silvery moon. Panic lashed her.

Full moon. Would she turn? Could she stop it, now that she'd changed? Maggie choked back a panicked sob. Desire burned in his gaze. Nicolas took a step toward her.

He'd make love to her, and then the beast inside her would be freed at last. What would happen then? Would she turn into that loathsome creature that relished violence? Everything she hated would claim her. Maggie felt real fear, not at the fierce arousal in Nicolas, but the beast inside her clamoring to be freed. To run wild, claim him as a lover and then be set free.

To kill, and injure. No! Shivering, she leapt to her feet and stared at the moon. No way to control this. She didn't know how. Only one person she knew did.

Nicolas. The very man who wanted her in his bed. Maggie reached out a quivering hand.

"Help me," she begged. "Nicolas, I can't turn again...the moon... Please, I don't know how to stop this, the beast inside me. I'm so scared. I can't turn into a wolf. I can't control this."

Hard arousal on his face faded. Nicolas hung his head, clenched his fists. He lifted his head and then released an eerie, spine-tingling howl at the moon.

But when he stopped, the signs of desire had faded, replaced with a man fully in control.

"Maggie, Maggie. There is nothing to fear. Please, come to me."

He advanced toward her, his arms outstretched. She collapsed against him, burying her face against his chest. No matter what else he did, Nicolas had promised to keep her safe. She trusted in that promise.

Even if it meant keeping her safe from herself.

"Please, please, I don't want to change into a beast," she whispered.

His hand stroked her hair. "Shh," he whispered soothingly. "Hush, Maggie, caira. I won't let anything happen to you. Look at me. Am I turning? Do you see a wolf here?"

She had earlier, in the fierceness of his gaze, the raw hunger in the beast burning to be set free. But as she raised her head, she saw only Nicolas's warm brown gaze and concern furrowing his brow. Wind teased the edges of his thick dark hair.

"Maggie, you won't turn if you don't want to. There's nothing to fear. I'll show you."

Maggie rested her head against his shoulder, feeling weary and spent. She believed him. Trusted him. The wildness gone from his expression, Nicolas rocked against her if she were fragile porcelain he wanted to cherish.

He'd almost done it. But the raging desire had been forced down when he'd seen her fear. Damn, he never wanted her to look at him like that again. He'd fight his way through a legion of Morphs first. Maggie hated and feared her wolf nature.

He'd leashed the beast inside, only to show her how tight control always won. Nicolas smiled grimly. It took all his strength to pick her up and comfort her, instead of sweeping her inside, tossing her on the bed, covering her body with his and thrusting deep inside her at last.

A sense of awe and peace wrestled with raw animal hunger. He stroked her hair, marveling at his newfound feelings. Before, he'd always used women for his own pleasure. Today for the first time, he put another's needs before his own.

This felt strange and a little scary. But it also felt good, like he could sink into it forever.

Early the next morning, Maggie paced outside as Baylor walked Misha before leaving for the airport. Thoughts chased each other around relentlessly. Was she making the right decision in leaving with Nicolas to go to another safe location to hone her skills?

She went into the living room and stopped short. On the long leather couch, Nicolas stretched out. Lines furrowed his brow. He looked exhausted. She remembered how he had held her, and wondered if he'd slept.

Intrigued, she inched closer. His full lower lip eased open as he breathed deeply, one arm flung over his head. Dark lashes feathered his hard cheeks. Maggie leaned close, shocked to see a crystalline tear slip out of his eye.

She reached out with her mind, wanting more than anything to slip into his thoughts. Images flashed before her. Pain. Hurt. Loneliness. Nicolas felt as alone as she had.

Her heart twisted. Maggie touched the teardrop with one finger. Very gently she brushed it away.

Her breath caught as she heard Baylor and Misha bounding up the driveway. Nicolas's eyes snapped open. He sat up abruptly, and frowned.

"Why are you hovering over me?"

Because you needed me. Intuitively sensing he'd resent her witnessing that tear, she didn't dare voice the thought. Instead Maggie shrugged. "I'm waiting for them. They're back."

Nicolas bolted upright, fisting his eyes. He sprang off the couch as if fearing to be caught sleeping. Baylor came inside, patting Misha. But he didn't unhook her from the leash. Instead he eyed Nicolas with a wary look. Nicolas folded his arms over his muscled chest and glared back.

Ignoring the masculine tension lacing the air, Maggie bent down to hug her dog. She stood, giving Baylor explicit instructions on Misha's care.

"I'll take good care of her, Margaret." He gave

her a speculative look. "And take good care of yourself. Remember, we are your family. We'll always be there for you and you can trust us, unlike some. We would never turn on you."

Nicolas said nothing. But tension coiled his muscles, like a wolf ready to spring. Maggie shot him a troubling look.

"I don't play games, Baylor. If there's something you want to say, say it and stop being so elusive."

Instead, the Draicon went to her, leaned close and sniffed. Nicolas growled. Baylor stepped back, but kept his gaze locked on her.

"You haven't mated with him yet. I can't smell him on you. So you probably haven't seen it yet. Ask Nicolas about the tattoo, Margaret. Ask him what it means and where he got it. That's all I'm going to say. But be careful."

He turned and led Misha back to her carrier, speaking over his shoulder. "Sometimes even the friendliest wolves can turn on you when you least expect it, if it's in their nature. Remember that. You can't change a killer."

Chapter 10

She dozed in the car as he drove. Nicolas stole glances at her now and then as he sped toward their destination. His right hand drifted up and rubbed the tiny black eagle hidden on his nape. Ever since joining Damian's pack, he kept his hair long and the tattoo hidden.

Baylor had seen it when they'd fought. He knew what it meant.

Maggie did not. He hoped she wouldn't question him on it. Not yet. He couldn't tell her the truth, not until they mated and he felt secure of her.

He'd told Maggie only part of the truth.

Yes, he'd teach her to fight, to defend herself, and learn all about her Draicon heritage. After he mated with her.

The little cottage in the woods would serve as a love nest, giving them the necessary time to mate. Matings were delicate. A couple did not always exchange powers the first time. It took the right amount of emotional commitment during sex and intensity of orgasm to achieve a mating lock. Then they'd be joined together physically while exchanging memories, magick powers and emotions....

Weaknesses. Like Maggie's weaknesses. Her unwillingness to kill, her gentle nature that cloaked the Draicon lurking inside her.

His fingers tightened to white knuckles. Maggie's weakness, Damian's ultimate cure. Time grew short. Even now, if they achieved a mating lock and exchanged magick powers, it might be too late to save Damian. Then there was the delicate matter of his banishment.

A grim smile touched his mouth. He'd dutifully obeyed pack law, but a raging army of Morphs would not keep him from returning once he felt certain of a cure for Damian.

Of course, other males like Baylor would challenge him. He'd need all his strength, and fighting abilities honed for the return. He could not risk any softness.

Soft, like Maggie. Gentle and giving, like Maggie.

For years he trained to ward off emotions. He must not lose control or show any form of weakness before the pack. He was Draicon, wolf, strong.

You are not really pack, Nicolas.

Baylor's ancient taunt rang in his mind. Nicolas stole a glance at Maggie. If she knew his true origins, would she be as mistrusting as others?

During the joining process, he would stay dominant, not pliant and giving as other males did. It was possible. He'd quizzed another male, Kyle, before leaving New Mexico. Surely it did lessen the emotional fulfillment of the joining, but he could live with that.

As long as he maintained his precious control.

Nicolas spotted the turn off I-75 for U.S. 441 and made a hard right. Twilight gathered in the shadows as he drove down the highway, then turned onto the lonely two-lane road toward the cottage. The small cottage in the equally tiny town of High Springs suited his needs perfectly. More isolated than the big house in Melbourne and harder for Morphs to find, the cottage was sheltered by the woods and offered more privacy.

Darkness descended like a blanket. Only the

light of the full moon spilling through the dense thicket of trees cut through the inky blackness.

No signs existed to show him the way. He had memorized the map. A grim smile touched his lips. Unlike mortal men, he had an excellent sense of direction.

The vehicle's headlights picked out a rough stretch of dirt road. Nicolas turned right onto a single lane. Thick pines and maples flanked the roadway for a quarter of a mile, then the land-scape opened up, showing the grayish outline of a small cottage.

Their new home for the next week. He pulled up on the graveled drive and shut off the engine, rolling down the window to let in the fresh, piney breeze.

He turned to Maggie, who made adorable growling sounds. Sleep smoothed the worry lines from her face, highlighting her innocence. Long auburn lashes feathered her pink cheeks.

She wasn't a traditional beauty. Her beauty lay in her tenacious personality and devotion, her inner strength and a surprising courage for one who refused to defend herself. He wished she dared to confront the memory that ripped away her Draicon heritage, but perhaps the strength she'd inherit from him in the mating lock would enable her to do so.

His gaze drifted over the firmness of her breasts thrust against the stiffness of the cheap linen store-bought blouse, the new jeans encasing her curvy legs, hugging her rounded hips. Nicolas reached over, nuzzled the slender column of her neck, nibbling at her delicate, shell-like ear. Desire surged in his blood, thick and hot.

He pushed it down.

Nicolas reached in, picked her up as easily as if she weighed no more than her dog. She felt soft and warm and deliciously feminine in his arms. He wanted her more than his next breath.

But for her sake, he'd wait.

Maggie felt herself lifted and hooked her arms around Nicolas's neck. She squinted, shocked at how easily she could see in the darkness. The cottage he walked toward was square, with brown paint and a dull brown shingled roof. A wood rail fence ran around the edges of the land, ending where the forest began. Beneath a tall oak was a wooden swing built for two. A long wooden porch and sheltering tin roof ran the length of the home. Rocking chairs and wood Adirondack chairs lined the porch. Charming, quaint. Like Grandma's cottage in the woods.

She remembered the Big Bad Wolf, wanting to eat the little girl.

"If you want me to, I'll do exactly that."

The smoky desire in Nicolas's voice filled her with delicious heat. She shifted in his arms as he opened the door.

"No key. No one dares to come here. The magick wards off all intruders, but Draicon." He set her gently down on her feet, stroked her hair. "Which proves my point, Maggie. If you were not one of us, you couldn't enter. As soon as you reached the driveway, you'd become so violently ill you'd be forced to turn around. The suggestion of food poisoning would erase any suspicion from your mind."

Maggie ran a hand up his chest, relishing the hardness beneath her fingertips. He'd done so much to keep her safe, putting her needs before his own. The wolf inside her howled with a different need than to run wild and free. Her fingers slipped up the strong curve of his neck, testing the hard pads of muscle on his thick shoulders.

His big body was like chiseled marble. Suddenly she wanted to test his weight, feel him mount her and be inside her.

Nicolas pushed her hand away. His eyes were tormented.

"Go inside, Maggie," he said thickly. "Make yourself comfortable. I need to check the property."

"This time of night? I thought you said it was safe."

"It is. I'm not."

Swallowing hard, she watched him start to tug the shirt over his head. "Inside, now," he growled. "I need to run with the moon before I take you and release this wildness inside me. It's your first time and I want to be gentle."

Taken aback, she stared. "How…did you?"

"I can tell," he said shortly. "I can't smell another man on you."

Instead of entering the cottage she watched him remove his shirt. Moonlight gilded the rippling muscles of his biceps, the thick hair on his chest. Stubble shadowed his jaw, though he had shaved before they left this afternoon. He kicked off his shoes, removed his socks. Nicolas growled again and turned his back as he tugged down his jeans. Fascinated, she saw the outline of his heavy testicles dangling between his outstretched legs.

"Go inside," he said in a strangled tone.

Maggie watched the smooth halves of his muscled ass as he loped off toward the forest.

She showered, dried her hair and then hung the damp towel on the wood peg beside the vanity. Dressing in a thick white robe, she went into the bedroom. Simple, rugged masculine furniture in earth tones filled the room. The cream-colored walls were bare except for a detailed painting of a lone wolf standing on a hillside, howling at the silver globe of a full moon.

She had to smile a little at the irony.

Maggie sat down on the bed and ran a caressing hand over the carved pine headboard. Big as a football field, the bed felt soft and yielding. A shiver of anticipation raced through her as she thought of Nicolas's big body covering hers.

This is where we'll make love.

Restless and edgy, she sank onto a wicker rocker by the bank of ceiling-high windows and gazed outside. Two thick pines sheltered the house's left side. Aztec grass lined the redwood boardwalk leading from the gravel parking lot. Cabbage palms, looking incongruous besides oak trees, rustled their spiny branches. Someone had attempted to plant roses near the love seat swing beneath a sprawling oak tree.

Maggie went outside into the moonlit night and sat on the porch step.

The cottage was in the middle of a large expanse of field, guarded on three sides by tall pines, live oaks and sugar maples. Tree frogs chirped nearby, sounding like a miniature orchestra. Near a jasmine bush, a rusty windmill bird feeder gently swung back and forth.

The other night, he'd made it clear what he intended. No words, just one significant glance sweeping her from the top of her brows to the tips of her toes. As if he was famished, and she were a five-course gourmet meal.

I'll never leave you alone for long, sweet Maggie. I'm always with you, always. The husky masculine voice in her head made her jump. The night showed only shadows. A deep throbbing pulse began between her legs. She squirmed, her arousal growing to a fever pitch.

A large shadow detached itself from a tree and approached. She smelled forest, pine. Nicolas. A band of moonlight caressed his naked body.

Her hungry gaze roved over his powerful chest, the sculpted muscles banding his arms and legs and the dark nest of hair surrounding his thick arousal. Maggie swallowed hard. He was big. Definitely magnum-sized.

Suddenly a stab of fear coupled with her sharp desire. Maggie pushed past it.

"What are you doing out here?"

His deep voice seemed thick and husky. Maggie stood and faced him.

"Waiting for you."

She knew what would happen. Though she was a little afraid, her instincts urged her forward.

"Are you ready for me?" she whispered.

The dark hunger on his face gave her the answer.

Nicolas held out a hand. "Come inside, Maggie," he softly ordered. "It's time. It's long past time."

He waited, his palm outstretched, his manner that of a determined man. Maggie took his hand as he led her inside. Nicolas closed the door behind her. Turned around, an intense expression marking his face. Dark, hungry. His body taut, coiled energy ready to spring.

A little shiver went through her. He meant to take her. Tonight. Here. Now.

He would not be denied his mate any longer.

Taking her hand, he led her to the dimly lit bedroom. Slowly Maggie removed her clothing, watching him study her. His eyes widened as she stood naked before him. Approval twined with arousal on his face. His neck chorded as his entire body seemed to thrum with tension. Maggie's gaze dropped to his fingers, flexing and bending, and the taut control he exercised stunned her.

Nicolas remained silent, his gaze hot and intent. His thick ebony hair hung in unruly long waves about his face. But he remained motionless, his naked body like golden chiseled marble in the lamp's pale yellow glow.

He was waiting for her to make the first move.

She needed this, needed him. No matter what the consequences, she had to mate with him and end this ceaseless yearning.

Maggie pressed her mouth against his. His lips were firm and warm and he made a startled sound, then gathered her against him. Nicolas herded her backward toward the bed. They tumbled onto it, still kissing. Stubble abraded her soft skin as he drank in her mouth.

His mouth slid over her skin, trailing fire. Lips kissed the curve of one breast, then settled on her hardened nipple. Nicolas suckled her gently, flicking his tongue over the crested peak. Maggie arched, holding his head to her as he teased her with his tongue.

He released her nipple with a slow popping sound. Nicolas raised his head and smiled.

Then he began kissing her again. Maggie made a protesting sound. "I need to touch you," she said, grasping his shoulders.

"Later," he murmured. "I need to taste you."

Kiss after kiss he placed over her soft belly, licking her belly button, working his way downward. He was marking her body with his mouth, she realized. Placing his scent all over her, so every male Draicon would know she was his.

Maggie smiled. When she had a chance, she would mark him as well, letting every female Draicon know he was hers.

He kissed her slowly, thoroughly. She made little moaning sounds as she twisted and writhed beneath him. Her arms snaked up, slid about his neck, pulling him closer. Nicolas murmured that odd word she didn't understand.

"What does 'caira' mean?"

"It's an endearment. It means 'forever one,' in our ancient language."

The soft tenderness in his voice undid her. He'd been right all along. This was more than mere sexual attraction, but a bonding of two spirits. The part of her that longed to finally give in, give them both what they craved, gave a tiny sigh. And surrendered.

His mouth feathered over her skin slowly, inch

by slow inch. His firm, warm lips showered hot pleasure as he wrapped his arms about her and kissed his way down her body.

Nicolas ran a hand along the curve of her hip, skimmed across the flat of her belly and delved between her thighs. With consummate skill, he stroked her cleft. Maggie undulated her hips in silent need as he thrust a finger inside her. Her flesh clenched around him as he gently stroked, culling the moisture needed to make her ready for his entry.

"Ah, caira, you're so damn tight," he muttered.

He withdrew his finger, kissed her belly button. Licked his way down toward the juncture of her legs. Moisture pooled there. Gasping, Maggie raised her head as he parted her thighs and settled there.

Then he bent his head, and licked her. Moaning, she stiffened as his hands settled on her legs, kept them spread wide.

His mouth settled on her moist center. Sharp, delicious heat curled through her as he slid his tongue over her cleft. Maggie whimpered as he kissed and tasted her. Need arrowed through her. Need of him, inside her. Need to couple with him and join together at last, like two missing pieces finally made whole.

The heat built and her body tensed until she shattered, orgasm spilling through her in an explosive cry.

"Nicolas," she screamed.

He slowed and kissed her, staying with her then raised his head. Nicolas wiped his mouth with the back of his hand.

"You're ready now, caira."

"No, I'm not. My turn."

She sat up, and with a strength that surprised her, pushed him backward. Her wolf howled inside with approval. Amusement flared on his face as Maggie began exploring his body with the rapt fascination of a scientist and the heated arousal of a woman. She kissed a lean hip, ran a hand over his taut belly and delighted in the muscles quivering beneath her touch. Maggie nuzzled his collarbone then traced a line over his broad shoulder with her mouth. She licked velvet flesh over hard muscle and sinew, tasting the slight salt of his skin. Awe spilled through her at the vast differences between male and female. His was a warrior's body, built like a wrestler and thick with muscle, while her body was softer and pliant.

"Turn over," she ordered, barely recognizing her voice for the thickness lacing it.

"As you wish."

Nicolas turned onto his stomach as Maggie straddled his thick, muscled thighs. She ran a loving hand over silky hair on his legs, marveling at the strength in his limbs as she pressed against his hard flesh. Then she slid her palms over the smooth globes of his firm buttocks and then up the ridges of muscle on his back. Pushing aside his long hair, she kissed the back of his neck, loving the groans she culled from him. A tiny mark on his nape caught her attention. She pushed his hair back and went to inspect it but suddenly he tensed and just as easily as she'd pushed him back, he slid beneath her and flipped her onto her back.

"Now," he growled. "It's time."

Intensity radiated in his gaze as he settled his muscled body between her opened legs. Bracing himself on his hands, he stared down at her. "Caira, ah, caira."

She felt his rigid length probe at her wet, tight opening. Maggie stiffened in real alarm.

"Shh." He stroked her hair. "It's all right, sweet Maggie. Just relax. Relax."

It wasn't going to work. She was too tense and too small. But she wanted this.

Nicolas laced his fingers through hers, locking their hands together. He pushed forward. Burning pain laced her. She grit her teeth. *You've felt worse healing his wounds.*

Pressure increased. Maggie gripped his fingers as if he were an anchor. His heavy weight pinned her to the mattress. She writhed, helpless and open to him. Nicolas rose up, his gaze burning into hers.

"Now, Maggie," he said thickly. "You're mine, forever."

He pushed hard and deep inside her. Caught by the sudden shock of pain, she yelped. Nicolas caught her cry with his mouth. A single tear trickled down her cheek. He tore his mouth from hers, chased the tear away with his tongue.

Locked deep inside her, Nicolas remained motionless, his hands pinning hers down, his body keeping her captive. The burning pressure between her legs eased, replaced with a curious, delightful friction. He began moving, as her inner muscles clasped the male intruder eagerly, caressing him. Nicolas tensed and groaned. A bead of sweat rolled off his forehead and spilled onto her breasts like a teardrop.

Then something happened. A feeling grew inside her, like water pouring and filling her.

His dark eyes widened. "It's happening," he murmured. "Relax, Maggie. Don't fight it."

Tears shimmered in her eyes as she clutched him, silently holding him to her. The emotions raging wildly through her were so intense, she could barely stand it. It felt like the whole of her had opened out and poured out of her, replaced with primitive male satisfaction coupled with such tenderness and humbled awe she wanted to weep.

His emotions, she realized. She was feeling Nicolas's emotions.

Then he pulled back on his haunches and the feeling faded. His face alight with fierce desire, Nicolas spread her legs open wide. Maggie braced herself as he thrust deeply, holding her legs open wide. He stiffened, then his body shook as he released a deep groan. She felt his seed shoot inside her, then he collapsed atop her. Stroking his damp hair, Maggie welcomed his heavy weight.

Something had happened, and more than making love. Something wonderful, and slightly frightening.

"Almost," he murmured, sliding off her and kissing her temple. "Not quite, but it started. We just weren't ready yet."

They lay in drowsy contentment as Maggie curled against him, her head pillowed on his broad shoulder. Her fingers slid through the damp hairs on his chest.

"I know so little about you," she mused. "Tell me about your ranch in New Mexico."

She felt him stiffen slightly. "It's some distance from pack territory. I hadn't lived there in years until my banishment. I used to raise quarter horses, but sold them off and abandoned the ranch. Made a bit of money, which I put into investments. I had spent most of my time at the hunting lodge the pack owns. It's in the mountains, and many of our people have settled there since the Morph attacks increased."

"Do you miss it?"

His deep chest rose and fell. "Sometimes. I had converted the barn into a workshop where I did woodwork, but since I was spending so much time at the pack lodge, Damian had a workshop built for me on pack territory."

"Woodwork? Carvings?"

"Furniture. I like working with my hands. Haven't done so in a while. No time."

"Why not?" Maggie raised herself up and peered down at him. Auburn curls curtained her face. "You can't spend all your time prowling about for Morphs and caring for the pack."

He cupped her cheek. "It's who I am, Maggie.

I have a duty to the pack. I'm the warrior who keeps them safe. I have knowledge of the enemy few others claim."

"Even a warrior has to rest now and then."

He remained silent so long she wondered if he'd heard. Then Nicolas turned suddenly and clutched her so tightly she nearly yelped.

"There is no rest for me," he muttered. "I can't."

"You can with me." Maggie stroked his head, wishing she could erase the haunted look in his dark eyes.

What really bothered Nicolas?

Chapter 11

Sunshine speared through the opened wood blinds the next morning. Maggie awoke, drowsy and feeling replete. One hand splayed over Nicolas's muscled chest, her leg hooked over his hard thigh. A Nicolas pillow. She moved slightly, wincing at sore muscles and a deeper soreness between her legs.

The musky scent of sex, spicy maleness and fresh air filled the room. Maggie snuggled deeper into the Egyptian cotton sheets. An hour's more sleep couldn't hurt.

"No. Time to rise, caira."

Dark brown eyes blinked sleepily, as he smiled at her. Maggie felt a sense of peace at his husky voice.

"Are you risen?" Impishly, she grabbed him. A strangled groan fled him.

A squeal erupted as Nicolas rolled her over, straddled her body. A hank of dark hair hung down on his face. Desire darkened his eyes. Stubble shadowed his taut jawline. He looked dangerous.

Just as quickly, he slid off her. "You're too sore," he murmured, tracing a line on her cheek. "I can wait."

"I can't." She rolled atop him, surprised at her strength. Now that she'd acknowledged her wolf, everything seemed heightened. Strength. Hearing. Smell.

Nicolas's unique masculine scent of woodsy pine and green meadows…

Maggie kissed the line of his jaw. He stroked a line down to the base of her spine. She explored, rolling him onto his stomach and caressed his thick, silky hair. Nicolas made a muffled sound of pleasure.

She lifted the hair at the nape of his neck. Nicolas stiffened.

"Don't."

Maggie ignored him and studied the small black mark she'd spotted earlier. The eagle soared upward, but tiny black droplets dripped from its talons. Inked on his neck, the tattoo looked intricate and mysterious. Almost like a gang symbol.

The thought disturbed her. She kissed the tattoo

as if she could remove the anguish she sensed it caused him.

Nicolas jerked away as if her lips were hot irons. He rolled over and mounted her, kneeing open her thighs. His gaze was dark and fierce.

She lay submissively beneath him, sensing aggressive male tension coiling inside him. He pushed inside her in a single hard thrust. Silently she endured, feeling hot pleasure as his muscled body slid over her soft one. Maggie spread her legs open, and hooked her hands around his neck.

The hard look of cruel lust on his face faded. Nicolas stared down at her, something flickering in his gaze. She pushed into his thoughts as he pushed his body into hers. Joining them intimately as flesh to flesh, thought to thought.

Scaring her. Maggie. No. Be gentle, not rough. What the hell am I doing?

Maggie moaned and strained toward him, pulling him closer.

I'm not scared, Nicolas. I'm tougher than that, she whispered into his mind. *Give me all you have and release it.*

He did.

So tight, warm and silky. A wet, hot glove squeezing his cock. Nicolas braced himself on his hands and thrust deeply. *Ah, Maggie,* he said silently. *My Maggie.* She took all he gave and met him equally.

He felt her inner muscles tense around him as her grip about his neck tightened. He delved into her mind, the friction heightening to an explosive crescendo. His balls ached and drew up. Nicolas felt her emotions, thoughts and essence begin to flow into him like a trickling dam even as his cock swelled inside her. Maggie's sheath clamped down like a vise in exquisite pleasure.

It was happening, he realized in excited wonderment. The mating lock. Something inside him drained, flowing out of him. He threw up a mental gate, barring part of himself from entering her and allowing in only a thin trickle of her essence.

Then he felt her loosen slightly around him, as if she sensed his mental withdrawal. Nicolas raised himself up on his hands to lock gazes with her as he felt his climax approach.

"Come on, caira, sweet Maggie, come for me, come for me, yes, you can do it, you can do it," he said softly.

She gave a soft cry beneath him and her sheath squeezed him as her body shook. Nicolas let himself go, a guttural groan grating from him as he climaxed with her.

Like soft raindrops splashing onto cold metal, he felt a trickle of her gentle essence filter into his spirit. Nicolas lowered himself atop her, panting heavily. Sweat slicked their bodies together.

"Incredible," he murmured.

She blinked in drowsy satisfaction. "You were."

Part of him felt disappointed they hadn't achieved it yet. Perhaps later. Sometimes raw, frenzied sex brought on the mating lock. Maybe when she learned to embrace her wolf and not be afraid. Perhaps a little of his strength had flowed into her, enough to teach her to go beyond her fears.

In the meantime, they just had to keep trying. Nicolas rolled off her, trembling with spent passion, and smiled inwardly.

He greatly anticipated trying again, and again.

A while later, Maggie decided love wasn't quite enough. Nicolas had been content to absorb energy through lovemaking, but she'd lived too long as a human. Breakfast was necessary.

Nicolas hunted through the refrigerator and shut the door. He parked a lean hip against it. Maggie watched him, arousal rising already at the firmness of his body, the bands of muscles showing through the tight T-shirt.

"What's after breakfast? A drive into town?" she asked.

"No. We're going to fight."

"We just made love and you want to go to war?"

"Training. Fighting. Mastering the skills you need as a Draicon warrior to fight Morphs." He pulled a chair close to her, straddled it and rested his forearms across the back. "One reason why I brought you here, caira. This cottage is temporarily protected from Morphs finding us. The more magick we use, the thinner the shield becomes. We have a week at the most before the protection dies out entirely." His bright gaze burned into hers. "Including a mating lock. Just as your parents did before you, Maggie. Did they ever teach you about sex among our kind?"

"You mean the birds and the bees?"

A roguish grin touched his mouth. "More like the *canis* and the *lupus.* Just like real wolves, caira. Only in our kind, it's necessary to exchange magick powers."

Unbidden memories surfaced. "It's about sex," she recalled.

"I can see I'll have to start at the beginning," he muttered. "Millennia ago, our people grew too powerful and decided to divide ourselves and halve our powers. When we find our mate, it's literally finding our missing half, the missing half of our magick. This is why you and I can communicate on a telepathic level, Maggie. When we achieve a certain sexual fulfillment, our bodies will lock together and we'll exchange powers. Two becoming one again, as it was in ancient times."

He leaned closer, enough for her to smell the faint scent of soap, and clean skin and his familiar woodsy, very male scent. "Biologists call it a copulatory tie in wolves. It already began when we made love," he said softly.

"I thought it was just from absorbing energy through sex."

"No, it's more." Nicolas cupped her face in a tender gesture. She smiled at him.

"So you'll inherit my healing abilities, which is my magick, and I'll receive some of your strength and courage. What else will I get in return?"

He pulled back, looking cautious. "Most couples share the same magick, and the mating lock merely strengthens their powers. Not us. You'll inherit my ability to fight, sense and smell when the enemy approaches. Kill them swiftly."

Acid soured her stomach. "I don't want to kill."

Turbulent emotions flashed on his face. "You must. Maggie, something happened to make you block out everything you are, everything you're meant to become. You and I are a mated pair because we each balance out the qualities we both need. Your gentleness and healing, and my ability to protect and defend. You were born with the instinct as wolf to fight. Yet you lost it somewhere in childhood."

Lost in thought, she remained silent. The memory was there, flickering close to the surface like a grainy movie image. Letting it surface proved too dangerous.

"If it's any easier, think of the Morphs as germs. They're hurtful and will harm you."

Big, toxic human germs that bled bright red blood. Blood, flowing, oozing onto concrete… staining…

Maggie closed her eyes, opened them. "I can't. I won't."

"You will," he said quietly. "I'll teach you. Simple, basic techniques. Knives are best. In hand-to-hand combat you can kill them by stabbing them in the heart."

"Teach me self-defense techniques." Maggie pushed back from the table. "I will not pick up a knife to hurt someone."

"You don't need a dagger," he said softly. "You're Draicon. All you need are your fangs. Those can sink into flesh and your jaws can snap a man's neck instantly."

Maggie wrapped her arms about her, shuddering, as he stalked out of the kitchen. The door banged behind him.

"I can't do this!"

"You can. Try again."

Behind the house in the expansive backyard, they worked. A cooling breeze stirred dead leaves, sent the smell of fresh pine wafting through the air. Maggie had twisted her unruly curls into a bun. Sun beat down upon her neck. Nicolas stood back, watching her lunge at a CPR dummy nicknamed Kane hanging from the branch of a tall live oak.

An hour ago, he'd telephoned Baylor. Baylor assured Maggie that Misha was with him in New Mexico and safe with the pack. Knowing Misha was safe had eased her mind, but practicing at hurting others made her tense all over again.

Maggie found it difficult to overcome her revulsion at violence. She grit her teeth. If she didn't learn control, how could she prevent herself from turning into a wolf again?

"Think of the Morphs attacking Misha. Think of your dog bleeding on the ground."

His words snapped something inside her. Hands curled into fists. Maggie rushed at the dummy again, the heel of her hand rising up to make contact with the dummy's chin.

Nicolas gave an approving nod. He took a long slug of water. Fascinated, she watched a bead of water slide down his stubbled jaw, his strong throat muscles working as he swallowed. Nicolas backhanded his mouth.

She stared at her hand, deeply troubled. Her firm vow of nonviolence wavered, like wind touching the glassy surface of a still lake. *Maybe fighting techniques like this would have saved my parents.* The thought, shared openly with him, haunted her.

"No, it wouldn't have," he spoke aloud. "The ones who killed your parents weren't mortals. I tracked down the police report from your parents' deaths. Their bodies were found but no sign was found of their attackers. Except one oddity. Nearby pools of blood were tested and contained unusually high acidic content."

She felt a sudden sickness in her stomach as he continued. "Morph blood. When you walked back to your car that night, Maggie, the ones trailing you were disguised as humans, blending in to kill and then drain energy from victims. A blow to the throat would have no more effect than a gnat bite."

"Mom and Dad died protecting me." The surfacing memory haunted her. "They warned me, 'Run Maggie,' as the men were hitting them, kept hitting them…and the blood, so much blood on the sidewalk… Dad couldn't change, he and Mom hadn't shape-shifted in years because they didn't want anyone to track us down. His magick was too weak. Magick, they'd always called it, now I can admit that. It wasn't a carnival trick, but real, living magick. I went back to my father and I tried so hard, my hands on his chest," she whispered.

Nicolas gripped her upper arms, his touch firm and anchoring. "What happened to the killers, Maggie?"

She pressed a trembling hand to her temple. "Please, stop."

He gathered her against him, stroked her hair. She rested against him, relishing his comforting touch. Wind caressed the curls spilling from her topknot, dried the tears tumbling down her cheeks. Maggie fisted away her emotions.

"Let's try this again," she said harshly. "I want

you to teach me how to control this beast inside me, Nicolas. Control it so I never have to worry about it taking over me again."

His gaze turned hooded. "You can't force yourself never to change, Maggie. It's part of who you are. Repress the wolf and it will surface again when your guard is down. When your rage boils over and explodes, the wolf will emerge."

"Then teach me to leash it, Nicolas. Teach me to keep it at bay. I don't want to change. Not ever again."

Nicolas rubbed the back of his neck. "Maggie, all you see is a beast that threatens to take over you. Your wolf is as much a part of you as your hands and feet. It's been lying dormant for years and dimmed all your natural senses. When you finally acknowledge your wolf, you open yourself up to all the wonderful powers it offers. Your senses heighten. You feel the call to run wild and free. Your strength doubles. When you willingly embrace your Draicon self, you'll see the advantages. Your wolf will alert you to danger. You need your wolf now more than ever."

She had trouble believing him. Her wolf was a beast that only caused pain and destruction. It clawed to be free and turn her into something she loathed.

He stepped back with a wary look as the idea raced through her mind. She studied him thoughtfully. No, not a killer. He was strength, loyalty, determination. Some of those qualities he'd endowed her with when they'd made love. Maggie looked deep inside and found a glimmer of strength and courage. She could control her wolf, with his help.

Wind lifted the dark hair from his muscled neck as he stepped forward. With his broad shoulders, lean waist and lethal grace, Nicolas looked the strong warrior. Yet he was much more. She sensed a hidden wellspring of sensitivity inside him.

He cupped her chin, lifting her troubled gaze to his warm brown one. "Think of controlling your wolf as training a dog. You set the rules."

"Does this mean I'm not really housebroken?"

Nicolas threw his head back and laughed. The deep, rich sound warmed her. "Come on. I'll show you."

Minutes later, they stood on the long wood porch, at the head of the stairs leading down to the open field bracketing the thick forest. Maggie stripped off her shoes, jeans, thick black sweatshirt and underwear. Cold air hit her naked

flesh. Gooseflesh erupted over her body and she
wrapped her arms about herself. Nicolas stripped,
watching her quietly. He seemed at home in the
cold.

"In time, you'll adjust as well. Are you ready?"

She nodded, averting her gaze from him, using
all her concentration necessary for the change.

His muscles tightened as his dark gaze swept
over her naked body. Nicolas closed his eyes,
fisted his hands. When he opened them again, the
intensity had faded.

"Control, Maggie. It's all about controlling your
body and your emotions. I've spent a lifetime
mastering both. First you have to allow yourself
to shift into a wolf. Give yourself permission and
do it while all your emotions are even."

Dropping to all fours, she gave him an expectant
look. He drew in a harsh breath. "Dammit, this is
going to be hard…" He swallowed again. "You
don't have to drop down like that. Just keep the
image of a wolf in mind. Will yourself to change,
let the beast inside free. Think of running wild,
roving over hills, running with the moon. Allow
yourself to be free at last. Feel the power of your
wolf and let it go."

Maggie closed her eyes. A deep craving arose
inside her. She thought of letting it loose to run

free. Her arms lifted to the air. She embraced the ancient instinct.

The change happened slower this time. Maggie felt every intense feeling, as if her spirit burst forth. Fur rippled along her arms, torso. Bones lengthened. She opened her mouth to exclaim her excitement to Nicolas. A loud howl came forth.

Senses sharpened. Maggie could scent ancient rabbit scat, taste the fear of a deer pausing in its grazing in the forest. Nicolas's familiar scent slammed into her. Wolf knew this scent. Good. Familiar. Pack.

Her mate. She loped over to him as he dropped to one knee. Nicolas stroked her luxurious pelt as she lowered her muzzle. Instinct warned her this was a dominant male demanding respect. Her ears flicked back as her tail lowered.

"You see, caira? Nothing to worry about. You can control this."

She watched as he shifted into his wolf form. He spoke into her mind. *Let's run.*

Maggie followed Nicolas as he raced toward the meadow's edge. She inhaled a faint but pungent odor of dead raccoon. There, floating on the wind, something stronger, closer. Rabbit.

Maggie put her nose to the ground and trotted. Nicolas circled around and loped close behind her. Her nose twitched as she scented a rabbit. Ignoring his warning in her mind, she gave it chase. The small gray rabbit zigged and zagged across the open meadow. Maggie bounded after it, joy rippling through her.

She followed it into the woods until she sensed a familiar scent approach. Maggie turned with a snarl.

Nicolas nipped her hindquarters in warning. Maggie yipped.

Never ignore me. When you're wolf, you pay attention. There are all manner of dangers here. Wild boar. And human hunters.

The caramel gaze locked with hers, dominant and proud.

Maggie lowered her head. Nicolas trotted over. She exposed her muzzle to him, resting on his backside. He rubbed against her with great affection.

Side by side, they loped back to the cottage. Nicolas shifted back. Naked, he stood regarding her. "Now, change back," he ordered.

Focusing, she thought of her human form. Nothing. She lifted her head, howled her frustration. Maggie licked the back of Nicolas's outstretched hand. Taste, remembering the salty, masculine taste of them as they made love....

She found herself crouched over in human form, licking Nicolas's hand. Raindrops misted her hair. This time, she barely felt the cold.

Maggie felt a rising triumph.

"Nothing to it," he said softly, his hand reaching up to caress her cheek as she stood. "And when you feel the emotions raging out of control, such as anger, and you're afraid to let the wolf go, concentrate. Think of something utterly mundane."

"Like how some men think of baseball when they're trying to slow down during sex?"

He gave a strangled laugh. "Something like that."

Maggie didn't want to think of baseball. His scent swam in her nostrils. The exhilaration of changing without anger provoking her stimulated her senses. She wanted to taste him again, mark him with her scent.

Taking his palm, Maggie gave it a long, slow lick. Nicolas trembled as if trying to restrain himself.

She didn't want restraint. She wanted him, wild and free, as her wolf had been free.

Desire and something deeper swam in his velvet gaze.

More. Maggie ran her hand over the taut muscles on his body. Raging sexual need consumed her. Her body felt on fire with need for her mate. She burned. It felt almost painful.

A soft breeze caressed her naked skin. She felt wild, free and incredibly alive. Desire burned in his gaze.

"Caira," he said thickly.

She felt it as well, a need so sharp it consumed her. Nicolas started for her. She danced away, laughing.

"Not so fast. Let's see if you can run that fast on two feet."

Darting away, she tore off for the house. Maggie sensed Nicolas hot on her heels. She ran faster, exhilarated, her wolf still howling inside. Into the house, hooking a left into the living room then the bedroom when Nicolas pounced.

He tackled her, sending her flying backward on the bed. They wrestled a minute, rolling as Maggie laughed. Then Nicolas rolled her over, straddling her. His crooked smile faded with the intensity of his gaze.

"I can't be gentle with you," he growled. "Not now."

Panting, Maggie stared up at him. She knew what he wanted.

As an answer, she kneaded the firm flesh of

his taut buttocks then slid from under him and flipped over on her stomach.

His hungry growl echoed her own as his warm hands stroked a line down her back. Maggie arched her back, leaning into his caress.

His hands on her hips, Nicolas pulled her onto all fours. She felt him position himself behind her. His rigid length prodded her soft opening. Maggie arched and moaned, undulating her hips. He pushed inside a little, teasing, then withdrew.

Nicolas leaned over her, his chest hairs rasping over her overly sensitive back. He cupped her breasts, thumbing the nipples. She felt wild and carnal, animalistic in her need.

With a low snarl he thrust deep inside her. She gasped, trying to absorb the shock of taking all of him at once. He leaned close and thrust, withdrew and created a rhythm. Maggie snarled herself, desperate to be free, to touch him. But he held her firmly, controlling each deep thrust, intensifying the pleasure until it mounted and built. She felt ready to explode.

Then his hand reached down to her cleft. Deftly he flicked once, twice.

She screamed as the climax shattered her. Quivering, she wanted to collapse onto the mattress.

"Oh, no, I'm not done with you yet," he whispered into her ear as he thrust into her. She felt herself open to him like a flower, exposing everything. Then she felt him tense as his hands gripped her hips. His cock seemed to expand and stretch her beyond limits.

Suddenly he stopped, as climax shimmered just beyond her reach. Maggie howled with frustration as he withdrew. Nicolas pressed a gentle hand onto her backside, which was slick with sweat. She fell on the mattress.

"I want to kiss you. Turn over," he ordered.

She did and he slid over her, framing her face with his warm, strong hands. Nicolas kissed her deeply, his tongue thrusting in and out as she wriggled beneath him. He drew back, parted her legs and pushed into her, angling his thrusts to give her the most pleasure. Maggie arched off the mattress as the tension built. She felt taut as a bowstring. Trailing his mouth down her throat, he suddenly bit her neck. She screamed and wrapped her legs about him.

"Now, caira, now, come for me, now," he growled.

Arching, she climaxed and felt her sheath clamp down on him as he swelled inside her. Nicolas released his seed as a harsh roar ripped from him.

Her vision blurred with tears from the power of the emotions pouring from her, and into her.

He locked inside her even as his seed kept pouring into her, his essence. Everything. A little scared of the intensity, she wanted to pull back and hide, but he murmured soothingly into her ear.

"Maggie, my Maggie, don't fear it. Look, caira, look at us."

Colors swirled and sparkled, dancing like iridescent butterflies. Maggie gasped in awe and began to weep. Wonderment overcame her. She felt her very spirit flowing out of her, pouring into her mate. Strength filled her. Nicolas's immense strength and power. His magick.

She opened herself fully, giving him all her healing powers. Her tearful gaze locked with his intent one. She sensed Nicolas struggle against the powerful emotions pouring into and out of him. A single, small droplet of water leaked out of the corner of his eye and his expression tightened as he blinked furiously. Maggie sensed he held back the smallest bit. He was blocking her, putting up a small barrier, like concrete blocks piled in the middle of a raging river. Nicolas hung over her, kissing her neck as they melded together.

Nicolas carefully turned around and rolled over

so she lay atop him. He stroked her hair, murmuring endearments as she trembled in his arms.

Many minutes later, she felt herself loosen around him. Very carefully, he pulled out, leaving her feeling bereft and empty.

He opened his arms with a solemn look. "Oh, Mags, come here."

A little cautious, she lay against him, wondering what he'd seen deep inside her that put that aching note in his voice.

"You're scared," he whispered to her. "So scared and you think, if you hide, you won't have to face what happened when you were younger. You've been hiding your whole life behind your science, technology, logic. Hiding away from your true self because it scares you. Don't hide anymore. Come with me, and be who you are destined to become. You can't hide anymore. You're in this and there's no place to hide."

He caressed her cheek. A haunted look entered his dark eyes. "Have you ever been so lonely, Maggie, that you feel as if the world had died and left you behind? No one understands, no one cares, you're not even a speck of dust, not noticeable. Then along comes someone you know, who is there for you, and your world goes from being a cold, stone hearth and burnt ashes to a crackling fire and friendship. That's pack, Maggie. Family. With pack you are never alone, you're tied to them irrevocably unless you do something that banishes you. And that kind of loneliness is like a knife stabbing in little thrusts, over and over."

His gaze grew intense. "Until you meet your one, true mate, your draicara, the one who is meant only for you. And the loneliness fades and even pack isn't as all important as your mate and bonding to her at last. That is our life, Maggie. You feel it, too. I know you do."

"With you, I feel like I can be anyone." Maggie paused, touched his cheek. "A wolf. I'm not afraid anymore of who, or what, I was meant to be."

He closed his eyes, trembling as she caressed his face. A thought entered her mind and she sensed it had escaped him like an elusive tendril of smoke.

I am very much afraid. Because I don't want to lose you, Mags. I can't. Part of me will die with you.

This vulnerability of his touched her. He guarded it just as he guarded her.

She had never felt safe, protected. Or had been able to fully let go. Always on her own, guarded and wary, as if an instinctive caution guided her. Now resting against Nicolas, she felt cherished, protected and safe. This felt right. It felt like coming home after a long, weary journey.

Except Nicolas hadn't fully opened to her. And since he hadn't, it meant he didn't fully possess her empathic abilities to heal. If he tried healing a catastrophic illness, just as she'd healed her dog, it might kill him.

She lay awake for a long time, deeply troubled by the thought.

Much later, as Maggie slept, Nicolas slid out from beneath the covers. He padded out to the kitchen and fished in a drawer for a sharp knife.

Clenching his teeth, he drew the blade across his palm. Blood welled up, black in the darkness. Just as quickly the cut closed together. Nicolas watched in rising excitement as the wound healed. It worked. He'd inherited Maggie's healing abilities.

He cleaned the knife and put it away. Now he could heal any one of his sick pack members. The disease would not thwart him or kill him.

Nothing could stop him now.

Chapter 12

The next morning, the tender closeness they'd shared during the mating lock seemed to evaporate. Maggie's stubbornness grated on his nerves. Nicolas leaned against a tree trunk, rubbing his tattoo. It seemed to burn against his fingers. He'd shown her how to toss daggers as they practiced using a tree trunk. Maggie had excellent aim, her knives arrowing straight to the target. Then he demonstrated the intricate maneuvers needed in human form to stab a Morph through the heart.

She refused to practice. Maggie refused to even try. It was as if she'd never absorbed any of his warrior abilities.

Hitting a tree trunk with knives was more like a game, she said. Hitting a target was different. Emotions blazed in her deep blue eyes. The passion exhibited in bed last night flared now in mute defiance.

Nicolas took position before the CPR dummy. Unsheathing both daggers, he held them loosely with a practiced hand. "Like this. Loosen your wrists."

Barely concentrating, he flicked back his hands, released. The daggers sank into the dummy's chest. Several slits marked the target. His marks. Not hers.

"Try it now."

She broke her silence, folding her arms across the navy sweatshirt. "No, Nicolas. I won't do it. I won't kill so there's no point in learning."

Trying for the logic she liked so much, he pointed out that the Morph leader had clearly marked her for death. "Kill him and you dispatch the army, Maggie. Kane is the key to destroying them. You'll find no peace until he's dead. He'll search for you and use everything he has to cut you down. Everything. He will come after you himself."

A frown line dented her lovely brow. "I know. I can't keep running, but...can't you see, Nicolas? I've spent most of my life training myself to invoke peace. How can I change?"

How? Like he had learned to change. Out of

necessity, Nicolas learned to kill. "You do what you must. Faced with danger, you have to protect yourself. Remember, Kane is a germ and you're a white blood cell. He's a disease that needs to be eliminated."

Wind ruffled the curls framing her heart-shaped face. Her velvety lips pursed in a troubled moue. Nicolas tensed himself against a desire to kiss away that look. "Then why can't you kill him for me, Nicolas? If Kane is such a threat, and you're skilled in killing them, do it yourself. Baylor said out of all the males in the pack, you've downed the most Morphs."

Her eyes searched his as she studied him. "Hasn't he ever come up against you?"

His heart dropped into his stomach. "Kane has never tried to kill me." That much was true. Nicolas erected a shield to guard his thoughts.

Because I can't kill him, Maggie. If I kill him, I become what I fear most. And nothing will stop me. He turned to the immediate problem.

"Enough of this, Maggie. What was in your past is gone. You're Draicon now, and my mate. Every single Draicon must protect the pack. You will learn to kill Morphs." His firm voice brooked no argument.

"Like hell I will!"

"Would you let them kill you?"

"I'd find another way to defeat them," she stated. "And I'd stay out of their way until I did. I'm a vet and I know animals. There must be a way to destroy them without violence. I will not use violence to destroy evil. Not again."

Her inward gasp of breath alerted him to the disturbing memory she faced. Maggie pressed her hands against her temples. He slipped into her thoughts, did not find the shattering images of blood and bodies he'd expected. Instead he found a brick wall.

"Maggie, you need to remember. Only when you remember can you get past it," he said softly, watching her.

A barely perceptible shudder racked her delicate body. "I can't, Nicolas. Somewhere in my past is a memory filled with violence. I've spent the rest of my life pushing through it. I won't be like that again. It was brutal and bloody."

"Life can be brutal and bloody. You have to learn to fight back. I did. I proved myself and my worth to the pack."

He learned the hard way, carved a pathway to acceptance with his daggers and his strength.

Blue eyes deep as a quiet sea focused on him. "Nicolas, you're more than the image you project.

You're more than a warrior who's fought hard. You're kindhearted and noble and sensitive with the soul of a poet. Maybe you've never let anyone else see that. But I see it. The others should know all of you, not just the surface part of you. If you'd let them see deep inside you, they'd know what I know."

Alarm raced through him. Maggie dug beneath his layers and saw what he didn't dare show to anyone else. The pack didn't need a poet. They needed a warrior.

He had to steer her away from this dangerous thinking. "The only person who needs to go deep inside is you, Maggie. You must learn to defeat the enemy, and you have to remember what's in your past that's stopping you from learning," Nicolas growled.

"I don't need to remember anything. And I don't need this." With a firm flick of her wrist, she sent the dagger sailing downward. It stabbed the earth and quivered.

Nicolas studied the defiant thrust of her lower lip. She would not. Gentle-natured, stubborn Maggie would defy him. He could not break through that barrier blocking out her past. Not even with the mating lock. She'd erected her own block from him, just as he had with her, he thought ironically.

But he knew how to push past it, propel her into battle.

When the first Morph scout arrived, he'd put the plan into action.

Outside on the wood deck, they ate a hearty dinner of lightly grilled beef. Nicolas topped off her wineglass with the bottle of merlot he'd found on the wine rack. Rose twilight filtered through the thick pines, dappling the ground. Wind brushed the thick grass at the forest's edge. The late October chill felt delightful.

It felt peaceful and yet Maggie had never felt so tense before. Her wolf strained and whined to be free. It warned of danger and alerted her for predators.

Ridiculous. No predators existed here. Nicolas assured her the cottage was protected from intruders. The magick spell warding off Morphs would last as long…

As she and Nicolas didn't practice too much magick.

Her fork fell to the glass table with a loud clatter. Nicolas glanced up.

"Nicolas, we are safe here, aren't we? I mean,

this magick we've emitted with our shifting, has it done anything?"

Nicolas toyed with his food. "I'm not certain. The shield around the house is strong, but it's never been tested. It depends on the level of power used."

"How can you tell how powerful the magick is?"

He raised his intense gaze to meet hers. "Morph magick is dark and emits no colors, but most powerful Draicon magick produces iridescent sparks. Our mating certainly compromised the shield's integrity."

Remembering the brilliant flare of colors when they made love, Maggie's appetite faded.

His reassuring smile offered little comfort. "We'll be gone tomorrow, caira. Long before the Morphs can track us. Try to relax."

She speared another forkful of beef, but kept scanning the fields beyond the cottage. Twilight attracted animals to the straggling, sad garden. On the field's edge, she saw a flicker of movement. Maggie set down her fork and sniffed the air. She caught Nicolas's delicious masculine scent, the smell of meadow and a faint musky smell of deer.

The animal cleared the forest and stepped into the meadow. It began cropping the grass.

"It's only a deer." Maggie sat back, sighing with relief.

Nicolas raised a black brow in question.

"I guess I'm suspicious of every animal that walks nearby. I think it wants to jump me."

"Even me?" He smiled at her.

"Especially you. You always look like you want to jump me," she teased.

His smile faded into an intense look. "I do."

The dark promise in his eyes sent delicious shivers coursing through her. Maggie glanced at the deer again, which advanced as it grazed. She frowned as it drew closer, obviously unafraid of the humans eating their own dinner nearby.

"That deer is awfully large for a southern species. I've never seen one like it."

Maggie's senses went on full alert. The pretty doe flicked its ears forward. It licked its nose, then opened its mouth.

A ray of dying sunlight glinted off pointed, razor-sharp teeth.

Horror speared her. Maggie gasped as scales erupted over the deer's soft golden fur. The deer writhed and twisted, elongating into a scaly reptilian creature.

She stared in shock at the twelve-foot crocodile as it began crawling toward them.

Daggers had already materialized in Nicolas's hands as he jumped to his feet and ran to the deck's edge. "It's a Morph scout. Stay here. I'll kill it."

The shout of protest on her lips died as Nicolas jumped off the deck and ran toward the invader. It hissed, opened its jaws. She shouted a warning as the croc swung around to attack. Massive jaws closed on Nicolas's arm. Her mate dropped his daggers and screamed as the croc bit down, tearing open his skin.

Maggie cried out as well, her wolf clamoring for freedom. Nicolas had never screamed in agony. Tears blurred her vision.

She must save him. Maggie jumped off the deck and raced forward, ignoring Nicolas's weakened protests. Reptilian eyes stared at her as the crocodile swung around, jaws open, showing rows of sharp teeth. Nicolas lay on the ground, moaning. Always he fought in silence, a lethal machine mowing down Morphs.

He was seriously hurt. Dying maybe. Maggie fought for control of her emotions. She picked up one abandoned dagger. The crocodile turned, smacking her with its massive tail.

Toppling to the ground, Maggie dove into a roll as Nicolas had taught her. She sprang up.

Rushing forward, she grabbed the croc's tail and flipped it over. Maggie jumped on its chest, pinning it down.

The dagger sank into the soft underbelly and into the heart. Black blood spurted. Maggie cried out as the acidic fluid splashed over her face, her chest and hands. It burned. She grimly fought down the pain, continued twisting the knife.

The crocodile emitted an unearthly scream, writhed and shape-shifted before her horrified eyes. Soulless eyes, thin stringy hair, a walking nightmare.

Then it finally lay still. Rolling off the Morph, Maggie watched warily as it disintegrated into gray ash.

Staggering to her feet, she watched her burns turn pink, then fade entirely. Her healing powers grew stronger each day.

"Brava," Nicolas said softly.

Maggie's mouth fell open as he stood. Nicolas casually stood. The ragged tears in his arm had vanished.

He had her healing abilities now. She'd totally forgotten. He hadn't. Instead, he used the attack to provoke her into killing.

The realization burned worse than the Morph's blood.

"You…faked it!"

"On purpose." Nicolas regarded her through his hooded gaze.

"How could you? Are you that careless that you'd let that thing kill you? Or me?"

"There was no danger," he said calmly. "I smelled the scout long before the deer appeared in the meadow. I know them, Maggie. I knew one would appear tonight. I'd never let you come to harm."

"Why the hell did you do it?" She was shouting now, her emotions boiling over.

"To prove to yourself you could kill the enemy, Maggie. You did. You said you couldn't. You were wrong."

"Bastard," she whispered. "I thought you were dying. I thought you needed me."

His expression remained blank. "I can take care of myself."

"Obviously. So you don't need me. You have my empath powers now, Nicolas. You can go back to New Mexico without me. In fact, you can go straight to hell."

Nicolas had always prided himself on his intelligence and ability to reason. He'd never thought of himself as an idiot. Until now.

Maggie had run off. Acres of undeveloped land and forest gave her plenty of territory to roam. Searching for her, he prowled the woods. Thin strands of Spanish moss dripped from live oak branches overhead. Green lichen stamped the thin trunks of Australian pine trees. The smell of fresh earth swam in his nostrils. He picked up her scent, which zigged and zagged all over the woods.

He'd assumed killing a Morph to protect him would awaken her killing instincts. It backfired. Cursing, he'd spent the night looking for her. The morph scout would be followed by a horde by early morning. If he didn't find Maggie…

Swallowing hard, he pushed aside the thought. Nicolas reached out mentally to her. No answer. Emotions stripped him bare. Again he tried, opening himself up to his mate.

Nothing.

Fear for Maggie clawed up his spine. He'd never felt this spiraling, out-of-control feeling before. Emotions were dangerous. They made strong warriors weak, exposed vulnerabilities, clouded clear thinking. He couldn't afford the luxury of emotions, or falling in love.

Nicolas ground to a halt. Love? He choked back a self-deprecating laugh. He, the Draicon determined never to grow close to another, who guarded himself from involvement, had done the unthinkable. He'd fallen in love with his mate.

How stupid of him to assume he'd mate with her and keep himself separate. He couldn't afford to fall in love. Anyone close to Nicolas became a target for his enemies to use.

His jaw tightened. Nicolas continued loping through the woods. Maggie could be used against him if his feelings were discovered. Silently he vowed to keep them hidden and secret.

At all costs, Maggie must be kept safe. Even at the price he might pay—losing her.

He'd wanted to turn her into a killer to save the pack. Hooray for Nicolas. And did he once ever consider her feelings?

Nicolas rubbed his tattoo again. He thought he was doing the best thing for the pack, but what of Maggie? He was forcing her to turn into something she loathed and feared.

Just like something you loathe and fear?

The treacherous thought chased itself around in his head. Nicolas groaned. So desperate had he been to shut her out, and leash his growing feelings for her, he'd failed to consider her needs.

No longer. As soon as he found her, she'd come first. If he found her.

I must.

Dawn crept through the thick foliage, spearing the pines with thin light. Nicolas rubbed his tattoo, frustrated and scared. He had to find her. Images of Maggie ripped apart by Morphs haunted him.

Beside a scrawny pine, he sank to his knees. Nicolas closed his eyes, tried reaching out to his mate again. This time he poured all his emotions into the call.

A faint answer raised his hopes.

Nicolas opened himself up, listening with all his heart.

Dread filled him at Maggie's pitiful cry.

She had returned to the cottage, looking for him. And now the Morphs were coming in her direction.

Wolf ran faster than his human form. Nicolas stripped and shifted. He bounded toward the cottage, inwardly sending her reassurances. Fear drove him onward.

He could only hope he wasn't too late to save her.

They were coming.

Maggie whipped her head about. Nowhere to hide. Oh, God. The sounds of thousands of teeth whirring and chomping increased, mocking the gentle chimes of a church's bell in the distance.

Angry at Nicolas, frightened at her violent tendencies, she'd run off and spent the night wandering the woods in her wolf form. Running, until she'd found an abandoned barn. Then she'd changed back, and cried herself to sleep.

When she awoke, Maggie realized how foolish she'd acted. Running away solved no problems. She'd spent her whole life running and hiding.

She'd hide no more.

Upon her return to the cottage, she showered, dressed and went outside to look for her mate. Ready to answer his call, she turned to the forest.

And heard the sound, like a buzz saw through the yellow green meadow.

The Morphs were heading straight for her. She sent out a mental cry for help to Nicolas, then searched around. No time to flee. They'd find her.

The screeching sound trebled. Closer still. Too late to head for the road.

Maggie, the pine trees. Roll in the mud to mask your scent then climb the tree.

Nicolas's voice, laced with urgency, sounded in her mind. She darted around the house's side. Dropping to the muddy ground, Maggie did a fireman's roll, coating her body with thick wet earth.

She slapped mud on her hands, covered her face and then reached for the low branches. Her hands shook. Her muddied sneakers missed the first branch, sending her tumbling back to the earth.

Hurry, caira. Hurry. Stay calm. Climb. Steady. I'm here with you.

Maggie gulped down a calming breath and listened to Nicolas's soothing reassurances echoing in her head. She grabbed the first branch, using the sticky sap to gain a foothold. Up she climbed, her heart thundering, her hands shaking so badly she barely could grip the next branch. Up, up, never looking down, until reaching the top.

Perched on a sturdy limb, she hugged the trunk. Dared to look down.

Maggie bit back a shocked gasp.

Lines of crouching creatures marched through the meadow. They ploughed through the grass, leaving brown stubble in their wake. Sharp teeth gnashed, whirred, clicked. If they reached her, they'd cut her to ribbons.

Oh, Nicolas, I'm so scared.

Hang on, baby. I'll be there in a minute. I'm close now.

Horror crawled up her spine. *No! If you arrive now, they'll see you! They'll kill you. Stay away.*

No, Maggie, I'm coming....

Stay away or I'll jump. I swear it. I won't sit in this tree, safe, and watch you die for nothing. Stay!

Silence. Maggie bit her lip so hard she nearly drew blood.

A large red bull ant crawled up the trunk, paused near her hand. Maggie didn't dare move. Her leg muscles cramped. She remained still, blending with the tree, letting the sap and mud absorb her scent. The ant crawled onto her hand. She bit back a scream. Not a Morph. Just an ant. Just an ant.

The ant inspected her hand, marched up her wrist, explored the reddish-brown mud coating her arm. Maggie flinched.

Pincers bit down, through the mud. She winced, but did not move. The ant continued biting. Maggie ignored it, stared as the whirring mass of things advanced. On four spindly limbs they crawled, their naked bodies covered with sallow, saffron skin. Their male genitals hung grotesquely large between their legs. Eyes were pitch-black and soulless. But their teeth were yellow, razor sharp and triangular. Maggie stuffed a fist into her mouth. What kind of things were these?

Then they stood on two legs and she nearly lost her grip and tumbled to the ground.

This was the natural form of the Morph.

Noses lifted to the air, they sniffed, then like a stream, poured inside the house.

As if scenting the danger, the bull ant released its grip. It scurried away from Maggie, away from her arm and down the trunk.

One creature came outside. It approached the tree and tapped long talons against it. Maggie held her breath.

It pounded the trunk. Branches shook. The Morph glanced up. Maggie didn't dare swallow. She only hoped the thick coating of mud disguised her.

Apparently satisfied, the Morph stepped back. She peered down, saw it watching the ant crawling down the tree trunk. A long tongue snaked out of the Morph's mouth. Pop! The ant vanished, the tongue receded.

The Morph licked its large, greasy lips. Nausea rose in Maggie's throat. She fought it down as the Morph vanished into the cottage.

Then a long, eerie howl split the air.

Maggie craned her neck to see.

A large gray wolf stood near the cottage. It loped toward the tree. *Jump, Maggie, jump!*

She trusted. Maggie climbed down, jumped the last five feet. Pain exploded in her leg then just as quickly faded. She ran for Nicolas.

Morphs poured out of the cottage, shifting into wolves as they ran. They were gunning for him, a pack of wolves with fangs showing. Their hatred scented the air.

Shifting into his human form as he ran, Nicolas raced toward her. Naked, he tackled her to the ground. He covered her body with his own as the wolves attacked.

She struggled to be free as they fell upon him. He did not wince or even flinch, but bore their blows. Growls and snarls filled the air. She shut her eyes, terrified for her mate. The metallic smell of fresh blood mixed with the scent of mud. Tears clogged her throat.

A distant shout sounded. Maggie strained to hear.

Hush, caira. Lie still.

Maggie obeyed, bewildered as she heard the wolves whine, then their paws padded over the soft ground. They were leaving.

After a few agonizing minutes, Nicolas rose off her. She gave a startled cry as she examined the bloody gouges lining his back. They had clawed at Nicolas trying to get her. But he'd shielded her with his body.

As she watched, the claw marks faded, then vanished. Nicolas regarded her with a worried look. "Are you all right, caira?"

Maggie touched his unshaven cheek. "I'm sorry for running off," she whispered. "I was just so angry. Confused."

He closed his eyes as he leaned into her caress. "It's my fault. I'm the one who's sorry. I pushed you into something you don't want. Forgive me."

Nicolas drew his arms about her in a savage embrace. She pressed against his trembling body. "Let's start over, Nicolas. Both of us. Go to New Mexico, let me meet the pack. And put an end to this. There has to be a way out that doesn't involve violence. I'll find one. I know I can."

"I trust you," he muttered into her hair. "I don't want to lose you again."

She raised her head, deeply troubled. The Morphs had taken off, silently vanishing like mist. The leaden sky promised rain today, and a damp breeze stirred the trees.

By all rights, Nicolas should be dead. If they wanted to kill her, why hadn't they killed him?

"I don't understand." She wiped mud off her

face as she peered at her grim-faced lover. "Why didn't they kill you?"

Nicolas said nothing. But the determined set of his jaw warned her he still harbored secrets. And he didn't wish to share them with her. She remembered what Baylor had said, and shivered.

What exactly did his mysterious tattoo symbolize? Who was Nicolas, really?

Chapter 13

On the way to Atlanta's Hartfield International Airport, Nicolas made a quick stop. Maggie went to a medical supply store and purchased medical supplies, protective suits and sterile gloves. She was determined to treat the disease killing off the Draicon as a scientist, as well as a healer.

The flight to Albuquerque proved uneventful. When they arrived, Nicolas rented a car and drove north. They stopped at a grocery store and bought supplies, then headed to his ranch a few miles away from the pack's lodgings in the Pinyon Valley. Here they'd spend one precious day alone before joining the pack. Maggie fretted that the pack needed her, but Nicolas had stayed her protests with soft assurances.

He needed her more. His stark confession ended her protests.

The home had plush pinewood love seats and easy chairs with Southwest prints. A heavy pine coffee table and a rag rug were set before a river rock fireplace. Two brass reading lamps with aspen, leaf-designed lampshades sat beside the easy chairs. Floor-to-ceiling windows overlooked the valley below. The bedroom had a pine four-poster as big as her truck, a stone fireplace and a door leading out to a small porch.

Pine and cinnamon scented the air. The fragrant scent combined with the heavy masculine furniture and the small touches of whimsy, such as stuffed bears tucked into the corners, made the cabin feel like home. Maggie looked around with interest.

"It's mine," he said, setting down her bags. "Thirty good acres of prime land. The nearest neighbor is five miles away. I bought this years ago as a private retreat. Lots of wildlife, fox, deer, rabbits and it's far away enough from civilization for me."

They ate a light dinner Nicolas cooked. Perched on a bar stool at the center island, she watched him whip eggs into an omelet, add freshly grated cheddar cheese, onions and peppers. They toasted each other with glasses of pinot noir. Over the rim of his crystal, Nicolas gave her a crooked, endearing grin, reminding her of when they'd first met at the bar in Florida.

Conversation consisted of equally light talk. Nicolas's face lit up as he talked about home and how he longed to make the ranch a real home again someday.

"Lots of open space, fresh air. A good place to raise children," he said softly, his hand sliding over hers.

They finished dinner and spent time before the fire making long, slow leisurely love. Nicolas loved her with a quiet intensity, as he knew this was their last time together before returning to the Draicon. Flames crackled in the fireplace as he kissed her naked body, his lips trailing warmth. The fur rug beneath her felt soft and warm, contrasting sharply to the hard male body settling over hers.

The next morning, light snow danced around in the wind. Grayish light showed through the windows. Maggie snuggled deeper under the goosedown quilt as Nicolas raised his head.

He watched dawn's graying light touch her sleeping face. Dark lashes feathered her rosy cheeks. Fresh air, time alone with him had removed the strain and stress from her features. His trembling hand reached up to gently sweep her silky curls away from one cheek.

His feelings threatened to spill over. Nicolas threw up a mental wall, not daring to share himself mentally with her. Pain rolled through him. He had to teach her to fend for herself, reassure himself that she could survive among the pack on her own…if he were gone. Nicolas rolled over and hugged Maggie to his side, feeling an almost devastating sense of complete loss.

He couldn't lose her. Not now. "Maggie," he whispered, caressing her hair. "My beautiful Maggie."

Her eyes fluttered open, and he drowned in their sea-blue depths. Nicolas drew her close as Maggie nuzzled his neck. She curled against him, sharing her body heat. She was warm and soft, silky female flesh yielding against him. Cold air whistled through the slightly opened window. She splayed her fingers over his chest, making him shudder with renewed desire.

Reality would come soon enough. Too soon.

Pinyon Valley, home to the Draicon. Years ago the pack had moved here, fleeing the comfortable heights of Colorado's Rockies for the quietness of northern New Mexico. Nicolas explained that the pack had once moved every forty years to keep mortal suspicions at bay since the Draicon aged slowly. Now they moved to keep their children safe from the Morphs.

Grayish sagebrush, dense forests of pinyon, ponderosa pine and juniper grew on the foothills and valleys. The plains seemed barren and the mountain slopes thick with brilliant golden aspen. The grasslands and meadows were sparsely populated but for ranches peppering the seemingly endless valley. Rising above the foothills were majestic mountains wooded with thick trees.

Hidden on a mountainside cloaked with thick firs and aspens, the large pinewood hunting lodge now served as the Draicon's main quarters. Most pack members lived separately, but when Damian fell ill, the pack moved as a unit into the lodge. They needed the closeness of each other when their leader lay dying.

Nicolas drove the Ford Escape rental up a dirt road. Birds called to each other in the trees. Clouds scuttled overhead, driven by a light wind. Maggie rolled down her window to inhale the fresh, pine-scented air. Memories tugged. Good memories.

"My father used to take me for long walks in

this area," she murmured, lifting her head to let the wind brush her curls.

Nicolas glanced at her. "You're remembering. Good. The pack may remember you, or may not. I'm uncertain as to what Baylor told them, so be on your guard."

She frowned. "Why does he detest you, Nicolas? He seems determined to bait you at every step."

Those broad shoulders lifted in a shrug. "I once had sex with his girlfriend, before they had a relationship. It was nothing more than sex after a fight with Morphs and I needed the energy. Probably he still resents it."

Doubts filled her. Baylor's animosity simmered from more than mere jealousy. The Draicon harbored a strong sense of family and pack. She sensed it had more to do with that.

The dirt road opened to a large, grassy meadow and a graveled drive. A split rail fence separated the property from the woods beyond. Nicolas parked in front of the enormous log building. Large floor-to-ceiling windows looked out over the meadow. Though the immense house resembled a sumptuous vacation spot, she sensed it was fortified heavily, like a fortress.

He climbed out, grabbed their bags. "Come on. No sense in delaying this. They're waiting for us."

"How can you tell?"

"I can smell them," he muttered.

Nicolas pressed his palm over a flat scanner besides the large double doors. Nothing happened. A muscle ticked in his jaw as he tried again.

"Dammit. They still have me locked out."

Not a very welcoming sign. Maggie gave her brightest smile. "It's me, Nicolas. They're unsure of what to expect. I am a stranger, for the most part."

Her loud knock sounded more confident than she felt. What felt like minutes later she heard a brisk tread on the floorboards inside and the slide of several locks.

The door opened outward slowly.

A friendly faced young woman stood on the threshold, holding out her hand. The welcoming smile on her face contrasted to the thick doors that barred them shut.

"Hi. I'm Katia. You must be Maggie."

Before Maggie could respond, the other female stepped forward and enfolded her in a giant bear hug. Her strength surprised Maggie.

"I'm so glad you're here, and Nicolas is back. It's awful. Just awful. Everything is falling apart," Katia whispered.

Then she rubbed at her brimming eyes, fostered a brave smile and gave Nicolas a brief, but affectionate hug. "Come on in. I'm giving you a bedroom upstairs. The sickroom is down in the basement. Damian's room is on the third floor and isolated from the others."

Nicolas shot Maggie a questioning look as he picked up their luggage and entered the lodge. Katia was crumbling inside. How many others felt the same? Maggie's compassion surfaced. She squeezed Nicolas's hand after he set their bags down in the hallway. The pack needed them. She felt certain of it.

They walked down the carpeted hallway into a large, open room flooded with natural light. In chairs, couches and sitting at several small tables around the room, sat dozens of ordinary-looking people.

The pack.

Everyone looked up at the same time.

Nicolas kept a light, but proprietary grip on Maggie's waist as she studied the people. One woman juggled a curly-haired baby boy on her lap. The toddler laughed and pointed at Maggie with a welcoming smile. The mother bent her head, shushed him. A man with a bristling crew cut and sharp features came over, took the baby from her and sat beside the woman, his attitude protective.

No welcoming smiles here, or even a friendly nod. She felt thrust into a crowd of hostile strangers. Looking at them all, imagining them changing into their wolf forms, she felt even more alienated. This was a family who bonded together, played together, raised their children in close proximity and hunted together as wolf. She was the outsider.

They were different. She sensed it. The fine lines of beauty in the women, the hard edges of the men, doused her eagerness. Maggie felt as confused and alienated as she had when she'd been thrust into the cold, antiseptic world of foster care. She didn't fit in.

Even here, with Nicolas? He'd insisted this was her family, her pack, her home.

Yet nothing felt familiar. Maggie steeled her spine, lifted her chin. No one would see how their brimming hostility hurt. No one.

Sudden warmth crept into her mind. Images of hearth, family and home flooded her. Nicolas. She felt the reassurance of his steely arm around her waist. His confidence raised her own. Maggie lifted her chin, studying the crowd. The initial hostility seemed to ease, replaced by curious looks.

A towheaded boy playing on the floor beside a leather easy chair tossed something. Maggie's heart raced. A dog toy. Suddenly a brown shih tzu dashed from behind the chair, claws scraping the carpet. The dog ground to a halt. She turned toward Maggie, her tail beating the air. A bark of utter joy split the room's dead silence.

"Misha!" Maggie broke free of Nicolas, ran forward. Her dog scampered and bounded straight into her arms. Furious licks of her face greeted her, lapping the tears streaming down her cheeks.

This alone was worth everything. She'd healed Misha. Maggie stroked the silky fur, marveling at her friend's excellent health. Whatever feelings the pack harbored toward her, they'd taken excellent care of her dog.

She looked up and saw something startling.

The hostile gazes were not centered on her, but Nicolas. He stood proudly, shoulders straight, taking in the rancor lasered at him.

She wasn't the source of their suspicion. The pack members began leaving their seats and approaching.

"Maggie, stand up. Let them get to know you," Nicolas instructed.

Maggie stood absolutely still as the others gathered near, eyeing her critically. Nicolas spoke soothing words into her mind. *It's all right. I'm here.* She knew this process was essential to her gaining pack acceptance. They came to her, running their hands over her, sniffing. One lifted her hair and sniffed behind her ear. Another nuzzled the top of her head. The women especially looked her over. Not human, she reminded herself, forcing her hands to relax. This was Draicon, pack acceptance.

One male did more than inhale her scent. He brazenly lifted her hand, kissed it in a courtly manner. Nicolas lifted his upper lip in silent warning. The male backed off, looked down.

She saw Baylor enter the room, closing off another door. The urbane Draicon approached, flashing her a warm smile. It faded as he turned his gaze on Nicolas.

"So you're back," he said flatly. "It's good to see you, Margaret. Your blood has helped Damian. He's still critically ill, but it bought him some time."

Relief smoothed Nicolas's expression. Baylor went to Katia, pulled her against him. "As for you, Nicolas…"

Katia laid a finger on his lips. "Please, stop. Now's not the time."

"Rules are rules," Baylor said, removing Katia's hand. "Nicolas broke them. He was banished."

"I know the rules," he said softly, his gaze never leaving the other male. "I helped implement them and followed them when I left the pack. The rules state my acceptance is conditional upon returning with the missing empath, Margaret. Don't test me, Baylor."

Others looked at her with open interest. The male who had kissed her hand stared with bold aggression. "Legend says you are the one who will destroy our enemy, Kane, the Morph leader. Have you fought? Can you survive the wounds of a Morph or will they kill you?"

"I'm tougher than you are," she shot back, locking gazes until the male dropped his. Damn, they were aggressive. She smelled their underlying fear laced with deep worry. Baylor had been right. The pack was falling apart.

Treading lightly was better than coming on strong. The Draicon wanted and needed reassurances. Maggie tried for a comforting, confident smile. "I've survived a Morph attack. Their blood burns, but my body heals too quickly."

Katia looked at her solemnly. "Baylor told us what happened. You healed your dog. Can you heal our people of this disease? We have some who fell sick tending to Damian. They're not as ill, but need your touch."

Her natural curiosity took over. "Only the ones tending him fell ill?" That meant the disease *was* transmitted by touch—only from species to species.

"Yes. Jake and Caren, our two best scientists, took the blood you sent and tried making an antibody. They injected Damian with it, but it hasn't healed him, only bought him some time. And it hasn't healed the others."

A fat tear rolled down Katia's cheek. "Now they're sick as well. Everyone who's come into contact with Damian is sick. Even Aurelia, who's been nursing him."

Maggie became decisive. "It must be transmitted through contact, not airborne. I've brought gloves and HAZMAT suits. Burn all the clothing and linens Damian's been in contact with. We can't risk anyone else falling ill."

"And what about the ones who already are sick?"

The hard edge in Nicolas's voice warned of his worries for her. She touched his arm reassuringly. "I'll do what I must. Damian is holding his own for now, but if the others aren't cured, they'll grow worse. I'll heal them now, before they do."

"Maggie," he said tightly.

She turned and cupped his cheek. No words were needed between them, but she said them aloud so others would hear.

"Nicolas, the pack needs you as much as they need me. There's no real leadership here since Damian fell ill. The children are too thin. I can see food supplies are scarce. They need someone to lead them."

He closed his eyes, nodded. Then he opened his eyes, looking every inch what he had been. Fierce determination and quiet strength. Damian's second, next to take over the pack. Nicolas squeezed her hand. "Go, do what you must."

Her mate fixed a baleful look on Baylor and the other males. "Gather a group together. You need to hunt fresh game."

Baylor started to speak and fell silent under Nicolas's cold command. He turned and the other males began shuffling out of the room. Katia looked troubled, but smiled at Maggie and Nicolas. "Come on, I'll show you to your room."

She led them up a flight of wood steps to the second floor and down a long hallway. Windows lined the hall, giving an excellent view of the snow-dusted field surrounding the lodge.

A vantage point, Maggie realized. Every

window allowed them to see anyone approaching. The lodge was built more for protection than recreation.

Opening a door at the hallway's end, Katia gestured. "I hope you'll be comfortable here. Damian insisted you have some privacy. Everyone else is at the other end. I tried to make it as homey as possible. If you need anything, let me know. I'll have the guys bring your luggage up."

Maggie gazed around the cream-colored bedroom. A royal-blue patchwork quilt covered the antique king-sized bed. A ceramic blue pitcher filled with autumn leaves stood on an antique maple dresser and rag rugs added color to the pine floor. Lamps fashioned from train lanterns sat on twin nightstands. The lace curtains at the window added a delicate touch. Yet she could not feel comfortable here, not with the animosity brimming like a summer storm.

She preferred Nicolas's abandoned ranch with its tattered white goose-down comforter on a bed as big as a football field and the grimy windows that overlooked the forest's gentle slope leading down to the grassy meadows.

Nicolas paced the bedroom like a caged animal. "I need to talk to Damian. Why don't you settle in?"

"Settle in, when there's members of the pack who are ill? I'm heading downstairs."

As she turned to leave, he caught her arm. Something dark flickered in his caramel gaze. "Be careful in using your magick, caira. Even your powers may not be able to work on everyone. I smelled it in the air downstairs."

"Smelled what?"

His mouth flattened. "Death."

The moment she hit the carpeted basement steps, it hit Maggie. Gagging, she pressed a hand over her nose. Nicolas had been right. Her eyes watered with sorrow. The stench of illness was the same she'd recognized in Misha. In her dog, she'd thought it cancer. Now she knew it for its true nature, the stench of despair and hopelessness.

Following Katia, who was bedecked in a protective suit, Maggie climbed down to a large wood-paneled room. Twin beds arranged in dormitory style lined the room. At least a dozen females and some males lay in them.

It was worse than she'd envisioned. Healing these Draicon would sap her strength. But she must.

Flexing her hands, Maggie went from bed to bed as Katia explained the various stages of the disease. Most had the beginning stages. A few were moderate. She healed those who were least sick and worked her way through. She felt incredibly tired, and weak, but pushed on to the last, and worst, case.

Aurelia, Damian's nurse. The female Draicon moaned and tossed on her bed. Maggie felt tears well up at her suffering.

"I have to go…Damian needs me." Aurelia sat up, then moaned and fell back onto the bed.

Her loyalty to the pack leader deeply touched Maggie.

She looked down at the female Draicon curled into a tight ball. Compassion filled her. Maggie sat on the bed and gently laid her hands over Aurelia's heart. Pain encompassed her. Waves of violent, red pain. Maggie bit her lip and plunged on. Concentrating, she saw ugly blackened cells made healthy and whole.

Minutes later, she removed her hands. Her breath came in ragged gulps.

Her hands had turned a mottled gray. Nausea welled up. Maggie staggered to an empty bed and collapsed upon it.

This was harder than she'd ever imagined. But she'd healed the sick ones. All of them except Damian. She lacked the strength now to heal him.

For now, he must wait.

* * *

An hour later, a still-exhausted Maggie slipped into Damian's third-floor room. It wasn't hard to find. She followed his scent. Powerful, dominating, laced with the same sickness from downstairs.

Slowly she opened the door, and stepped inside. On a king-sized bed, the Draicon leader dozed. The same grayish color tinted his skin. His thick black hair was cropped short, unlike Nicolas's long locks. He had a strong, square face and a deceptively vulnerable mouth.

She sensed nothing was vulnerable about this Draicon.

Her hands lifted as if to heal but Maggie forced them down. She didn't dare risk trying to heal him while she was this weak. He was far too ill.

Drawing nearer, Maggie's heart turned over at the thinness of his face, the lines of pain ravaging it in sleep. She sensed he masked the agony while awake so as to not alarm the pack.

A noise at the window startled her. Maggie whipped around, but the door was too far away. The closet. She stepped inside, leaving the door ajar slightly and watched.

The window slid open without noise. A diminutive woman climbed over the sill and stepped inside.

A warm, calloused palm slid over Maggie's mouth at the same time a steely arm jerked her backward. She gasped in surprise, then scented Nicolas.

Why are you hiding in here? she mentally asked.

Keeping watch over Damian. I picked up this one's scent, knew she was heading here, he mentally spoke back.

Bewildered, she started to question him further. *Later,* he whispered into her mind.

They watched the elfin woman approach Damian's bed. Her skin was pale as porcelain. Shoulder-length dark hair framed her thin face. She had a tilted nose, high, elegant cheekbones and looked no more than eighteen.

Jamie, Nicolas spoke into her mind.

This was Jamie, the terror that had ravaged the pack with her disease? The mortal woman who'd brought down Damian?

Jamie stood by the bedside. Maggie tensed, ready to protect the Draicon leader with her own body if necessary. But Nicolas seemed relaxed and unafraid for Damian.

The woman hung her head a moment. When

she raised it, shock filled Maggie. A single large teardrop slid down Jamie's translucent cheek.

"Crying for me?"

The soft New Orleans drawl made Maggie and Jamie gasp at the same time. Damian's eyes were open, his gaze sharp. She wondered if he'd been sleeping all along.

The mortal stepped back, scrubbing at her face. Hot blood suffused her face.

"Me? Don't be a fool. I came to see if you were dead yet." Her sultry, mellifluous voice sharply contrasted the youthful look.

"Disappointed? I'm quite alive, thank you for checking." Amusement threaded Damian's voice. Maggie didn't understand.

"Since you're here, why not sit? Rest a bit. You look peaked."

He acted almost gentle and very unafraid of the woman who had stripped him of his strength and power.

Jamie stared at him, her lower lip jutting out. A wary look came over her as she parked herself on the edge of Damian's bed. She did look no more than a child, a confused, scared child. Maggie felt confused herself.

"The Morphs know Nicolas is back with Margaret. I came to tell you. They're planning to attack her the day after tomorrow. I heard Kane coordinating it. They'll attack this lodge in a swarm of bees. It's the fastest way to travel. They plan to infiltrate through the heating vents, then they'll shift into wolves. Don't care about the others, they only want to kill Margaret. Kane figures you're dead already."

Maggie's heart lurched. Nicolas gave her a comforting squeeze.

"Thank you for telling me," Damian said quietly. "Why are you telling me this?"

Her slight shoulders lifted. "I don't know. Maybe because I owe Nicolas one."

"How did you leave without them noticing?"

"They don't care much what I do anymore. I can come and go as I please." Jamie toyed with a lock of her hair. "They're not afraid of me leaving. Kane is certain I'll stay."

"Are you certain you'll stay? Why are you really here, Jamie?"

Damian's voice radiated command and demanded answers.

"They told me…" Jamie looked troubled. "Kane told me who you really are and what I did…what it means. Who I am. It's crap. Lies. They were just trying to torment me."

"It's the truth." Damian regarded Jamie with a

hooded gaze. "It's why I sent Nicolas after you with the lure I knew would tempt you beyond anything. He taught you magick, at my request."

Maggie made a startled sound. Nicolas was banished for following Damian's orders?

"You used me," Jamie blustered. "You knew I was a virgin. It was my first time and all I wanted...you screwed me and then left. You promised to teach me magick and you used it to get me into bed and then dumped me. I was a fool to trust you. Well, Damian, I got you back. Kane was more than happy to take me into his family and teach me all he knew. The Morphs have real power."

But a quiver threaded through her soft voice. Maggie sensed the girl's uncertainty.

"I did seduce you. But I didn't leave you, Jamie. I went to find out how to bring you back here." Damian gave a gentle smile. "I knew the truth would come as a terrific shock to you."

Jamie sprung off the bed. "Nothing shocks me. You're just a bastard, Damian. A shifter who uses mortal women for pleasure."

"Other women, perhaps. Not you. There is more between us."

"No," she whispered. "It was just sex. There's nothing between us, and never will be."

"It wasn't just sex, Jamie. You can't deny it. Try to run and hide. It won't change the truth," Damian said softly, watching her.

"I'll deny it all I can. No one can tell me what to do." Jamie whirled around, anguish and anger twisting her pretty face. "Not the Morphs and not you. No one."

With lithe grace, she bounded across the room, vaulted over the windowsill and vanished. Shock filled Maggie. Jamie had just leapt three stories down, just like a pixie.

Nicolas removed his arm and opened the closet door. Maggie blinked at the bright sunlight flooding the room. Damian didn't even glance up.

"Should I go after her?" Nicolas asked.

Damian sighed as he toyed with the quilt's edge. "Leave her be. She's safe, for now. They still think of her as their puppet."

"This isn't the first time she's been here. Is it, Dai?"

The pack leader closed his eyes a minute. "No. The pack doesn't know, either."

"I would never tell," Nicolas assured him.

Nicholas clasped Maggie's hand, his palm warm and strong. Nicolas pulled her forward, sliding a protective arm about her. "Damian, this is Margaret. Maggie."

"Hello, Maggie." Damian had sharp eyes, green as a turbulent sea, but his smile was kind. "Thank you for coming back to us. We've sorely missed you."

His gaze flicked away for a moment. "I'm deeply sorry we lost your parents. Richard and Carla were good people. I knew they only left out of fear for you."

His warm, deep voice sent waves of reassurance through her. Though he sat up in a sickbed, he radiated authority. Definitely the alpha male of the pack.

She glanced up at Nicolas. His entire manner seemed more relaxed and confident than downstairs. He too radiated the confidence of an alpha male instead of the subservience of a beta. Confusion filled her. Why then, wasn't Nicolas leading his own pack?

Too many questions swirled in her mind. She focused her attention on Damian.

"Nicolas wasn't my beta when you and your parents were still with the pack," Damian answered her unspoken question.

"I was without a pack. Damian took me into his."

"After he saved my hide." Damian sat back against his pillows, his color growing sallow. A grimace crossed his face. He made no effort to hide it. Maggie realized the extent of his pain.

She went to his side, felt his pulse. Thready and weak. His skin felt ice-cold and clammy. She found a bowl and filled it with warm water, and began bathing his brow.

"I thought you were from Colorado. When did you live in New Orleans and how did you meet my parents?" Maggie asked, deeply curious about the pack leader.

"I spent my boyhood in the bayou. When the Morphs killed off my parents and our pack, I left and found distant kin who needed a leader, including your parents."

"Who is Jamie to you?" Maggie wrung out the cloth.

"A mortal," he said drowsily. "Someone I met in New Orleans when I went back there a while ago. Mmm, this feels good. Nicolas, don't give her up. I want her to stay."

"So do I," Nicolas murmured. He stayed her hand as Damian's eyes fluttered shut.

"Let him rest. Come on, let's get settled."

Chapter 14

Healing the pack members stripped Maggie of much-needed energy. Nicolas brought her to the kitchen for food, hoping to replenish her. He didn't want sex now. Maggie was too inquisitive. Experience taught him that he lowered his natural defenses during lovemaking. Sex with her brought his emotions to the surface.

After they ate, she rested while he went outside on the wood deck. Nicolas braced his hands on the pine railing. A wrought iron table and chairs in a corner commanded an excellent view of the sloping snow-dusted meadow and forest. Once the cushions had been bright green and bedecked with blue stripes. Time and sunlight faded the cushions. They looked sad and neglected.

Like the pack did, he thought.

Tension rifled through the lodge. It felt as tranquil as a battlefield.

Every hour he worried more that things would spin out of control. He'd promised himself and Maggie no more killing or violence. But the pack didn't know that.

They'd expected him to deliver into their hands a killer trained to dispatch Morphs and Kane, the leader. His acceptance was conditional upon those terms.

Where would he be without his pack? Nicolas stared at the rolling meadows, the verdant green of the firs and the white aspens. He remembered the days of roaming alone, the gut-crunching loneliness so sharp he howled into the night. Pack was necessary for survival. He needed this pack, and Maggie.

Yet if Maggie discovered the truth about him, would she grow as fearful as the others? Just as some others did now, would she look at him with wary suspicion, expecting him to turn traitor?

He waved his hands in the air. Colors swirled in the air as a lethal dagger materialized in his hand. Nicolas examined the blade. Honed and gleaming, it represented his life. He'd killed the enemy over and over to prove his loyalty to the pack. Nicolas, the pack's fiercest warrior and destroyer of Morphs. Sometimes he wondered if he knew anything other than violence, death and blood.

Until Maggie came into his life, he didn't.

The realization slammed into him with the force of a bullet. Nicolas threw the dagger downward. It landed on the wood deck, quivering from the violence of his toss.

He was tired of death and killing. He wanted a hearth, home, family. He wanted Maggie, and her stubbornness, her gentle touch, her peace.

Once he only achieved that balance with music. Finally the music had died as well in his relentless quest to search and destroy their enemies.

No one was around. Nicolas climbed down the deck steps with his accustomed surreptitious caution. He walked to a small outbuilding in the distance, close to the western edge of the property. The square building was about the size of a three-car garage. Nicolas took the key above the door frame, unlocked the padlock and went inside. Two double-paned windows allowed in thin light.

The first room was used for storing winter equipment for the pack. Skis, snowshoes and shovels neatly lined the walls in racks. Nicolas fished a key out of a pail holding rock salt and unlocked the door to the second room.

He flicked the switch. Light flooded the room.

There were no windows in this room. Nicolas disliked the idea of someone spying on him so he
had installed a ventilation system to draw in fresh
air from outside. Worktables long in disuse were
covered in dust. Saws, chisels and other tools
looked neglected. The interior smelled of old saw-
dust. In the middle of the room sat a half-finished
rocker. Nicolas crept over to the corner, sorting
through a cache of old horse blankets no one
used. Very gently, he lifted the instrument from
its hiding place.

The case was cracked leather, but when he
opened the lid, the guitar sat gleaming in the
dim light. Nicolas sat on the cold wood floor and
settled the instrument into his lap. Elusive peace
settled over him.

Very softly, he began to play. He didn't dare
allow others to hear him. Music soothed his tur-
moil and settled his troubled thoughts. He imagined Maggie as he strummed an old folk tune.
Maggie, with her tousled auburn curls, the sunny
smile on her mobile mouth, her earnest expression. His Maggie.

After a few minutes he packed the guitar away
and hid it again. If anyone from the pack spotted
him, it would arouse suspicions. Nicolas, playing
music? What had happened to the warrior who

fought to keep them safe? Was he growing soft? Weak? Weak Draicons couldn't resist the allure of power the Morphs offered.

Weak Draicons were dangerous to the pack.

Once someone had caught him singing and commented on it. Nicolas had never forgotten the male's careless laugh about how singing love songs tarnished his fierce warrior's image.

Outside, the temperature had plummeted. Small flakes drifted down from the leaden sky. Early snow, nothing unusual. He stole back to the lodge, brushing light powder off his jeans.

In the kitchen, Katia sat on a bar stool, talking with Aurelia. Aurelia, who had been like a mother to him, and had been dying. Joy bounded through him. He stole up and enveloped her in a hug.

"Nicolas!" She pulled back, cupped his face with affection. He inspected her features, relieved to see she looked healthy. "Maggie, your Maggie, healed me. Healed all of us who were ill. She's amazing, Nicolas. Thank you for bringing her back." The older female gave his hand a tight squeeze.

He looked around with interest, expecting to see his mate. "Where's Maggie? Is she up yet?"

Katia glanced away. "Baylor and the others

found Morph tracks on their hunt for food. When they came back with the game, they took Maggie with them to go hunting. They were looking for you but…"

Nicolas's heart dropped to his stomach.

"They said now was a good time to see how well you trained her, Nicolas. She is the one foretold to kill our enemy, isn't that so?" Aurelia looked confused as she pushed back a hank of graying blond hair.

His mouth flattened. "Legends aren't always truth. Sometimes they become greater than the people themselves."

And I should know that, he mused. His own image, projected in stories told to frightened children, had been legend.

"She should return soon. I doubt they'd take her far, her first hunt. I know they should have brought you along, but…" Katia's voice trailed off. Both females looked deeply troubled.

Understanding flashed through him. Led by Baylor, the males were starting to separate Maggie from him. They still didn't trust Nicolas, but they needed Maggie. Enfolding her into their brotherhood would drive a wedge between him and his mate.

Rage filled him. He wanted to tear, rip, maim

those who dared to spirit away his mate. Nicolas threw back his head and released an earsplitting howl.

Katia and Aurelia cried out and backed away. Fear twisted their faces. He looked at them and saw in their eyes the beast they thought he was. Nicolas drew in a calming breath and thought of his music. He remembered Maggie's gentleness, her passion in making love.

Finally he was able to control his emotions. Nicolas held out his hands.

"It's all right. I'm going after her."

"Please don't, Nicolas. Maggie needs to spend some time alone with the pack. Let them get to know her."

"Through fighting, Aurelia? Through killing? Just as all of you grew to know me?" He rubbed his tattoo in frustration. "Maggie is nonviolent. I had to teach her how to kill Morphs. But I made a big mistake. She's not meant to be a killer."

The two females stared at him. "But she must," protested Katia. "She's our last hope."

There had to be another way.

"Leave her be for now, Nicolas." Aurelia laid a gentle hand on his arm. "Let her get to know the males first. Perhaps you are wrong about her

destroying Morphs. She may return just as triumphant as you were when you went on a hunt."

He doubted it. But for Maggie's sake, he hoped
Aurelia was right.

Hours later, as he sat by the crackling fire in the
great room, Maggie returned.

Nicolas watched his mate shuffle inside as if a
great weight dropped on her slender shoulders.
She unsheathed her two daggers. Crimson droplets splattered on the stone hearth. Methodically
she cleaned her weapons, sheathed them, then
dropped the belt on the floor. Staring into the fire,
her expression appeared blank and unfocused.

She did not acknowledge Nicolas or anyone
else. His heart twisted.

He'd taught her how to kill so she could become
the weapon of legend, foretold to destroy their
enemies. Maggie did not acknowledge the approving slaps on her shoulder, the nods of respect
from the males. She remained quiet, emotionless.

A robot trained to kill.

He ached to see beyond the stone wall she'd
erected to shut others out. Nicolas went to her
side, crouched down and took her hand. It felt
chilled, the skin not warm and soft as when

they'd first met, but rough, as if she'd physically grown a hard shell around her body.

"Mags, look at me," he ordered softly.

She turned slightly, enough for him to glimpse the barrenness in her eyes. Once they were filled with life, determination and love. Now they showed only the reflection of flames crackling in the fire.

"We killed more than two dozen. I speared a few in the heart, as you showed me."

Detachment flattened her voice. Nicolas squeezed her hand, hurting from the pain he knew she'd hidden deep inside. He'd achieved his goal and forced her to acknowledge her Draicon heritage. But at what price?

"More than a few she nailed. Good fighting. Never seen anything like it. Didn't even flinch when their blood splashed her hands. She just kept on fighting."

Respect rang in Baylor's voice as the other males grinned and nodded in agreement. Nicolas took both of Maggie's hands into his, turning them over and examining them. No trace showed of the burns from the Morphs' acid blood.

"Were you badly hurt?" he asked.

A little shake of the head. "You push past the pain and just focus on the kill. Remember, they're evil. Germs that must be eradicated. They're bacteria and you're a white blood cell, surrounding the enemy and destroying them, no matter what your own personal cost."

His words, tossed back at him in this flat voice. Nicolas winced, grieving at the loss of the Maggie he'd known before he'd taught her to fight. Before the mating...

Alarmed, he drew back, dropped her hands. The mating. When they'd exchanged magickal powers, emotions, memories. His warrior's strength. Her healing.

His killing nature.

He swore softly. What the hell had happened to her?

Nicolas reached out, felt her thoughts. Drained. Exhausted. Numb.

Nicolas outlined her soft mouth with his index finger. "Maggie, Maggie," he said softly. He touched her lips with his in the barest of kisses. She barely responded to the gentle pressure. Deeply troubled he touched her cheek. Chilled, as if his Maggie had turned into a frozen block of hard ice.

"You're tired, needing refreshment," he murmured. "Come with me, darling. I'll keep you warm. I'll never let you grow cold again."

Baylor and the other males gathered around. Nicolas smelled them before he heard them.

"Maggie, we were headed into the kitchen for dinner. You need to replenish your energy," Baylor said.

A low growl rumbled in his chest. Nicolas drew Maggie close. "She's not going with you anymore," he shot back, lightly stroking her spine.

Maggie did not respond as Nicolas nuzzled the top of her head. Before the night was over, she would respond to him. "Maggie will restore her energy with me."

Baylor folded his arms across his chest. "She's too spent," he challenged. "We can care for her needs better than you, Nicolas. Go back to playing your guitar."

So he had been heard after all. Nicholas's chest felt hollow.

Other males murmured, cleared a space as if expecting the pair to openly challenge each other.

"Back off," Nicolas said softly. "Maggie is my mate, Baylor. My responsibility. If you're foolish enough to challenge me on this, wait until I care for her."

"You're too dangerous for her, Nicolas, music or no music," Baylor retorted.

His smile was all teeth. Nicolas felt his canines

descend. "Music can be dangerous," he agreed. "Right now I'm fighting the urge to bash you over the head with my guitar."

His bold, open stare stated his aggressive threat. Baylor finally lowered his gaze, shuffled back. Nicolas stalked toward the bedroom, his arm securely about his mate's waist.

In their bedroom, he slowly undressed her. She stood mutely, like a large child, her gaze dull and unfocused. Pain sluiced through him as he delved into Maggie's thoughts and saw horrific images. Blood, bodies, glee at inflicting violence on the faces of the Draicon and the Morphs, until Morph and Draicon merged into one indistinguishable dark mass. In that battle, they had become one and the same.

Steeling himself, he pushed further into her dark memories of the hunt. He saw Maggie hang back, then cry out as the Morphs advanced and Baylor and the other males egged her on, urged her to attack. Yet she stood there helplessly until a Morph launched itself at her.

Each time the creature sank its sharp teeth into her arm, the wound immediately healed. She seemed indestructible. Cries echoed in her mind, the urgent shouts of the Draicon to kill their enemy, slay them... *Help us, Maggie, help us, we're dying....*

In her mind Nicolas saw Maggie lift the daggers in her hands and plunge them over and over and over, a frenzied, uncaring robot trained to destroy. Blood coated her hands, her fingers. She looked down at those slender digits, dripping with warm, wet crimson and something inside her died. Numbness overcame her. She had ceased to feel, or think.

Swearing softly, he pulled out of her thoughts.

Maggie had turned into what he himself had become. An indifferent killing machine.

Never again.

Nicolas guided her over to the bed and gave her a gentle push. She lay on her stomach like a wax doll. He shed his clothing and looked around the room uncertainly.

On the oak dresser sat a bottle of cinnamon-flavored massage oil. Nicolas grabbed it and straddled Maggie's back legs. He squirted oil into his palms and rubbed them together. The sharp scent of spice filled the air.

She did not move.

Very slowly, he ran his palms up the curve of her spine, working in the oil, murmuring to her in low, reassuring tones. He praised her beauty, her gentle compassion in healing others, reminding her of the Maggie she had been. Erasing the ugliness of the violence she'd inflicted. Strong fingers that could crush a man's windpipe were extraordinarily gentle as he kneaded out the knots in her tensed muscles.

Beneath him she stirred slightly.

He flipped up the bottle's cap and drizzled oil onto her rounded bottom. Droplets slid into the delicious crevice of her ass. Maggie undulated her hips and whimpered.

Good. But he wanted more.

With one finger, he traced the droplet's journey, very gently working the oil into her bottom. Now she openly moaned with pleasure. Nicolas skimmed a finger down into her feminine cleft and slid it back and forth.

Up, down. He stroked, culling her own moisture, pleased at her response. He breathed in her sexual energy and returned it to her, feeding her his own raw hunger of her. Nicolas slipped the finger deep inside her sheath.

Maggie's bottom arched upward in a nameless, ancient feminine plea.

He withdrew, gently turned her over and worked the oil into her front. His fingers flicked over her taut nipples. Nicolas watched with pleasure as they grew hard as tiny pearls. His groin felt heavy and his body hammered for release, but he ignored his own need.

This was for her. Maggie came first.

Unable to resist the temptation of those rosy little pearls, he lowered his mouth to one. Nicolas flicked his tongue over it, then suckled her.

Now Maggie wriggled beneath him, cradling his dark head to her chest. Her legs spilled open as her hips pumped upward.

Still not enough. He wanted her mindless with pleasure, begging for it, oblivious to everything but him. Make her forget. His mouth left her breast and showered hot kisses down her belly, licking and nibbling her satiny skin.

Opening her legs wide, he put his head between them and tasted her arousal.

Maggie screamed as his tongue flicked over her, swirling as if she were a hot cinnamon Maggie treat. Over and over he caressed her, his hands pressing her thighs wide open for him. he breathed in the erotic pleasure she felt, and felt her tense as her orgasm approached.

Nicolas gave another long lick. She cried out his name and her body jerked off the bed. Iridescent sparks burst into the air.

Pure masculine satisfaction filled him as Nicolas watched her fall back onto the mattress, her body quivering. She lay there with a look of languid pleasure. Smoky passion drenched her deep blue eyes as she opened her arms.

"Nicolas, I need you," she whispered.

He covered her, thrust hard and fast and she came again. Only then did he allow the shuddering tension to explode. Nicolas threw back his head and cried out her name as his big body shook.

Panting, he dropped onto her, his hot breath coming back as he lay facedown in the pillow. Maggie's thighs trembled against his as she gently stroked his sweat-slicked back.

Nicolas rolled off, taking her with him. She pillowed her head on his dampened shoulder. Something warm and wet trickled down his arm.

She was crying. His heart turned over, even though he knew the emotional release was necessary.

He never wanted to be the one to make her weep. Nicolas buried his face into her soft curls and spoke.

"Maggie, sweetheart, you don't have to kill anymore. I promise you, to my last dying breath, I won't force you to do it and I'll make damn sure no one else forces you to as well." He dropped a gentle kiss atop her forehead. "You're extraordinary, my special, wonderful Maggie, and I wouldn't change a thing about you."

"I can't do it again, Nicolas." Her muffled sob against him stung like a dozen knife wounds. His grip about her tightened, as if he could ward off all the demons chasing her.

"I did it before and I will not do it again." Tears dripping onto his shoulder like warm raindrops.

"It was me, Nicolas." Maggie wiped her cheeks. "When I was twelve, I was walking back to our car with my parents. They jumped at us from nowhere. My parents pushed me aside to protect me, screamed for me to run. I couldn't move. I watched them fight them, these creatures, they kept shifting and shifting. There were too many... five of them. They killed my parents. Then they turned to me and laughed...."

"You were only a child," he said softly, stroking her hair.

"I ran to my father and tried healing him, it had worked for a few animals I found on the roadside hit by cars. But I couldn't do it. I looked up at these things, and I..."

She took in a shuddering breath. "All this rage and anger and grief rose up. I didn't even think. I tore off my clothes and I changed into a wolf.

I attacked them. I killed two before they could shift, and then the three others, they attacked, but as they wounded me, my wounds just healed. I just kept striking and striking at them until they were dead. And then I shifted back. There was so much blood, so much…"

"And you saw what you had done. You killed five adult Morphs."

"I blocked it out. I changed back into my clothing and ran. The police found me wandering the street a few blocks away, crying and crying."

"There was nothing wrong with what you did," he insisted. "You changed, Maggie and the trauma of your first shift, watching your parents die, and the attack made you bury everything inside. You defended your family, Maggie. What you did was right and good."

"It's who I am, but more than that, I'm a healer, Nicolas," she said slowly. "I can't be both a killer and a healer. I don't want to kill."

He lay in bed a long time, his arm draped about her as Maggie slept. His thoughts chased each other like a dog chasing its tail. Maggie could not hunt anymore. She deserved to retain her gentle, healing nature. Before his eyes, she was changing. And what of him? What if in trying to suppress any softness, his dangerous edge came out?

The darkness swirled inside him. Baylor insisted he was a caged beast clawing for freedom. He belonged with the Morphs. One day, he would destroy members of his own pack, Baylor always warned.

Nicolas turned to Maggie. His heart ached. What if he accidentally unleashed his darkness on his mate?

Maybe it was best if he left before any such thing happened. Though mated and bonded, they could separate. Eventually, Maggie would forget him if he left. The months on his own had taught Nicolas strength. He could handle the loneliness if it meant keeping her safe from the beast craving to claw free. She could seek another mate.

The thought pierced him like one of his daggers.

In his arms, Maggie stirred. She snuggled closer, resting her head on his shoulder. Nicolas kissed her forehead. "I don't want to lose you," he whispered, burying his head into her hair. "But I don't want to hurt you, either, caira. I can't bear it."

After Maggie destroyed the Morph leader, and that particular threat was gone, he should leave the pack. Leave her, before he hurt her.

It made sense. It was logical, as Maggie herself

was logical. But even as his mind assured him he had made the right decision, the treacherous tear slipping out of the corner of his eye fiercely denied it.

The pack males attacked him en masse the next morning.

"Getting domesticated, Nicolas? We noticed you haven't been hunting. Maybe you've lost your touch and don't like killing Morphs. Makes us wonder where your loyalty lies."

At Baylor's sneer, Nicolas went still at the counter. He'd been making a casserole with salsa, cheddar cheese, potatoes and scrambled eggs for Maggie. She still hadn't accustomed herself to eating raw meat yet.

"I'm not soft on anything," he replied, giving the mixture another stir.

"You were dangerous before," Baylor said softly, advancing toward him. "Now you're a double threat. You have her healing abilities. If you turn on us, you can wipe out our people. You'll be a Morph with the power to heal yourself and your kind. We won't be able to kill you. Maybe we should kill you now. Eliminate the threat."

Other males muttered uneasily.

Anguish speared him. "I'd never turn on the pack."

"Then prove it. Damian's accepted you back as our beta. But I won't accept you and neither will the rest until you bring us proof you're pack again. Bring us back evidence you killed Kane."

His stomach gave a sickening twist. Nicolas dropped the wooden spoon onto the counter and turned. *So it comes to this. I knew I couldn't avoid it forever.* "It's not my destiny to kill the Morph leader," he said, sweat trickling down his back. "It's Maggie's."

"Making your mate kill for you? You're weak, Nicolas. Weak Draicon are most likely to turn Morph. You don't deserve to come back to us." Baylor's smile didn't meet his eyes. "You don't deserve Maggie, either. She's got courage, unlike you. I think I'll claim her for myself."

Jealous rage roared through him. Nicolas growled and clenched his fists. "We're mated. Are you challenging me for her?"

"A challenge? You couldn't survive one. Face it, Nicolas, you're too soft. She needs a real male in bed. All you know how to do is cook. Go back to the Morphs where you belong, traitor. Maybe you can cook for them."

Nicolas snarled and lunged for Baylor.

Other males leapt back in startled gasps. He ignored them.

Baylor's punch landed square in his solar plexus. Too enraged, driven by jealousy and adrenaline, Nicolas grimly fought back. Over and over he thrashed at the younger male, the red haze in his mind urging on. Then a familiar female voice reached out and yanked him out.

"Nicolas, stop it, stop it!" Maggie pulled at his shirt. Snarling he turned to her, then stopped. Stricken, he stared at his mate in horror.

"I almost hit you," he whispered in shock. "Maggie, what's happening? What if I hurt you?"

Maggie couldn't bear to see what they were doing to him. Tears blurred her eyes. The pack only saw Nicolas as their warrior, a fighter who killed. They didn't know his tenderness, his affection and the deep wells of courage and loyalty he had.

All they saw was a bloodied killer.

She knew he was so much more.

"You could never hurt me," she told him.

She reached up and touched his face. He flinched. Nicolas turned his head to see Baylor on the kitchen floor. One eye had swollen purple. Blood streamed down his temples.

"Nicolas, oh…" Maggie slid her arms around his waist. She looked up at the pack males assisting Baylor to his feet. A protective snarl lifted the corner of her mouth.

"Get him out of here and leave us alone."

They filed out of the kitchen, Baylor sagging between two for support. Maggie turned back to Nicolas. "Nicolas, you don't have to prove anything to them. Violence isn't the answer."

"It's the only answer. You don't understand, Maggie. The only way I can earn their respect is through fighting."

He pulled away, his dark eyes haunted. "You don't understand. They're always waiting to test me, watching for any sign of weakness, that I'll slip."

"Give yourself a rest, Nicolas. Haven't you done enough for the pack all these years? You deserve a chance at peace more than any other male. You're their family as much as Baylor is. Why do they always challenge you?"

"There never will be any peace for me, Maggie. They challenge me because they're afraid I'll turn on them one day. And maybe I will. Because they're not really my true family. I wasn't born into this pack, Maggie. I have no relatives here. But one of my close relatives is the enemy they hate the most. The enemy the pack needs you to kill. They don't realize I can't."

Strain etched his features, and tension coiled his powerful body as if he were ready to leap forward in battle. The true battle hadn't been waged with the Morphs, she slowly realized. It warred within him, just as she fought the rage her wolf demonstrated when her parents were killed.

A terrible suspicion crested as he turned away. Nicolas braced both hands on the countertop, avoiding her gaze.

"The Morph leader, Kane. He isn't merely my enemy. He's my real family, the uncle who raised me. Baylor and the others want me to kill him to prove my loyalty, but the day I kill Kane is the day I turn into a Morph, too."

Chapter 15

Maggie stepped back with a look of horrified shock. Nicolas rubbed the back of his neck. Weary resignation settled over him. So it came to this. He'd tell her and if she rejected him, at least she knew the truth. He strode to the kitchen doors, quietly closed them.

"Sit. It's a long story, and not a pretty one."

The backs of her legs connected to the chair he pulled out. Maggie gripped the chair's armrest. Deeply ashamed, and hiding his thoughts, Nicolas did not look at her.

"My parents and Kane lived with another Draicon pack in Montana when I was only twelve. Back then there were Draicon packs all over the United States. Now there are only a few of us. My parents and Kane were tired of being low in rank. They banded together and killed my grandfather, the pack leader, and became Morph and formed their own pack. They took me with them to live, assuming I'd join them when I grew older. We roamed the northwest as they destroyed mortals, Draicons, every living thing, a killing machine mowing over life. I saw their destructive evil. But it wasn't all death. Kane tempted me with what he knew I craved most—the power of shape-shifting. He showed me how he could take to the air as an eagle, or even frisk in river waters as an otter. I wanted that power. Badly."

She pushed back her chair and stood as if to go to him. Nicolas held out a hand like a traffic policeman. He couldn't bear her pity now. He'd shatter like glass.

"Stop it, Maggie. Sit down."

She sat.

"What did you do?" she asked in a normal tone.

"I was seventeen, Maggie. Filled with rage and pain and confusion. I wanted to belong, but detested the evil they wrought. I ran off."

"You were a lone wolf, so to speak."

He gave her a wry smile. "On my own, afraid to seek out others of my kind. I began killing Morphs in my journeys, ones I didn't know. Then one day I saved a Draicon from a Morph attack. In return, he invited me to join his pack and become his beta. Damian lived in Colorado then, but was taking the pack south to New Mexico where things were quieter. In exchange for the position, I taught the others everything I knew about their enemies. How to kill them by stabbing them through the heart. Where they roamed, how they acted. All their weaknesses. But some males never quite trusted me. I always had to prove my loyalties to show I wouldn't turn against them."

"The tattoo, it's their mark, isn't it? That's why you didn't want me to see it."

"Kane marked me when I experienced my first change into a wolf as Draicon. He knew I always longed to soar like an eagle. So he made the mark on me so I'd always remember the freedom they have to fly. But the eagle's talons drip blood, the price paid for turning Morph. When the longing rises in me, it burns. It was my uncle's way of tempting me to turn."

Emotion clogged his throat, making it difficult to speak. He stared at grains of sugar dusting the countertop. Someone had forgotten to clean up after themselves.

"So there you have it. The pack doesn't know Kane is my uncle. Only Damian does. But they fear I'll turn into a Morph because I lived among them. Now you know what I am. I'm a walking time bomb, according to Baylor. I'm a great warrior, according to Damian. And I'm a double-edged sword, according to others."

"And what do you see yourself as?"

Her question threw him off. Nicolas raised his head.

"I don't know," he said honestly. "For so long I've seen myself in their eyes that I don't know who I am anymore."

She stood and went to him. Her palm slid over his in a light caress. "I know who you are, Nicolas. You're a courageous, loyal friend to Damian. You have immense inner strength to resist the evil you lived among for all those years. You're my mate, and I'm proud you chose me. I'd want no one else."

Maggie paused and slid her fingers over his hand. "I love you, Nicolas. I love you for who you are, not the image of what you want others to see. I always sensed you had this inner struggle going on, and that's why you withheld yourself when we achieved the mating lock. I wish you'd open yourself up fully to me. Share everything, Nicolas. There's nothing you can say or do that would make me walk away from you as they would."

He said nothing, relishing her soft caress.

Maggie believed in him and trusted him. Maybe it was about time he did the same.

At what price? What if he turned on her as everyone thought he'd eventually turn? He couldn't bear to hurt his draicara.

Nicolas thrust her hand away. "Leave me alone," he snapped. "You think you know me but you really don't. You have no idea what I could do, Maggie. I mated with you not because I wanted to, but I was ordered by Damian. Mate with you and bring you back here. Those were my orders and like a good soldier, I followed them. I've fulfilled my duties to the pack. So back off and go tinker with your microscope. That's what matters most to you."

Hurt flashed in her sea-blue eyes. He winced inwardly, knowing he'd placed it there.

"No, Nicolas. What matters most to me now is you. I just wish you could read that inside me as well as you read everything else."

Maggie turned and left.

Nicolas paced outside, mindless of the snowflakes blowing into his face. It had snowed steadily for the past hour. Maggie was downstairs, having set up her lab in the basement now that it was no longer used as a sickroom. She took samples of the blood and compared them.

Practical Maggie, always trying to find a cure through science.

Her grit and iron will humbled him. The pack had taken to her, but still, he had seen the sidelong looks. He'd heard the whispers.

They were still suspicious.

The pack wouldn't fully accept Maggie until she healed their leader. Damian was so close to death Nicholas feared for her to try. What if he lost her?

Nicolas jammed a hand through his hair. Maggie was key to destroying Kane. Desperation drove him to believe in her mythical abilities. Surely he could not kill the Morph leader.

But he could heal Damian. Heal Damian and spare her the pain, and possibility she might die because Damian was so ill.

Nicolas spread his hands out, studying them. Surely he possessed all her healing abilities. He could rid Damian of the Morph disease.

Now was the time to find out.

Steeling his spine, he headed inside the lodge, toward Damian's room.

Maggie perched on a stool, peering into a microscope at blood samples. She tried to concentrate, but Nicolas's words echoed in her mind.

Nicolas used her to achieve his own purposes. That truth stung.

But she'd glimpsed inside him and seen the pain he carried. Why couldn't he open himself up to her? He'd shut her out during the mating lock and now he was shutting her out emotionally as well.

It was about damn time he stopped. About time she started asserting her own needs. She had come this far to come home...

The slide slipped from her fingers and fell to the counter with a clatter. Home. Here, among the Draicon, she no longer felt alienated and at odds, as if her carefully organized life would shatter if she took one wrong step. Despite the friction in the lodge, Maggie felt comfortable here. She was one of them. And what if Nicolas had never forced her to look inside and see who she truly was?

Would she have spent the rest of her life never knowing who, or what, she was?

Maggie searched deep inside herself. She had been living a lie, and Nicolas brought out her true nature. He accepted her, faults and all.

If he was only concerned with performing his duty and returning her to the pack, he could have forced her to hunt as the pack males had. Instead, Nicolas had showered gentle, loving care on her, his touch reassuring and soothing. He took her into his strong arms and promised her she'd never have to kill again.

Not the actions of a male interested only in following Damian's orders.

She had to talk to him, and stand by him. Nicolas shut everyone out, but dammit, he wasn't shutting her out. He needed her.

Maggie jumped off the stool and ran upstairs.

She checked the living room, the kitchen, outside. Nothing. But in the hallway, Baylor mentioned seeing Nicolas head up to Damian's room.

A horrible misgiving overcame her. As she stepped onto the stairs, a giant shock wave of pain slammed into her. Maggie staggered against the wall, crying out.

The pain welled from deep inside, and vanished. But she knew the source. Nicolas.

"Nicolas, oh, no, Nicolas!"

Her cry brought Baylor and the others running.

"What is it?" he asked sharply.

Gathering her composure, she ignored him and raced upstairs, the pack members right behind her. Maggie tore down the hallway toward the wing leading to Damian's room. Baylor beat her there and threw open the door.

He stared at something curled up in the corner of his room.

Maggie's heart raced. Nicolas.

She ran toward him. He lay curled in a tight ball, hands clutching his stomach. He was moaning.

"What the hell's wrong with him?"

She ignored Baylor, reached out for her mate. Nicolas did not respond.

"Baylor! Everyone! Look!"

Only the excitement in Katia's voice made her turn. In the large four-poster, the Draicon leader sat up, his color no longer grayish. His face was pale and thin, but the lines of pain ravaging it had vanished.

Nicolas had healed him, she realized with sudden dread. Nicolas healed Damian before she could. He hadn't realized he never inherited her full healing abilities because she in her stubbornness didn't tell him.

Now he was paying the price.

Her mate lifted his face. "Had to...pack wouldn't...accept you...otherwise...too risky for you...couldn't lose you...Maggie," he rasped.

Very gently she lifted him. His body felt like a block of ice. Remembering how sick she'd felt after healing Misha, Maggie knew what she must do.

Nicolas would not want other males seeing

him like this. Every fiber in his body would protest the pack witnessing his weakness. Maggie
marched out of Damian's bedroom, ignoring the
stream of excited, hopeful Draicon pouring into
their leader's bedroom. She headed straight for
their bedroom, kicked the door shut. Very gently
she laid her mate on the bed.

"Maggie, let us help him," Katia implored
through the closed door.

"Go to hell," she snapped.

Friend or not, she couldn't trust Katia. Instinct to protect her mate drove her on. Maggie
undressed him, tucked Nicolas beneath the
covers and stroked his forehead. He moaned and
thrashed. Pain twisted his handsome face. Grayish skin tones alerted her to the disease's powerful grip on his body.

He lacked the antibodies to fight the disease
and eradicate it as she had.

Maggie climbed into bed and lay besides him,
holding Nicolas tight. "Please, Nicolas, fight it.
Don't leave me," she whispered.

Rocking back and forth, she laid her hands on
him. Willed herself to heal him, inside and out.
Taking all her strength, Maggie poured it into
her mate. She opened herself fully to him, seeing
him made whole and strong again. She spoke into

his mind words of love she hadn't dared voice, and saw the disease in her mind chased away by whole, growing new cells. White-hot agony lashed her, but she persisted.

At long last he opened his eyes. His color had returned and his thin, cracked lips were no longer blue.

Maggie buried her face into his shoulder and wept.

She felt his hand gently stroke her hair.

"Don't cry, caira, please don't cry."

Clinging to him, she gulped down her sobs. "I thought I'd lost you." Maggie sat up, swiping at her tears. She punched his rock-solid bicep lightly. "Don't ever go pulling anything that asinine again or I'll murder you!"

Nicolas grinned, holding his arm. "You just healed me and now you're going to kill me? You make no sense."

His look sobered. "What happened? I thought I had your healing abilities."

"You didn't absorb them all during the mating lock because you blocked me." Maggie outlined his lips with one finger. "I sensed it, but didn't tell you because I was too proud."

"We both made a mistake." He took her finger and kissed it.

The Empath

"Then let's remedy it, Nicolas." Never had she felt so certain of anything.

His gaze searched hers. He nodded. She undressed.

Nicolas turned and slid his arms about her. His mouth descended on hers.

He drank in her mouth, tasting her satiny lips, wanting to climb inside her heat and become one with her.

When he pulled away, the same desire shone in her blue eyes. Nicolas feathered kisses over her cheeks, nuzzled her neck and explored her satiny skin with his hands. He kissed the tiny hollow of her neck, hooked his hands into her silky curls. He charted her body with his mouth, mapped it with his touch, marveling at her pale, soft skin against his big, sun-darkened hands.

Maggie undulated beneath him and parted her legs, opening her arms.

Nicolas mounted her, panting with need and hunger.

"Now," she said in a deep, sultry voice.

He entered her hard and fast.

"Maggie." He groaned aloud as he raised himself up on his hands and moved inside her. The friction was exquisite, her tight inner muscles squeezing him. A crystalline bead of sweat rolled down his forehead, dropped on her breast. He locked his gaze to hers, intent on melding them together as one, matching his pleasure to hers. Nicolas withdrew, thrust hard and deep. She made a tiny gasp. Her deep blue eyes rounded with wonder.

Lacing his fingers through hers, he pinned her wrists to the mattress. His sweat-slicked body moved over hers, skin against skin. One flesh, one body, one mind. Minds merged and swirled, exchanging thoughts, ideas.

Memories.

Pack, family, home. Running wild, wind caressing fur as they ran over the hills. He thrust deep into her, pouring himself, his essence, his life, into his mate. Maggie. Making her his own with each exquisite thrust, sealing them together in the flesh and spirit. Nicolas opened his eyes, gazed at her features, her parted, kiss-swollen mouth, passion clouding her sea blue eyes.

He opened himself fully to her, letting her inside. Nicolas allowed her to see every dark corner, every deep crevice.

He felt her power flowing into him, her gentle, healing strength and marveled at the newness of it.

Iridescent sparks swirled around in rainbow

colors. Nicolas felt himself swell inside her as her tiny muscles bore down upon him.

The mating lock.

He rolled, taking her with him so she rested atop him. He smoothed her hair and kissed her face. Something wet rolled down his cheeks. This time, he didn't attempt to stop the tears, but let them come.

This time, he felt like he had come home at last.

Chapter 16

They had little time to plan before the Morph attack.

Maggie insisted on searching for a way to annihilate their enemy without violence. The pack had no means of fighting an all-out attack when the Morphs could clone themselves into an animal army. Nicolas agreed. He stated his case before Damian, who had recovered dramatically and began restoring order to the pack. Damian held a meeting and firmly told the pack Nicolas's role in saving him.

Downstairs in Maggie's lab, they took samples of Damian's blood and examined it. Maggie worked steadily, refusing to sleep. She knew she had to find a means to destroy the Morphs soon. First she needed to know how the disease was transmitted.

"How exactly did Jamie infect you?" She asked Damian this question as she withdrew the hypodermic needle.

The pack leader sighed and squeezed a fresh ball of cotton over the puncture mark. "I'd rather not say…"

Nicolas gave him a censuring look. "No use being secretive now, Dai." He turned to Maggie. "Damian kissed her."

She nearly dropped the vial of blood. Goggle-eyed, Maggie stared at Damian.

"It's not what you think," he explained, looking troubled. "She sent me a note saying she needed to talk. As I've told you, I'd met Jamie in New Orleans."

"You had sex with her," Maggie said accusingly.

Damian nodded, looking more thoughtful than regretful. "I needed to see her afterward, and when she sent me that letter, I agreed to meet her on neutral ground. We had words and then I kissed her. After, she laughed and told me she had her revenge for how I'd abandoned her. I tried pursuing her, but she took off."

"Ran? Why didn't you run after her?" Nicholas asked.

Damian smiled grimly. "No, not running. She

took off, literally into the air. She'd joined the Morphs and they gave her the magick ability to fly. That's when I knew…"

"You were screwed. Literally," Nicolas shot back.

A low growl rippled from the pack leader. "Jamie's different from most humans. Many mortals possess the ability to work magick and can do so with the right instruction. Very few can fly. The ability must have been in her and the Morphs' dark magick activated it."

Judging from the guarded looks Damian exchanged with her mate, there was more. Maggie opted against asking questions. Instead she prepared another slide of Damian's blood.

When it was ready, she studied it under the microscope. The microscope showed exactly what she'd suspected since allowing herself to see the disease as more than a scientific reality.

"It invades the host like a staph infection through simple skin contact. That's what makes it so contagious and why anyone caring for Damian was infected. Some forms of bacteria can live for months in clothing."

She pushed back on the rolling stool and gestured for Nicolas to look. "It's how they infected Misha. All they needed to do was brush it against her nose or mouth and *bam!* Jamie must have infected Damian when she kissed him. It's actually not a virus, but more a cleverly disguised bacteria."

Nicolas frowned as he squinted into the scope. "I thought bacteria could be killed with antibiotics. Giving Damian antibiotics should have at least slowed its progress."

"Even some bacteria, like *staphylococcus aurea,* are resistant to antibiotics. This particular bacteria we're dealing with is a toxin that's carried by a section of Morph DNA. Normally Damian's natural resistance would have combated it, but they intricately cloaked the Morph DNA by wrapping Jamie's human female DNA around it. His body must not have recognized the human female DNA and allowed it to invade his immune system."

Damian gave a wry smile. "That's me. Always allowing females to invade me."

"Once it entered his system, it adjusted and banded to his DNA. Literally it cloaked itself so it could be passed on to the other pack members. That's why he was infected first. Just as pack members have a scent marker unique to this pack, the bacteria needed Damian's DNA to get past the pack's immune system and infect other members. Everyone here has a strain of DNA unique to this pack that's strongest in Damian, the alpha. Either they inherited it through their parents or it bonded with them when they achieved a copulatory lock with their mates."

"It explains why I was never infected," Nicolas said slowly. "I'm not pack. You are, but we hadn't mated yet."

"Misha became infected, but she couldn't infect me because I never assumed my wolf form. Maybe they thought I would change, and become infected that way," Maggie mused.

Mouth flattening, Nicolas reached over and squeezed her shoulder as if to reassure her. She drew in a cleansing breath.

"Once it's inside the body, it acts just like a bacteria, only it appears more like a cancer because it devours healthy cells. The bacteria multiplies and poisons normal cells, absorbing them and eating them alive."

She looked at Nicolas. "I don't suppose you ever watched old fifties horror flicks."

"I tried to avoid them when I could," he muttered. "Especially the hokey werewolf ones. They were very insulting to my intelligence."

"You're too sensitive," she teased.

His soft growl made her laugh. Nicolas grinned. Damian rolled his eyes.

"Well, there was this movie called *The Blob*. Steve McQueen starred in it. It featured this germ from outer space that infected a local doctor, and then consumed him. Ate him alive and it grew larger. The more people it ate, the bigger it got. It looked like a huge rolling ball of jelly."

"This disease acts like the blob?"

"As it moves through the body, it eats its way through healthy cells, turning them into killer cells just like it. That's why the body's normal defenses don't work. It feeds off energy the cells produce, and the more calories a victim consumes, the more energy the disease has to spread."

Maggie drummed her fingers on the counter. "What I don't understand is why the Morphs needed Jamie's DNA to infect Damian. It makes no sense. I could understand it if it were a Morph who was a close relative of Damian's or even his bonded mate who turned Morph. Damian's system should have recognized the intruder and shut it down before it infected him. Even if it were simple human DNA, his body would manufacture antibodies to combat the infection. How could a simple human female's DNA get past his defenses?"

A shuttered look came over Damian. "It wasn't just simple human female DNA," he muttered.

"Dammit, now this all makes sense, why they recruited her and needed her..."

"I don't get it."

"Never mind. It's not important now. What is important is that we find a way to use this against the Morphs. Can we?" Damian asked.

Maggie thought. "Now that we know how the disease infects, we need a plan."

"Then we'll make one," Damian said decisively. "Gather the others, Nicolas. We'll have a meeting and discuss this news."

They met in the enormous living room. Outside, large flakes of snow floated gently downward. Flames crackled in the fireplace and the smoky scent added a cozy touch to an atmosphere rife with bristling male tension.

To her surprise, Damian and Nicolas sided with her idea of finding a means to destroy the Morphs while avoiding an all-out war. Kane was the primary target.

"Maggie's made a good point. Kill Kane, the leader, and the Morphs will disperse like a colony of ants without their queen. They'll scatter," Damian pointed out.

Sitting in a straight-back chair close to the fire, Baylor shot Nicolas a meaningful look. "That's your duty, Nicolas. You're Damian's second, so it falls upon you to kill him. If the attack is planned for tomorrow, you need to act now."

Nicolas rubbed the nape of his neck. Maggie could almost feel the tension radiating from him. "This isn't as simple as it appears, Baylor. Killing Kane isn't as easy as it seems. He's well protected at all times. Yet we can't plan an all-out attack on them. There's Jamie. You have to separate her from them. We have to keep her out of danger and in an attack she could get killed in the confusion. Or they could use her as a shield to protect themselves."

A casual shrug indicated Baylor's feelings on the mortal woman. "She infected Damian. She deserves to die."

"No." Damian leveled a hard look at the other male. "Jamie is to be left alone and unharmed. Understand? No one hurts her. Either Nicolas or I will deal with her."

Baylor frowned. Maggie could understand his doubts, and the unrest among the pack.

Maggie reached out with her mind, touched Nicolas's thoughts. She found a swirling mass of emotions he struggled to contain. Fear the pack would discover his secret. Worry for her. Anger and disdain for Baylor.

She slid off the stool, thinking fast. There must be a way out of appointing Nicolas to dispatch his uncle without making anyone suspicious. She began pacing, thinking aloud.

"Look, eliminating Kane alone isn't the answer. Nicolas is right. He's studied them, knows their patterns just like I've studied animals and know their behavioral patterns. You don't use a sledge-hammer to kill a single queen bee. That won't kill the hive. You smoke them out so they become docile and…"

She ground to an abrupt halt. Excitement poured through her. "That's it, yes, has to be."

"What, Mags?" Nicolas jumped off the counter.

Maggie's mind raced over the knowledge she'd gained in her practice. "Animals, they're animals, so you deal with them as animals. They're hard to kill because they shift so quickly. But there has to be a life-form they prefer when they target a particular individual."

Nicolas began pacing behind her. "Yes. The easiest way for them to kill is their wolf form, the original Draicon form. Takes less energy, so if they can attack as a wolf pack, they will. It's only when they're presented with a situation that they need to breach a target's defenses that they shift."

"Like my home, when they invaded as ants," Maggie said, remembering.

"Or when they sneak up on a victim and cloak their numbers."

Maggie halted so fast Nicolas almost collided with her. "So if a situation presented itself that they could attack easily as wolves…then we could form a plan."

She swung toward Nicolas, forgetting Baylor, the other males, everything else. All her attention was focused on her mate. His strength. His knowledge. His cunning.

Nicolas always thought his only value and purpose lay in killing Morphs. He failed to see what she did—his resolve, deep loyalty and intelligence. He could strategize and shift plans while others were still arguing about what to hunt for dinner.

"Tell me everything you know about the Morphs and how they shift. What about how they feed? Do they have to remain in wolf form to feed?"

Nicolas shook his head. "They must reshift back to their original form to feed."

"And if they couldn't, if they remained, say in their wolf form, and couldn't shift, what would happen?"

Baylor and the others looked impatient, but understanding flashed on her mate's face. A slow smile lifted the corners of his mouth.

"They would die, eventually. The more energy they had expended in shifting to different forms, the more they'd need to feed, so they'd die faster."

"That's the answer. We don't kill them one by one. We lure them into a trap, making them shift. Then when they're in their wolf form, we neutralize them."

Baylor scoffed. "With what? An atomic death ray?"

"Anesthetic," she replied calmly. "Applied in a contained room, dispersed evenly, it would immobilize them and prevent them from shifting to their true forms. They would quickly starve to death. Diazepam is what we used with the wolves out West, but I'm thinking nitrous oxide. It's a gas."

Nicolas went very still. "And what exactly do you use to lure them into the trap?"

"Bait," Maggie replied serenely. "What they want the most. Me."

Every protective instinct surged in Nicolas. Maggie, using herself as bait? Putting herself in danger?

"Sounds like a good idea," Baylor mused.

"You're the one Kane wants the most and the best way to lay a trap."

"No," he interjected tightly. "Maggie, stay out of this."

"Nicolas…"

"Not you. Never." He fisted his hands. Baylor, who threatened to challenge him over Maggie, was ready to hand her over like a sacrificial lamb…or in this case, the sacrificial wolf.

"There's no other way."

"There must be. I won't allow you to endanger yourself." He dragged in a deep breath. "I'll dispatch Kane myself, if it means keeping you out of this."

Her eyes went soft with emotion. Maggie laid a gentle hand on his arm. Nicolas felt his wolf ready to explode, howl with fury. Grimly he leashed it.

"Nicolas, luring them en masse into a trap will work. Your killing Kane isn't an option."

"I'll make it an option." He closed his eyes, filled with anguish. His destiny became clear, as if a fog suddenly lifted. He'd kill Kane, eliminate the threat to Maggie and the pack, and then before he became too dark, would sacrifice himself.

Better that than watch Maggie be torn to pieces by his triumphant uncle if something went wrong.

His eyes snapped open. Resolve filled him.

Damian shot them both a troubled look. "Using yourself as bait may not work, Maggie. It's too risky and they also may sense a trap."

"Then do you have other suggestions?" She lifted her chin in challenge.

Damian looked thoughtful. "We could use Jamie. I sense she's…regretful. She may be able to lure them into a trap instead of you without arousing suspicion and then rescue herself at the last minute."

Nicolas saw his logic. Using Jamie not only made sense, but would be a first step toward lessening the pack's hostility toward her.

"Regretful? She tried to kill you. You can't trust her," Baylor snorted. "Do you want to invite her in and have her attack all of us? Another intruder who lived with Morphs and might turn, just like Nicolas?"

Damian whirled around, his green eyes snapping with fire. "Silence," he snarled.

A deadly quiet draped the room. Even Nicolas drew back.

The pack leader's low growl commanded respect. He stood and threw back his shoulders, his stance aggressive and bold. "Did I ask for your opinion?"

Baylor lowered his gaze respectfully.

"No, I didn't. Keep your muzzle shut and stop spreading dissension among our family."

Baylor's mouth opened.

"Close it or I'll close it myself with my fist," Damian ordered silkily.

Baylor shut his mouth, his eyes wide.

Damian faced them all, looking every inch the confident leader. He went to Nicolas and rested a hand on his shoulder. "When I took Nicolas in, I didn't do so out of pity. Nicolas saved my life from Morphs. He put himself in danger to do so for a stranger. He had nothing to gain and asked for nothing. I asked him to join us because I knew he was good for our family. I trusted him. Time and again he's proven himself and yet some of you still feel he will betray us."

He paused. "I trust him and that should be good enough for all of you. Nicolas is my second. I'd place my life into his hands over and over. He's shown his loyalty to me and all of you. He deserves respect, not haranguing.

"And any member who does otherwise, can leave." His icy green gaze swept over all of them. "I'd rather have Nicolas at my side than a legion of pack members who disrespect him. Because when you show contempt for Nicolas, you show contempt for me. I accepted Nicolas as my brother. Anyone who doesn't want to do the same, leave now."

The pack leader's hard glare challenged each member. No one looked him in the face, but all dropped their gazes. All except Nicolas, whose look of gratitude said more than words. Maggie sidled up to him and took his hand. He squeezed it and she relished the simple contact between them.

Nicolas had left his people, but never abandoned them. Loyal to the core, devoted to protecting them and keeping them safe. Just like he'd done to her. Even when they'd turned on him, he'd gone on doing his job, keeping the pack safe, protecting his leader. She'd never known anyone more capable of trust and deserving of love. Through all he'd put her through, forcing her to acknowledge who she really was, he'd never let go of his own fidelity.

His love.

Her life since her parents' deaths had been a series of farces. Playacting the role of a normal human when inside her true self screamed to be heard. For too long she'd denied herself. Nicolas forced her to turn inward, examine that which frightened her the most. In turn, Maggie learned to let go of fear and find peace at last. She couldn't hide any long from her true nature.

She, Maggie Sinclair, veterinarian, woman, tax-payer, was Draicon. Wolf. A powerful creature born to manipulate magick and heal injuries. No longer could she ignore her skills, or the driving need inside her to hunt, roam free and run with the moon.

She belonged. To a people, her pack. To some-one. Nicolas, her mate.

Just as Nicolas belonged, and Damian made that perfectly clear.

"All right then. Let's move on." Damian dropped his hand and paced to the room's center. "Forget about using Jamie. I will not risk her life and she's too...flighty."

Maggie stifled a smirk behind her hand as Damian winked at her.

"What Maggie proposes makes excellent sense—however, the Morphs aren't stupid. In their zeal to eliminate her, they may become care-less but we can't risk that. They could tear her to ribbons before we could storm in and save her," the pack leader continued.

She swallowed hard, seeing the scene as he laid it out. Her logical mind raced over possible alter-natives.

"Scent," Nicolas spoke up. "We could use her scent instead as the bait. They would detect it, think she's there and enter the room. Less risk to Maggie and they won't get as agitated or violent. Or sense a trap."

"Makes sense," she agreed. "But we'll need a lot of nitrous."

Damian gestured to a tall Draicon with graying hair sitting by the fire. "Owen is a dentist. He has access to plenty of it. But we need to plan the trap carefully. Let's get started."

The best-laid plans looked like they would backfire before they even got started.

Damian spread the outline of a plan out on the table in the basement. Nicolas's workshop was a perfect place to lure the Morphs. Once the Morphs assembled in the room, Nicolas would shut the door, locking them inside. Using the ventilation system, they'd pump in the nitrous oxide.

However, they all realized Maggie would have to be used as bait after all to lure them to the shack.

"The problem is, we have to use her to attract them to the building." Damian tapped the crude map. "Her scent won't be strong enough. Even if we cloak one of our males with it and disguise him as Maggie, the Morphs will see through it."

"You can go into the shop and there's a back door where you can slip outside, Maggie," Baylor pointed out. "We'll place clothing with your scent in the workshop so the Morphs still think you're inside."

"A tricky plan requiring careful coordination," Damian mused.

Nicolas didn't like it one bit. "I don't want to use Maggie."

"You have to, Nicolas." Maggie placed a gentle hand on his arm. "I'm the only one they want, and their senses are sharp. You can't disguise another male, or even a female, as me. My scent is too strong and they'll suspect. I'll carry a tranquilizer gun, and if I'm in danger, I can fire it. I won't be in any danger."

Damian shot him a questioning look. Nicolas sighed and rubbed his tattoo. "All right. But I'm with you right outside. If I even suspect you're in one iota of trouble, I'm coming in."

Too many factors existed for them to control. Nicolas didn't like it. Jamie was a loose canon who could ruin things at the last minute, Kane was far too clever and the Morphs knew how to work together as an army.

He only wished he could rid himself of this nagging feeling that something would go terribly wrong.

Chapter 17

Maggie kept assuring herself all would go well as she watched the males set up the canisters of nitrous oxide that would be pumped into Nicolas's wood shop. Around the shop, Nicolas hid articles of her clothing. Like bloodhounds following a trail, the Morphs would pick up her scent and be lured inside.

She had already laid a scent trail through the woods for the enemy to follow straight to the wood shop. The trap would surely work for most of the Morphs, but Kane was clever and elusive. At least the nitrous would prove harmless to Jamie if she arrived with the Morphs to attack. Damian remained tight-lipped about any possibility of her involvement.

Maggie stepped outside the shop to draw in a

lungful of cool autumn air. Dusk approached, heralding the promise of a cool, clear night. A perfect night to hunt. Her wolf craved to be free. It scented danger riding on the light breeze. Nicolas shut the wood shop door and joined her.

"I wish you would return to the lodge where it's safe." He slid an arm around her, nuzzling her hair.

"I wish you would quit worrying."

"The day I die," he muttered.

His concern warmed her, calmed her wolf that clawed to be free.

"Do you smell it?" Nicolas asked suddenly. "They're coming."

She stiffened, fighting the urge to set the stronger wolf free to fight. Seeming to sense her anxiety, Nicolas kissed her temple. "Remember, you control your wolf," he soothed.

Damian appeared, dusting off his hands. He searched Maggie's face. "Are you ready, Maggie?"

Nicolas turned and gripped Maggie's arms.

"I'll be safe." She gave him a quick kiss. "Trust me."

She ran to her hiding place behind a cluster of nearby scrub brush as Nicolas, Damian, Baylor and the other males climbed the trees to wait.

They had dusted their clothing liberally with Maggie's scent to cloak their own. Wind rustled through the pines. Maggie swallowed hard and waited. Tucked into the waistband of her jeans was a tranquilizer dart gun.

The swarm landed nearby and the Morphs shifted. In the growing twilight she watched, revulsion filling her as they shifted into their human forms. Maggie shuddered, imagining Nicolas turning into a Morph, his face reflecting the same twisted ugliness and greed for inflicting pain.

One lifted his long, thin nose and sniffed the air. Which was Kane? She craned her neck to search the crowd, but didn't risk peering out beyond the sparsely covered brush.

They started toward the wood shop, then halted. They glanced at each other uncertainly. A pack of about fifty, with sallow flesh and sunken features. Dead, black, soulless eyes.

Her scent alone wasn't luring them into the wood shop. Ignoring Nicolas shouting a warning inside her head, she darted out. Whirling, she faced them.

Seeing her, the Morphs growled. Maggie raced toward the wood shop. She pulled open the door to the building and ran inside. Opened the door to the wood shop, and stood there, waiting. Dry-mouthed, she shivered, cold fear piercing her bones.

The Morphs slowly filed into the shop, shifting as they did so. Wolves greeted her, fangs dripping with saliva. Eager for the kill, they loped toward her.

"Now!" Maggie screamed.

A door slammed. The pack turned, but it was too late. She saw the gas begin to fill the room. The pack howled and started for her.

Giggling from the heady intoxication, Maggie ran toward the back door, fumbled with the latch. She raced outside as Nicolas rushed up and threw a sturdy wood bar against the door, bolting it.

His fierce scowl didn't stop her from laughing. She leaned against the building.

"You look like you want to eat me alive," she gasped. "Big Bad Wolf."

His scowl turned into a worried look. Gently, he touched her cheek. "You could have been killed," he muttered.

"Doubtful. They didn't act very clever. Not like they had before. I wonder why." She gulped down lungfuls of fresh, chilled air, trying to clear her head.

Damian rounded the corner, concern lining his

brow. "Something's not right. I think Kane sent this group as decoys."

A rustling noise overhead turned their attention to the leaden sky. Expecting another swarm of bees, Maggie braced herself. Instead, she saw a small, pixyish woman. Clad in ordinary jeans, and a heavy gray sweatshirt and white sneakers, Jamie descended before them.

"I escaped to warn you. They tried locking me up, but I got away. Kane isn't inside," Jamie said breathlessly, her feet hovering two feet off the ground. "He smelled a trap and went to the lodge. He's going to kill them all, Damian. Including the women and children."

Damian cursed, and turned to the other males. "All of you, to the lodge. I'll be along shortly. Nicolas and Baylor, stay here a minute. I need your help."

As the other males ran off, the Draicon leader nodded toward Nicolas and Baylor. "Hold her."

They grabbed Jamie, holding her arms fast. Maggie's heart raced as Damian circled the mortal, waving his hands.

Ancient words filled the air in Damian's rich, deep voice. Maggie slowly understood.

"I bind you Jamie, with the power against doing magick and the power against flight. I bind you

Jamie, with the power against doing magick and the power against flight."

Iridescent sparks swirled around Jamie. Her body began slowly drifting back to earth.

Horrified shock spread on the mortal's face. Jamie thrust up her hands, beating the air as if trying to climb upward. "No, no, no!" she cried out.

Something like pity twisted Damian's features, but he grimly continued chanting. Jamie fell to earth, collapsing. Very gently, Damian helped her stand.

"Why?" she wailed.

"You're safe now. The Morphs won't want you now that you have no powers," he said, brushing back a tendril of dark hair as he gazed at her with a tender look. Jamie jerked out of his embrace.

She shot him a daggered look and began stalking up the hill toward the lodge. Damian jerked a thumb in her direction. "Go with her, Nicolas, Baylor. Guard her and keep her safe until my return. I'm going hunting for Kane."

Maggie watched the Draicon leader vanish into the forest. Nicolas and Baylor guarded Jamie's front and back. Maggie flanked the sullen girl. Jamie threw her baleful looks.

"So you're Maggie, the famous empath. I

warned Damian they were coming for you, and this is the thanks I get."

Maggie felt sorry for the grounded Jamie, who looked like an angry child.

"I don't know why Damian did it. But I do know you're special to Damian, and we're charged to keep you safe."

As they neared the split rail fence demarking the lodge's property, a figure stole out of the woods and approached from the right. Their little group whirled about. Maggie caught the scent of decaying flesh. Her heart sank as the Morph leader held out a long, thin clawed finger.

"Jamie," the low, silky tone chuckled. "It's you I want now. Traitor. You're dead."

From a few feet away, Kane regarded them with a sickly grin.

Fear twisted Jamie's delicate features as she stared at the Morph leader. Powerless, she was vulnerable. The Morph leader lunged toward her as she stumbled backward, hands in front of her face. Baylor charged forward. Nicolas leapt in front of Maggie and Jamie protectively. With his body, arms spread, he acted like a shield.

An unearthly howl split the air. Maggie watched in astonished shock as Damian charged through the woods and tackled Kane. Snarling, he wrestled with the more powerful creature, tangling with him. Nicolas hung back, wild frustration on his face.

Nicolas couldn't attack his uncle. If he killed Kane, he would become Morph as well. The Morph leader didn't fight back. Instead, he ran toward Jamie with a snarl. Damian started for Kane again, wrestling with the Morph and toppling him unconscious with a powerful blow. Baylor jumped on him as well, dagger drawn and ready.

"Kill him," Damian snarled. He jumped off and ran toward Jamie, grabbing her arm and herding her toward the lodge.

But even as Baylor lifted his blade to stab Kane, the Morph leader came to life. He grabbed Baylor's arm and twisted. A sickening crack of bone followed. Baylor howled and dropped the knife. Kane swiped the Draicon with a clawed hand, and Baylor lay still on the ground.

Kane rose, turning his attention to Maggie. Nicolas snarled and charged, but Kane sidestepped. A dagger suddenly materialized in his hand.

Her wolf howled. Instinct kicked in. Maggie withdrew the dart gun to defend herself when Kane shifted into a bee. He flew toward her, stung her arm. She cried out, dropping the weapon. Maggie twisted and turned, desperately swatting as the bees multiplied and started attacking her. Suddenly something sharp sank into her back over and over, burning like fire. She sank to the ground, moaning. White-hot pain laced her body.

She turned to find the Morph leader in his human form, grinning and holding a dagger wet with her blood. He snapped his fingers and the bee clones vanished.

She collapsed, hoping the Morph leader would think her dead. Darkness rushed up. She fought it, knowing she had to hang on for Nicolas's sake.

His Maggie was dead.

Seemingly satisfied, Kane turned toward his nephew.

"Maggie!" Nicolas screamed and ran toward her. Kane intercepted him. Twin daggers appeared in Nicolas's hands, his mind unconsciously summoning them by rote.

Kane giggled, the sound like fingernails against slate. "Kill me, Nicolas. It's what you want. I'm the one who's made your life a living hell. Kill me. Your mate is dead."

His voice dropped to a mocking whisper. "Kill

me and join us. You'll have everything you want. Your own pack, a family more powerful than you could ever dream of. You're a killer, Nicolas. You always were, you just turned your skills into fighting your own people. Violence is all you know. Join us now and return to us. You'll never be anything more than an assassin."

Nicolas clenched the daggers, struggling to control his fury.

"Maggie's dead, Nicolas. I killed her. You have nothing now. You are nothing."

Nicolas rushed forward with a snarl, lifting his weapons. Kane did not move.

No, Nicolas!

The soft entreaty in his head ground him to a halt. *I'm alive. Please, Nicolas, you can fight this. Fight it. You don't want to become like him.*

Every cell in his body urged him to sink the daggers into Kane's heart. End this now and end the threat to the Draicon. Anger propelled him on.

Maggie's quiet, soothing voice spoke in his head again. *I love you, Nicolas. I believe in you. Kane is wrong. You weren't destined to become Morph. You can control your own destiny just as I can. Just as you taught me to control my wolf.*

Please, stay with me. Let him live. You're not the killer he says you are.

A calming peace settled over Nicolas. He had Maggie, his beautiful, wonderful, courageous draicara. She mattered most to him. His heart.

She was right. He didn't belong to the Morphs anymore. This time, he chose not to kill.

Nicolas stepped back and symbolically opened his palms. The steel daggers fell to the ground.

"I won't kill you, Kane. You won't win. I'm not what you say I am."

Kane's features twisted in ugly anger. "Fool. You could have had it all. Now all you'll have is a grave."

Kane rushed forward, snarling, shifting into a wolf as his jaws opened wide.

Nicolas picked up Maggie's abandoned dart gun and fired. Kane howled as the dart landed on his flank. Then Nicolas dropped to the ground, covering Maggie's body with his own as he prepared to take the full brunt of his uncle's fury.

He would die, but Maggie might have a chance.

"Nicolas can't kill you. But I can."

The familiar voice of his pack leader shifted into a snarl that echoed down the mountainside. Nicolas lifted his head and stared in shock as Damian rushed forward, shifting as he ran. His wolf struck the Morph leader, taking him down. The spitting, howling fury that was the Draicon pack leader attacked.

Weakened by the drug and unable to shift, Kane released an unearthly scream.

In a minute, it was over. Damian in his wolf form rose off the dead Morph leader. He shifted back and stared at his ancient enemy. Kane slowly disintegrated into gray ash.

Nicolas placed his palms on Maggie, feeling the healing energy flee him. She struggled beneath him and he rose off her. He reached out a hand and pulled her upright. Nicolas went over to Baylor, and laid his hands on the Draicon.

Emitting a deep groan, Baylor struggled to sit up. He stared uncertainly at Nicolas, then clasped his arm.

"Thank you," he said brokenly, and Maggie knew the Draicon would always be in Nicolas's debt.

"Go back to the lodge, go see after Katia," Nicolas told him.

Gratitude shone in Baylor's eyes. "If there's anything I can ever do for you…"

"There is," Damian cut in, shrugging back into his clothing. "I have to leave the pack for a while and need Nicolas to assume leadership, if he's

willing to do so. He's going to need full coopera-
tion from you, and the others. Will you give him
your loyalty as you give it to me?"

The other male studied Nicolas with a look of
newfound respect. "Absolutely. And if anyone
dares to oppose him, I'll show them their place."

Nicolas nodded gruffly as Baylor clasped his
arm again. As the male ran off toward the lodge,
Nicholas raised a questioning brow at his leader.
"You're leaving?"

Damian sighed. "It will be fine, now that Kane
is gone. The Morphs lack leadership, and will
scatter. With you and Maggie, the pack will be
fully protected."

He seemed to struggle with his emotions as he
rested a hand on Nicolas's shoulder. "There's no
one I trust more than you. Will you do it?"

Part of him longed to take Maggie, run off
and leave. He no longer craved the acceptance
and closeness of the pack. But he knew Damian
wouldn't ask unless he truly needed him. And it
was his friend's strategy to make the pack embrace him, as they had already accepted Maggie.

"I will do it, with Maggie's help." He glanced at
his mate, who nodded.

"I have a feeling you're leaving to go after

Jamie, right?" Nicolas asked after Damian thanked them both.

A rueful look came over his pack leader. "She escaped as soon as I got her to the lodge. It's all right. I have an idea of where she went. She's safe from the Morphs now that she has no magick. I'll find her."

Maggie slid her palm into his, and he relished the warmth of her touch. "Why, Damian? Who is Jamie to you?"

Damian's jaw tightened. "Jamie is my draicara."

Slowly, the story came out. Damian had met Jamie in New Orleans and sensed something special about her. Yet he couldn't merge with her thoughts fully, probably because she was mortal.

"I had to leave and sent Nicolas to find her, with instructions to do whatever it took to keep her in sight."

"Including teaching her magick," she said, realizing.

"I found her all right." Nicolas rested his cheek against Maggie's soft hair. "I taught her magick, and she escaped and joined the Morphs."

"After she left and joined the Morphs, she totally blocked me out and I couldn't do anything to keep her safe. I must find her," Damian said.

"Go, Damian. Once you've found your mate,

you'll do anything to get her back into your arms, and once you do, if you're smarter than I am, you'll immediately realize there isn't a thing in the world you want to change about her," Nicolas said softly.

"It goes both ways," she murmured. "His strengths become your strengths and you find in yourself the power to become who you're meant to be."

Damian looked a little sad. "I wish it could be so for us as well." Then he gave a philosophical shrug and loped off back toward the lodge.

"Do you think he'll be all right?" she asked.

"Damian will. He'll find her." Nicolas caressed her cheek, his face growing soft with love. "Right now all I care about is you, Maggie. My Maggie. My love."

"You did it, Nicolas. You thought you couldn't resist killing Kane. You faced your greatest fear and won."

He caressed her face tenderly. "I did it because of you, Maggie. Your strength gave me strength, because you saw me for something other than what others did. You saw all of me."

Maggie looked at him with shining eyes. "We did it, Nicolas. You and I. The legend said I was the one who would destroy the Morphs, but it was us. You helped me realize who I am, and reconcile to my wolf. You gave me your strength and courage and they helped me overcome my deepest fears."

Enfolding her in a warm embrace, he rested his cheek against her silky hair. "When Damian returns, I want to go back to my ranch, Maggie. Make a real home for both of us, and start a family of our own."

Warmth filled her as she slid her arms around his waist. "I've always wanted a real family, Nicolas. I've been so alone since my parents died. Until I met you, I felt like I'd always be lonely and never find anyone to love."

"Never again. I'm yours, Maggie. You're all I want. If you'll have me, for good. I'm yours, forever."

Epilogue

She sat by the crackling fire, working on a cross-word puzzle. Across from her, Nicolas lay on the carpet. Rapt fascination stole over his face as he watched baby Angelica play with the colorful mobile over her head. Her chubby legs kicked as she squealed in happy delight.

Six months since Angelica's birth, they had made Nicolas's ranch into their private retreat. As soon as Damian returned, their contact with the pack had been limited, at Nicolas's insistence. They set about making their own family, long, lazy afternoons of making love on every part of the ranch, finally conceiving Angelica.

Maggie had contacted her business partner and sold him her share of the practice. The money and Nicolas's accumulation of wealth afforded them a comfortable lifestyle, but Maggie went back to the work she loved. The locals were delighted to have a veterinarian and she had focused on large animal practice. Nicolas hired help to work the ranch and devoted his time to watching Angelica and administrative paperwork. The hardened warrior who once only knew violence now spent his days in peaceful contentment bouncing his daughter on his lap as he pored over the books.

He picked the baby up, cooing to her. Angelica nestled against him, resting her head on his shoulder. Maggie's heart turned over at the way he gently cradled the baby, the serenity in his once troubled dark eyes. Beside her chair, Misha dozed peacefully.

"Baylor and some of the others are coming over tomorrow to work on the fence in the north pasture," Nicolas said, juggling Angelica.

Amazing how the pack had accepted him. The long standing rivalry between himself and Baylor had vanished, with the other male helping Nicolas while Damian was gone. Baylor offered his friendship and proved a big help now, repairing the neglected parts of the ranch.

Her gaze dropped to the crossword. "It's your turn. I need a six-letter word for family."

Shifting Angelica in his arms, Nicolas walked

over to Maggie and peered over her shoulder at the puzzle. "Easy enough. M-A-R-G-A-R-E-T."

"That's eight letters," she protested.

"Doesn't matter. That's family to me," he said, kissing her.

He had his own little family now. Nicolas found the peace he'd thought possible only in dreams. Maggie had spent her life running away from her true home. Nicolas had spent his life desperately trying to find his.

They were both finally home. And here they would stay.

* * * * *

"You ran because your instinct told you I'm your best damn chance of keeping safe. And I am."

Nicholas angled his head toward her. "Because I will keep you safe, to my last dying breath. You and I, Maggie, are destined to be together. It's not sexual chemistry, not the typical male-female kind. It's deeper, more important and lasting. So relax and stop questioning everything. In time, it will all make sense."

Maggie closed her eyes, trying to understand what seemed like utter nonsense.

She didn't believe in karma, the tooth fairy or soul mates. What she believed in right now was self-preservation. Having escaped one dangerous situation, she now had to get herself out of another one. Was Nicolas a knight to the rescue, or a dark night of the soul?

Dear Reader,

Imagine working as a veterinarian, oblivious about possessing a healing power that could save the animals you love. You yearn for something more, but are afraid to face the truth—you are not human, but a wild beast who craves the night. And your destined mate is hunting you down to make you his own and bring you back to the pack to save your people. This is Maggie, my gentle-natured heroine for *The Empath*. She is desperate to find a cure for the mysterious disease killing her beloved dog. It will take Nicolas, the pack's fiercest warrior, to bring the truth to light and force Maggie to realize their own destinies.

The Empath is truly a book of my heart. Though I'm multipublished, this is the first story evolving from a real-life experience. I began writing the book shortly after my husband and I were told our beloved Shih Tzu was dying from liver cancer. The story became my balm during those months when I knew we would eventually lose her. For eleven years, Tia had been my constant companion who always rested her head on my laptop while I wrote. Tia passed away in December 2006, but she will always live on in this book and in our memories and hearts.

I hope you enjoy Maggie and Nicolas's journey of strength, courage and passion. Maggie does embrace her incredible power to heal, but discovers the greatest power of all lies in the ability to love unconditionally.

Bonnie Vanak